THE MOON IS DOWN
and
THE LONG VALLEY

The Moon Is Down

John Steinbeck

P. F. COLLIER & SON CORPORATION
NEW YORK

PUBLISHED ON THE SAME DAY IN CANADA
BY THE MACMILLAN COMPANY OF CANADA, LTD.

TC

MANUFACTURED IN THE UNITED STATES OF AMERICA

TO

PAT COVICI

A GREAT EDITOR AND

A GREAT FRIEND

THE MOON IS DOWN

CHAPTER ONE

BY TEN-FORTY-FIVE it was all over. The town was occupied, the defenders defeated, and the war finished. The invader had prepared for this campaign as carefully as he had for larger ones. On this Sunday morning the postman and the policeman had gone fishing in the boat of Mr. Corell, the popular storekeeper. He had lent them his trim sailboat for the day. The postman and the policeman were several miles at sea when they saw the small, dark transport, loaded with soldiers, go quietly past them. As officials of the town, this was definitely their business, and these two put about, but of course the battalion was in possession by the time they could make port. The policeman and the postman could not even get into their own offices in the Town Hall, and when they insisted on their rights they were taken prisoners of war and locked up in the town jail.

The local troops, all twelve of them, had been away, too, on this Sunday morning, for Mr. Corell, the popular storekeeper, had donated lunch, targets, cartridges, and prizes for a shooting-competition to take place six miles back in the hills, in a lovely glade Mr. Corell owned. The local troops, big, loose-hung boys, heard the planes and in the distance saw the parachutes, and they came back to town at double-quick step. When they arrived, the invader had flanked the road with machine guns. The loose-hung soldiers, having very little experience in war and none at all in defeat, opened fire with their rifles. The machine guns clattered for a moment and six of the soldiers became dead riddled bundles and three, half-dead riddled bundles, and three of the soldiers escaped into the hills with their rifles.

By ten-thirty the brass band of the invader was playing beautiful and sentimental music in the town square while the townsmen, their mouths a little open and their eyes astonished, stood about listening to the music and staring at the gray-helmeted men who carried sub-machine guns in their arms.

By ten-thirty-eight the riddled six were buried, the parachutes were folded, and the battalion was billeted in Mr. Corell's warehouse by the pier, which had on its shelves blankets and cots for a battalion.

By ten-forty-five old Mayor Orden had received the formal request that he grant an audience to Colonel Lanser of the invaders, an audience which was set for eleven sharp at the Mayor's five-room palace.

The drawing-room of the palace was very sweet and comfortable. The gilded chairs covered with their worn tapestry were set about stiffly like too many servants with nothing to do. An arched marble fireplace held its little basket of red flameless heat, and a hand-painted coal scuttle stood on the hearth. On the mantel, flanked by fat vases, stood a large, curly porcelain clock which swarmed with tumbling cherubs. The wallpaper of the room was dark red with gold figures, and the woodwork was white, pretty, and clean. The paintings on the wall were largely preoccupied with the amazing heroism of large dogs faced with imperiled children. Nor water nor fire nor earthquake could do in a child so long as a big dog was available.

Beside the fireplace old Doctor Winter sat, bearded and simple and benign, historian and physician to the town. He watched in amazement while his thumbs rolled over and over on his lap. Doctor Winter was a man so simple that only a profound man would know him as profound. He looked up at Joseph, the Mayor's servingman, to see whether Joseph had observed the rolling wonders of his thumbs.

"Eleven o'clock?" Doctor Winter asked.

And Joseph answered abstractedly, "Yes, sir. The note said eleven."

"You read the note?"

"No, sir, His Excellency read the note to me."

And Joseph went about testing each of the gilded chairs to see whether it had moved since he had last placed it. Joseph habitually scowled at furniture, expecting it to be impertinent, mischievous, or dusty. In a world where Mayor Orden was the leader of men, Joseph was the leader of furniture, silver, and dishes. Joseph was elderly and lean and serious, and his life was so complicated that only a profound man would know him to be simple. He saw nothing amazing about Doctor Winter's rolling thumbs; in fact he found them irritating. Joseph suspected that something pretty important was happening, what with foreign soldiers in the town and the local army killed or captured. Sooner or later Joseph would have to get an opinion about it all. He wanted no levity, no rolling thumbs, no nonsense from furniture. Doctor Winter moved his chair a few inches from its appointed place and Joseph waited impatiently for the moment when he could put it back again.

Doctor Winter repeated, "Eleven o'clock, and they'll be here then, too. A time-minded people, Joseph."

And Joseph said, without listening, "Yes, sir."

"A time-minded people," the doctor repeated.

"Yes, sir," said Joseph.

"Time and machines."

"Yes, sir."

"They hurry toward their destiny as though it would not wait. They push the rolling world along with their shoulders."

And Joseph said, "Quite right, sir," simply because he was getting tired of saying, "Yes, sir."

Joseph did not approve of this line of conversation, since it did not help him to have an opinion about anything. If Joseph remarked to the cook later in the day, "A time-minded people, Annie," it would not make any sense. Annie would ask, "Who?" and then "Why?" and finally say, "That's nonsense, Joseph." Joseph had tried carrying Doctor Winter's remarks below-stairs before and it had always ended the same: Annie always discovered them to be nonsense.

Doctor Winter looked up from his thumbs and watched Joseph disciplining the chairs. "What's the Mayor doing?"

"Dressing to receive the colonel, sir."

"And you aren't helping him? He will be ill dressed by himself."

"Madame is helping him. Madame wants him to look his best. She"—Joseph blushed a little—"Madame is trimming the hair out of his ears, sir. It tickles. He won't let me do it."

"Of course it tickles," said Doctor Winter.

"Madame insists," said Joseph.

Doctor Winter laughed suddenly. He stood up and

held his hands to the fire and Joseph skillfully darted behind him and replaced the chair where it should be.

"We are so wonderful," the doctor said. "Our country is falling, our town is conquered, the Mayor is about to receive the conqueror, and Madame is holding the struggling Mayor by the neck and trimming the hair out of his ears."

"He was getting very shaggy," said Joseph. "His eyebrows, too. His Excellency is even more upset about having his eyebrows trimmed than his ears. He says it hurts. I doubt if even Madame can do it."

"She will try," Doctor Winter said.

"She wants him to look his best, sir."

Through the glass window of the entrance door a helmeted face looked in and there was a rapping on the door. It seemed that some warm light went out of the room and a little grayness took its place.

Doctor Winter looked up at the clock and said, "They are early. Let them in, Joseph."

Joseph went to the door and opened it. A soldier stepped in, dressed in a long coat. He was helmeted and he carried a sub-machine gun over his arm. He glanced quickly about and then stepped aside. Behind him an officer stood in the doorway. The officer's uniform was common and it had rank showing only on the shoulders.

The officer stepped inside and looked at Doctor Winter. He was rather like an overdrawn picture of an English gentleman. He had a slouch, his face was red, his nose long but rather pleasing; he seemed about as unhappy in his uniform as most British general officers are. He stood in the doorway, staring at Doctor Winter, and he said, "Are you Mayor Orden, sir?"

Doctor Winter smiled. "No, no, I am not."

"You are an official, then?"

"No, I am the town doctor and I am a friend of the Mayor."

The officer said, "Where is Mayor Orden?"

"Dressing to receive you. You are the colonel?"

"No, I am not. I am Captain Bentick." He bowed and Doctor Winter returned the bow slightly. Captain Bentick continued, as though a little embarrassed at what he had to say. "Our military regulations, sir, prescribe that we search for weapons before the commanding officer enters a room. We mean no disrespect, sir." And he called over his shoulder, "Sergeant!"

The sergeant moved quickly to Joseph, ran his hands over his pockets, and said, "Nothing, sir."

Captain Bentick said to Doctor Winter, "I hope you will pardon us." And the sergeant went to Doctor Winter and patted his pockets. His hands stopped at the inside coat pocket. He reached quickly in, brought out a little, flat, black leather case, and took it to Captain Bentick. Captain Bentick opened the case and found there a few simple surgical instruments—two scalpels, some surgical needles, some clamps, a hypodermic needle. He closed the case again and handed it back to Doctor Winter.

Doctor Winter said, "You see, I am a country doctor. One time I had to perform an appendectomy with a kitchen knife. I have always carried these with me since then."

Captain Bentick said, "I believe there are some firearms here?" He opened a little leather book that he carried in his pocket.

Doctor Winter said, "You are thorough."

"Yes, our local man has been working here for some time."

Doctor Winter said, "I don't suppose you would tell who that man is?"

Bentick said, "His work is all done now. I don't suppose there would be any harm in telling. His name is Corell."

And Doctor Winter said in astonishment, "George Corell? Why, that seems impossible! He's done a lot for this town. Why, he even gave prizes for the shooting-match in the hills this morning." And as he said it his eyes began to understand what had happened and his mouth closed slowly, and he said, "I see; that is why he gave the shooting-match. Yes, I see. But George Corell—that sounds impossible!"

The door to the left opened and Mayor Orden came in; he was digging in his right ear with his little finger. He was dressed in his official morning coat, with his chain of office about his neck. He had a large, white, spraying mustache and two smaller ones, one over each eye. His white hair was so recently brushed that only now were the hairs struggling to be free, to stand up again. He had been Mayor so long that he was the Idea-Mayor in the town. Even grown people when they saw the word "mayor," printed or written, saw Mayor Orden in their minds. He and his office were one. It had given him dignity and he had given it warmth.

From behind him Madame emerged, small and wrinkled and fierce. She considered that she had created this man out of whole cloth, had thought him up, and she was sure that she could do a better job if she had it to do again. Only once or twice in her life had she ever understood all of him, but the part of him which she knew, she knew intricately and well. No little appetite or pain, no carelessness or meanness in him escaped her; no thought or dream or longing in him ever reached her. And yet several times in her life she had seen the stars.

She stepped around the Mayor and she took his hand and pulled his finger out of his outraged ear and pushed his hand to his side, the way she would take a baby's thumb away from his mouth.

"I don't believe for a moment it hurts as much as you say," she said, and to Doctor Winter, "He won't let me fix his eyebrows."

"It hurts," said Mayor Orden.

"Very well, if you want to look like that there is nothing I can do about it." She straightened his already straight tie. "I'm glad you're here, Doctor," she said. "How many do you think will come?" And then she looked up and saw Captain Bentick. "Oh," she said, "the colonel!"

Captain Bentick said, "No, ma'am, I'm only preparing for the colonel. Sergeant!"

The sergeant, who had been turning over pillows, looking behind pictures, came quickly to Mayor Orden and ran his hands over his pockets.

Captain Bentick said, "Excuse him, sir, it's regulations."

He glanced again at the little book in his hand. "Your Excellency, I think you have firearms here. Two items, I believe?"

Mayor Orden said, "Firearms? Guns, you mean, I guess. Yes, I have a shotgun and a sporting-rifle." He said deprecatingly, "You know, I don't hunt very much any more. I always think I'm going to, and then the season opens and I don't get out. I don't take the pleasure in it I used to."

Captain Bentick insisted. "Where are these guns, Your Excellency?"

The Mayor rubbed his cheek and tried to think. "Why, I think—" He turned to Madame. "Weren't they in the back of that cabinet in the bedroom with the walking-sticks?"

Madame said, "Yes, and every stitch of clothing in that cabinet smells of oil. I wish you'd put them somewhere else."

Captain Bentick said, "Sergeant!" and the sergeant went quickly into the bedroom.

"It's an unpleasant duty. I'm sorry," said the captain.

The sergeant came back, carrying a double-barreled shotgun and a rather nice sporting-rifle with a shoulder strap. He leaned them against the side of the entrance door.

Captain Bentick said, "That's all, thank you, Your Excellency. Thank you, Madame."

He turned and bowed slightly to Doctor Winter. "Thank you, Doctor. Colonel Lanser will be here directly. Good morning!"

And he went out of the front door, followed by the sergeant with the two guns in one hand and the submachine gun over his right arm.

Madame said, "For a moment I thought he was the colonel. He was a rather nice-looking young man."

Doctor Winter said sardonically, "No, he was just protecting the colonel."

Madame was thinking, "I wonder how many officers will come?" And she looked at Joseph and saw that he was shamelessly eavesdropping. She shook her head at him and frowned and he went back to the little things he had been doing. He began dusting all over again.

And Madame said, "How many do you think will come?"

Doctor Winter pulled out a chair outrageously and sat down again. "I don't know," he said.

"Well"—she frowned at Joseph—"we've been talking it over. Should we offer them tea or a glass of wine? If we do, I don't know how many there will be, and if we don't, what are we to do?"

Doctor Winter shook his head and smiled. "I don't know. It's been so long since we conquered anybody or anybody conquered us. I don't know what is proper."

Mayor Orden had his finger back in his itching ear. He said, "Well, I don't think we should. I don't think the people would like it. I don't want to drink wine with them. I don't know why."

Madame appealed to the doctor then. "Didn't people in the old days—the leaders, that is—compliment each other and take a glass of wine?"

Doctor Winter nodded. "Yes, indeed they did." He shook his head slowly. "Maybe that was different. Kings and princes played at war the way Englishmen play at hunting. When the fox was dead they gathered at a hunt breakfast. But Mayor Orden is probably right: the people might not like him to drink wine with the invader."

Madame said, "The people are down listening to the music. Annie told me. If they can do that, why shouldn't we keep civilized procedure alive?"

The Mayor looked steadily at her for a moment and his voice was sharp. "Madame, I think with your permission we will not have wine. The people are confused now. They have lived at peace so long that they do not quite believe in war. They will learn and then they will not be confused any more. They elected me not to be confused. Six town boys were murdered this morning. I think we will have no hunt breakfast. The people do not fight wars for sport."

Madame bowed slightly. There had been a number of times in her life when her husband had become the Mayor. She had learned not to confuse the Mayor with her husband.

Mayor Orden looked at his watch and when Joseph came in, carrying a small cup of black coffee, he took it absent-mindedly. "Thank you," he said, and he sipped it. "I should be clear," he said apologetically to Doctor Winter. "I should be—do you know how many men the invader has?"

"Not many," the doctor said. "I don't think over two hundred and fifty; but all with those little machine guns."

The Mayor sipped his coffee again and made a new start. "What about the rest of the country?"

The doctor raised his shoulders and dropped them again.

"Was there no resistance anywhere?" the Mayor went on hopelessly.

And again the doctor raised his shoulders. "I don't know. The wires are cut or captured. There is no news."

"And our boys, our soldiers?"

"I don't know," said the doctor.

Joseph interrupted. "I heard—that is, Annie heard——"

"What, Joseph?"

"Six men were killed, sir, by the machine guns. Annie heard three were wounded and captured."

"But there were twelve."

"Annie heard that three escaped."

The Mayor turned sharply. "Which ones escaped?" he demanded.

"I don't know, sir. Annie didn't hear."

Madame inspected a table for dust with her finger. She said, "Joseph, when they come, stay close to your bell. We might want some little thing. And put on your other coat, Joseph, the one with the buttons." She thought for a moment. "And, Joseph, when you finish what you are told to do, go out of the room. It makes a bad impression when you just stand around listening. It's provincial, that's what it is."

"Yes, Madame," Joseph said.

"We won't serve wine, Joseph, but you might have some cigarettes handy in that little silver conserve box. And don't strike the match to light the colonel's cigarette on your shoe. Strike it on the match-box."

"Yes, Madame."

Mayor Orden unbuttoned his coat and took out his watch and looked at it and put it back and buttoned his coat again, one button too high. Madame went to him and rebuttoned it correctly.

Doctor Winter asked, "What time is it?"

"Five of eleven."

"A time-minded people," the doctor said. "They will be here on time. Do you want me to go away?"

Mayor Orden looked startled. "Go? No—no, stay." He laughed softly. "I'm a little afraid," he said apologetically. "Well, not afraid, but I'm nervous." And he said helplessly, "We have never been conquered, for a long time–" He stopped to listen. In the distance there was a sound of band music, a march. They all turned in its direction and listened.

Madame said, "Here they come. I hope not too many try to crowd in here at once. It isn't a very big room."

Doctor Winter said sardonically, "Madame would prefer the Hall of Mirrors at Versailles?"

She pinched her lips and looked about, already placing the conquerors with her mind. "It is a very small room," she said.

The band music swelled a little and then grew fainter. There came a gentle tap on the door.

"Now, who can that be? Joseph, if it is anyone, tell him to come back later. We are very busy."

The tap came again. Joseph went to the door and opened it a crack and then a little wider. A gray figure, helmeted and gantleted, appeared.

"Colonel Lanser's compliments," the head said. "Colonel Lanser requests an audience with Your Excellency."

Joseph opened the door wide. The helmeted orderly stepped inside and looked quickly about the room and then stood aside. "Colonel Lanser!" he announced.

A second helmeted figure walked into the room, and his rank showed only on his shoulders. Behind him came a rather short man in a black business suit. The colonel was a middle-aged man, gray and hard and tired-looking. He had the square shoulders of a soldier, but his eyes lacked the blank look of the ordinary soldier. The little man beside him was bald and rosy-cheeked, with small black eyes and a sensual mouth.

Colonel Lanser took off his helmet. With a quick bow, he said, "Your Excellency!" He bowed to Madame. "Madame!" And he said, "Close the door, please, Corporal." Joseph quickly shut the door and stared in small triumph at the soldier.

Lanser looked questioningly at the doctor, and Mayor Orden said, "This is Doctor Winter."

"An official?" the colonel asked.

"A doctor, sir, and, I might say, the local historian."

Lanser bowed slightly. He said, "Doctor Winter, I do not mean to be impertinent, but there will be a page in your history, perhaps——"

And Doctor Winter smiled. "Many pages, perhaps."

Colonel Lanser turned slightly toward his companion. "I think you know Mr. Corell," he said.

The Mayor said, "George Corell? Of course I know him. How are you, George?"

Doctor Winter cut in sharply. He said, very formally, "Your Excellency, our friend, George Corell, prepared this town for the invasion. Our benefactor, George Corell, sent our soldiers into the hills. Our dinner guest, George Corell, has made a list of every firearm in the town. Our friend, George Corell!"

Corell said angrily, "I work for what I believe in! That is an honorable thing."

Orden's mouth hung a little open. He was bewildered. He looked helplessly from Winter to Corell. "This isn't true," he said. "George, this isn't true! You have sat at my table, you have drunk port with me. Why, you helped me plan the hospital! This isn't true!"

He was looking very steadily at Corell and Corell looked belligerently back at him. There was a long silence. Then the Mayor's face grew slowly tight and very formal and his whole body was rigid. He turned to Colonel Lanser and he said, "I do not wish to speak in this gentleman's company."

Corell said, "I have a right to be here! I am a soldier like the rest. I simply do not wear a uniform."

The Mayor repeated, "I do not wish to speak in this gentleman's presence."

Colonel Lanser said, "Will you leave us now, Mr. Corell?"

And Corell said, "I have a right to be here!"

Lanser repeated sharply, "Will you leave us now, Mr. Corell? Do you outrank me?"

"Well, no, sir."

"Please go, Mr. Corell," said Colonel Lanser.

And Corell looked at the Mayor angrily, and then he turned and went quickly out of the doorway. Doctor Winter chuckled and said, "That's good enough for a paragraph in my history." Colonel Lanser glanced sharply at him but he did not speak.

Now the door on the right opened, and straw-haired, red-eyed Annie put an angry face into the doorway. "There's soldiers on the back porch, Madame," she said. "Just standing there."

"They won't come in," Colonel Lanser said. "It's only military procedure."

Madame said icily, "Annie, if you have anything to say, let Joseph bring the message."

"I didn't know but they'd try to get in," Annie said. "They smelled the coffee."

"Annie!"

"Yes, Madame," and she withdrew.

The colonel said, "May I sit down?" And he explained, "We have been a long time without sleep."

The Mayor seemed to start out of sleep himself. "Yes," he said, "of course, sit down!"

The colonel looked at Madame and she seated herself and he settled tiredly into a chair. Mayor Orden stood, still half dreaming.

The colonel began, "We want to get along as well as we can. You see, sir, this is more like a business venture than anything else. We need the coal mine here and the fishing. We will try to get along with just as little friction as possible."

The Mayor said, "I have had no news. What about the rest of the country?"

"All taken," said the colonel. "It was well planned."

"Was there no resistance anywhere?"

The colonel looked at him compassionately. "I wish there had not been. Yes, there was some resistance, but it only caused bloodshed. We had planned very carefully."

Orden stuck to his point. "But there was resistance?"

"Yes, but it was foolish to resist. Just as here, it was destroyed instantly. It was sad and foolish to resist."

Doctor Winter caught some of the Mayor's anxiousness about the point. "Yes," he said, "foolish, but they resisted?"

And Colonel Lanser replied, "Only a few and they are gone. The people as a whole are quiet."

Doctor Winter said, "The people don't know yet what has happened."

"They are discovering," said Lanser. "They won't be foolish again." He cleared his throat and his voice became brisk. "Now, sir, I must get to business. I'm really very tired, but before I can sleep I must make my arrangements." He sat forward in his chair. "I am more engineer than soldier. This whole thing is more an engineering job than conquest. The coal must come out of the ground and be shipped. We have technicians, but the local people will continue to work the mine. Is that clear? We do not wish to be harsh."

And Orden said, "Yes, that's clear enough. But suppose the people do not want to work the mine?"

The colonel said, "I hope they will want to, because they must. We must have the coal."

"But if they don't?"

"They must. They are an orderly people. They don't want trouble." He waited for the Mayor's reply and none came. "Is that not so, sir?" the colonel asked.

Mayor Orden twisted his chain. "I don't know, sir. They are orderly under their own government. I don't know how they would be under yours. It is untouched ground, you see. We have built our government over four hundred years."

The colonel said quickly, "We know that, and so we are going to keep your government. You will still be the Mayor, you will give the orders, you will penalize and reward. In that way, they will not give trouble."

Mayor Orden looked at Doctor Winter. "What are you thinking about?"

"I don't know," said Doctor Winter. "It would be interesting to see. I'd expect trouble. This might be a bitter people."

Mayor Orden said, "I don't know, either." He turned to the colonel. "Sir, I am of this people, and yet I don't know what they will do. Perhaps you know. Or maybe it would be different from anything you know or we know. Some people accept appointed leaders and obey them. But my people have elected me. They made me and they can unmake me. Perhaps they will if they think I have gone over to you. I just don't know."

The colonel said, "You will be doing them a service if you keep them in order."

"A service?"

"Yes, a service. It is your duty to protect them from harm. They will be in danger if they are rebellious. We must get the coal, you see. Our leaders do not tell us how; they order us to get it. But you have your people to protect. You must make them do the work and thus keep them safe."

Mayor Orden asked, "But suppose they don't want to be safe?"

"Then you must think for them."

Orden said, a little proudly, "My people don't like to have others think for them. Maybe they are different from your people. I am confused, but that I am sure of."

Now Joseph came in quickly and he stood leaning forward, bursting to speak. Madame said, "What is it, Joseph? Get the silver box of cigarettes."

"Pardon, Madame," said Joseph. "Pardon, Your Excellency."

"What do you want?" the Mayor asked.

"It's Annie," he said. "She's getting angry, sir."

"What is the matter?" Madame demanded.

"Annie doesn't like the soldiers on the back porch."

The colonel asked, "Are they causing trouble?"

"They are looking through the door at Annie," said Joseph. "She hates that."

The colonel said, "They are carrying out orders. They are doing no harm."

"Well, Annie hates to be stared at," said Joseph.

Madame said, "Joseph, tell Annie to take care."

"Yes, Madame," and Joseph went out.

The colonel's eyes dropped with tiredness. "There's another thing, Your Excellency," he said. "Would it be possible for me and my staff to stay here?"

Mayor Orden thought a moment and he said, "It's a small place. There are larger, more comfortable places."

Then Joseph came back with the silver box of cigarettes and he opened it and held it in front of the colonel. When the colonel took one, Joseph ostentatiously lighted it. The colonel puffed deeply.

"It isn't that," he said. "We have found that when a staff lives under the roof of the local authority, there is more tranquillity."

"You mean," said Orden, "the people feel there is collaboration involved?"

"Yes, I suppose that is it."

Mayor Orden looked hopelessly at Doctor Winter, and Winter could offer him nothing but a wry smile. Orden said softly, "Am I permitted to refuse this honor?"

"I'm sorry," the colonel said. "No. These are the orders of my leader."

"The people will not like it," Orden said.

"Always the people! The people are disarmed. The people have no say."

Mayor Orden shook his head. "You do not know, sir."

From the doorway came the sound of an angry woman's voice, and a thump and a man's cry. Joseph came scuttling through the door. "She's thrown boiling water," Joseph said. "She's very angry."

There were commands through the door and the clump of feet. Colonel Lanser got up heavily. "Have you no control over your servants, sir?" he asked.

Mayor Orden smiled. "Very little," he said. "She's a good cook when she is happy. Was anyone hurt?" he asked Joseph.

"The water was boiling, sir."

Colonel Lanser said, "We just want to do our job. It's an engineering job. You will have to discipline your cook."

"I can't," said Orden. "She'll quit."

"This is an emergency. She can't quit."

"Then she'll throw water," said Doctor Winter.

The door opened and a soldier stood in the opening. "Shall I arrest this woman, sir?"

"Was anyone hurt?" Lanser asked.

"Yes, sir, scalded, and one man bitten. We are holding her, sir."

Lanser looked helpless, then he said, "Release her and go outside and off the porch."

"Yes, sir," and the door closed behind the soldier.

Lanser said, "I could have her shot; I could lock her up."

"Then we would have no cook," said Orden.

"Look," said the colonel. "We are instructed to get along with your people."

Madame said, "Excuse me, sir, I will just go and see if the soldiers hurt Annie," and she went out.

Now Lanser stood up. "I told you I'm very tired, sir. I must have some sleep. Please co-operate with us for the good of all." When Mayor Orden made no reply, "For the good of all," Lanser repeated. "Will you?"

Orden said, "This is a little town. I don't know. The people are confused and so am I."

"But will you try to co-operate?"

Orden shook his head. "I don't know. When the town makes up its mind what it wants to do, I'll probably do that."

"But you are the authority."

Orden smiled. "You won't believe this, but it is true: authority is in the town. I don't know how or why, but it is so. This means we cannot act as quickly as you can, but when a direction is set, we all act together. I am confused. I don't know yet."

Lanser said wearily, "I hope we can get along together. It will be so much easier for everyone. I hope we can trust you. I don't like to think of the means the military will take to keep order."

Mayor Orden was silent.

"I hope we can trust you," Lanser repeated.

Orden put his finger in his ear and wiggled his hand. "I don't know," he said.

Madame came through the door then. "Annie is furious," she said. "She is next door, talking to Christine. Christine is angry, too."

"Christine is even a better cook than Annie," said the Mayor.

CHAPTER TWO

UPSTAIRS in the little palace of the Mayor the staff of Colonel Lanser made its headquarters. There were five of them besides the colonel. There was Major Hunter, a haunted little man of figures, a little man who, being a dependable unit, considered all other men either as dependable units or as unfit to live. Major Hunter was an engineer, and except in case of war no one would have thought of giving him command of men. For Major Hunter set his men in rows like figures and he added and subtracted and multiplied them. He was an arithmetician rather than a mathematician. None of the humor, the music, or the mysticism of higher mathematics ever entered his head. Men might vary in height or weight or color, just as 6 is different from 8, but there was little other difference. He had been married several times and he did not know why his wives became very nervous before they left him.

Captain Bentick was a family man, a lover of dogs and pink children and Christmas. He was too old to be a captain, but a curious lack of ambition had kept him in that rank. Before the war he had admired the British country gentleman very much, wore English clothes, kept English dogs, smoked in an English pipe a special pipe mixture sent him from London, and subscribed to those country magazines which extol gardening and continually argue about the relative merits of English and Gordon setters. Captain Bentick spent all his holidays in Sussex and liked to be mistaken for an Englishman in Budapest or Paris. The war changed all that outwardly, but he had sucked on a pipe too long, had carried a stick too long, to give them up too suddenly. Once, five years before, he had written a letter to the *Times* about grass dying in the Midlands and had signed it Edmund Twitchell, Esq.; and, furthermore, the *Times* had printed it.

If Captain Bentick was too old to be a captain, Captain Loft was too young. Captain Loft was as much a captain as one can imagine. He lived and breathed his captaincy. He had no unmilitary moments. A driving ambition forced him up through the grades. He rose like cream to the top of milk. He clicked his heels as perfectly as a dancer does. He knew every kind of military courtesy and insisted on using it all. Generals were afraid of him because he knew more about the deportment of a soldier than they did. Captain Loft thought and believed that a soldier is the highest development of animal life. If he considered God at all, he thought of Him as an old and honored general, retired and gray, living among remembered battles and putting wreaths on the graves of his lieutenants several times a year. Captain Loft believed that all women fall in love with a uniform and he did not see how it could be otherwise. In the normal course of events he would be a brigadier-general at forty-five and have his picture in the illustrated papers, flanked by tall, pale, masculine women wearing lacy picture hats.

Lieutenants Prackle and Tonder were snot-noses, undergraduates, lieutenants, trained in the politics of the day, believing the great new system invented by a genius so great that they never bothered to verify its results. They were sentimental young men, given to tears and to furies. Lieutenant Prackle carried a lock of hair in the back of his watch, wrapped in a bit of blue satin, and the hair was constantly getting loose and clogging the balance wheel, so that he wore a wrist watch for telling time. Prackle was a dancing-partner, a gay young man who nevertheless could scowl like the Leader, could brood like the Leader. He hated degenerate art and had destroyed several canvases with his own hands. In cabarets he sometimes made pencil sketches of his companions which were so good that he had often been told he should have been an artist. Prackle had several blond sisters of whom he was so proud that he had on occasion caused a commotion when he thought they had been insulted. The sisters were a little disturbed about it because they were afraid someone might set out to prove the insults, which would not have been hard to do. Lieutenant Prackle spent nearly all his time off duty day-dreaming of seducing Lieutenant Tonder's blond sister, a buxom girl who loved to be seduced by older men who did not muss her hair as Lieutenant Prackle did.

Lieutenant Tonder was a poet, a bitter poet who dreamed of perfect, ideal love of elevated young men for poor girls. Tonder was a dark romantic with a vision as wide as his experience. He sometimes spoke blank verse under his breath to imaginary dark women. He longed for death on the battlefield, with weeping parents in the background, and the Leader, brave but sad in the presence of the dying youth. He imagined his death very often, lighted by a fair setting sun which glinted on broken military equipment, his men standing silently around him, with heads sunk low, as over a fat cloud galloped the Valkyries, big-breasted, mothers and mistresses in one, while Wagnerian thunder crashed in the background. And he even had his dying words ready.

These were the men of the staff, each one playing war as children play "Run, Sheep, Run." Major Hunter thought of war as an arithmetical job to be done so he could get back to his fireplace; Captain Loft as the proper career of a properly brought-up young man; and Lieutenants Prackle and Tonder as a dreamlike thing in which nothing was very real. And their war so far had been play—fine weapons and fine planning against unarmed, planless enemies. They had lost no fights and suffered little hurt. They were, under pressure, capable of cowardice or courage, as everyone is. Of them all, only Colonel Lanser knew what war really is in the long run.

Lanser had been in Belgium and France twenty years before and he tried not to think what he knew—that war is treachery and hatred, the muddling of incompetent generals, the torture and killing and sickness and tiredness, until at last it is over and nothing has changed except for new weariness and new hatreds. Lanser told himself he was a soldier, given orders to carry out. He was not expected to question or to think, but only to carry out orders; and he tried to put aside the sick memories of the other war and the certainty that this would be the same. This one will be different, he said to himself fifty times a day; this one will be very different.

In marching, in mobs, in football games, and in war, outlines become vague; real things become unreal and a fog creeps over the mind. Tension and excitement, weariness, movement—all merge in one great gray dream, so that when it is over, it is hard to remember how it was when you killed men or ordered them to be killed. Then other people who were not there tell you what it was like and you say vaguely, "Yes, I guess that's how it was."

This staff had taken three rooms on the upper floor of the Mayor's palace. In the bedrooms they had put their cots and blankets and equipment, and in the room next to them and directly over the little drawing-room on the ground floor they had made a kind of club, rather an uncomfortable club. There were a few chairs and a table. Here they wrote letters and read letters. They talked and ordered coffee and planned and rested. On the walls between the windows there were pictures of cows and lakes and little farmhouses, and from the windows they could look down over the town to the waterfront, to the docks where the shipping was tied up, to the docks where the coal barges pulled up and took their loads and went out to sea. They could look down over the little town that twisted past the square to the waterfront, and they could see the fishing-boats lying at anchor in the bay, the sails furled, and they could smell the drying fish on the beach, right through the window.

There was a large table in the center of the room and Major Hunter sat beside it. He had his drawing-board in his lap and resting on the table, and with a T-square and triangle he worked at a design for a new railroad siding. The drawing-board was unsteady and the major was growing angry with its unsteadiness. He called over his shoulder, "Prackle!" And then, "Lieutenant Prackle!"

The bedroom door opened and the lieutenant came out, half his face covered with shaving-cream. He held the brush in his hand. "Yes?" he said.

Major Hunter jiggled his drawing-board. "Hasn't that tripod for my board turned up in the baggage?"

"I don't know, sir," said Prackle. "I didn't look."

"Well, look now, will you? It's bad enough to have to work in this light. I'll have to draw this again before I ink it."

Prackle said, "Just as soon as I finish shaving, I'll look."

Hunter said irritably, "This siding is more important than your looks. See if there is a canvas case like a golf bag under that pile in there."

Prackle disappeared into the bedroom. The door to

the right opened and Captain Loft came in. He wore his helmet, a pair of field glasses, sidearm, and various little leather cases strung all over him. He began to remove his equipment as soon as he entered.

"You know, that Bentick's crazy," he said. "He was going out on duty in a fatigue cap, right down the street."

Loft put his field glasses on the table and took off his helmet, then his gas-mask bag. A little pile of equipment began to heap up on the table.

Hunter said, "Don't leave that stuff there. I have to work here. Why shouldn't he wear a cap? There hasn't been any trouble. I get sick of these tin things. They're heavy and you can't see."

Loft said primly, "It's bad practice to leave it off. It's bad for the people here. We must maintain a military standard, an alertness, and never vary it. We'll just invite trouble if we don't."

"What makes you think so?" Hunter asked.

Loft drew himself up a little. His mouth thinned with certainty. Sooner or later everyone wanted to punch Loft in the nose for his sureness about things. He said, "I don't think it. I was paraphrasing *Manual*

X-12 on deportment in occupied countries. It is very carefully worked out." He began to say, "You—" and then changed it to, "Everybody should read *X-12* very closely."

Hunter said, "I wonder whether the man who wrote it was ever in occupied country. These people are harmless enough. They seem to be good, obedient people."

Prackle came through the door, his face still half covered with shaving-soap. He carried a brown canvas tube, and behind him came Lieutenant Tonder. "Is this it?" Prackle asked.

"Yes. Unpack it, will you, and set it up."

Prackle and Tonder went to work on the folding tripod and tested it and put it near Hunter. The major screwed his board to it, tilted it right and left, and finally settled gruntingly behind it.

Captain Loft said, "Do you know you have soap on your face, Lieutenant?"

"Yes, sir," Prackle said. "I was shaving when the major asked me to get the tripod."

"Well, you had better get it off," Loft said. "The colonel might see you."

"Oh, he wouldn't mind. He doesn't care about things like that."

Tonder was looking over Hunter's shoulder as he worked.

Loft said, "Well, he may not, but it doesn't look right."

Prackle took a handkerchief and rubbed the soap from his cheek. Tonder pointed to a little drawing on the corner of the major's board. "That's a nice-looking bridge, Major. But where in the world are we going to build a bridge?"

Hunter looked down at the drawing and then over his shoulder at Tonder. "Huh? Oh, that isn't any bridge we're going to build. Up here is the work drawing."

"What are you doing with a bridge, then?"

Hunter seemed a little embarrassed. "Well, you know, in my back yard at home I've got a model railroad line. I was going to bridge a little creek for it. Brought the line right down to the creek, but I never did get the bridge built. I thought I'd kind of work it out while I was away."

Lieutenant Prackle took from his pocket a folded

rotogravure page and he unfolded it and held it up and looked at it. It was a picture of a girl, all legs and dress and eyelashes, a well-developed blonde in black openwork stockings and a low bodice, and this particular blonde peeped over a black lace fan. Lieutenant Prackle held her up and he said, "Isn't she something?" Lieutenant Tonder looked critically at the picture and said, "I don't like her."

"What don't you like about her?"

"I just don't like her," said Tonder. "What do you want her picture for?"

Prackle said, "Because I do like her and I bet you do, too."

"I do not," said Tonder.

"You mean to say you wouldn't take a date with her if you could?" Prackle asked.

Tonder said, "No."

"Well, you're just crazy," and Prackle went to one of the curtains. He said, "I'm just going to stick her up here and let you brood about her for a while." He pinned the picture to the curtain.

Captain Loft was gathering his equipment into his

arms now, and he said, "I don't think it looks very well out here, Lieutenant. You'd better take it down. It wouldn't make a good impression on the local people."

Hunter looked up from his board. "What wouldn't?" He followed their eyes to the picture. "Who's that?" he asked.

"She's an actress," said Prackle.

Hunter looked at her carefully. "Oh, do you know her?"

Tonder said, "She's a tramp."

Hunter said, "Oh, then you know her?"

Prackle was looking steadily at Tonder. He said, "Say, how do you know she's a tramp?"

"She looks like a tramp," said Tonder.

"Do you know her?"

"No, and I don't want to."

Prackle began to say, "Then how do you know?" when Loft broke in. He said, "You'd better take the picture down. Put it up over your bed if you want to. This room's kind of official here."

Prackle looked at him mutinously and was about to speak when Captain Loft said, "That's an order, Lieutenant," and poor Prackle folded his paper and put it into his pocket again. He tried cheerily to change the subject. "There are some pretty girls in this town, all right," he said. "As soon as we get settled down and everything going smoothly, I'm going to get acquainted with a few."

Loft said, "You'd better read *X-12.* There's a section dealing with sexual matters." And he went out, carrying his duffel, glasses, and equipment. Lieutenant Tonder, still looking over Hunter's shoulder, said, "That's clever—the coal cars come right through the mines to the ship."

Hunter came slowly out of his work and he said, "We have to speed it up; we've got to get that coal moving. It's a big job. I'm awful thankful that the people here are calm and sensible."

Loft came back into the room without his equipment. He stood by the window, looking out toward the harbor, toward the coal mine, and he said, "They are calm and sensible because we are calm and sensible. I think we can take credit for that. That's why I keep harping on procedure. It is very carefully worked out."

The door opened and Colonel Lanser came in, removing his coat as he entered. His staff gave him military courtesy—not very rigid, but enough. Lanser said, "Captain Loft, will you go down and relieve Bentick? He isn't feeling well, says he's dizzy."

"Yes, sir," said Loft. "May I suggest, sir, that I only recently came off duty?"

Lanser inspected him closely. "I hope you don't mind going, Captain."

"Not at all, sir; I just mention it for the record."

Lanser relaxed and chuckled. "You like to be mentioned in the reports, don't you?"

"It does no harm, sir."

"And when you have enough mentions," Lanser went on, "there will be a little dangler on your chest."

"They are the milestones in a military career, sir."

Lanser sighed. "Yes, I guess they are. But they won't be the ones you'll remember, Captain."

"Sir?" Loft asked.

"You'll know what I mean later—perhaps."

Captain Loft put his equipment on rapidly. "Yes, sir," he said, and went out and his footsteps clattered down the wooden stairs, and Lanser watched him go with a little amusement. He said quietly, "There goes a born soldier." And Hunter looked up and poised his pencil and he said, "A born ass."

"No," said Lanser, "he's being a soldier the way a lot of men would be politicians. He'll be on the General Staff before long. He'll look down on war from above and so he'll always love it."

Lieutenant Prackle said, "When do you think the war will be over, sir?"

"Over? Over? What do you mean?"

Lieutenant Prackle continued, "How soon will we win?"

Lanser shook his head. "Oh, I don't know. The enemy is still in the world."

"But we will lick them," said Prackle.

Lanser said, "Yes?"

"Won't we?"

"Yes; yes, we always do."

Prackle said excitedly, "Well, if it's quiet around Christmas, do you think there will be some furloughs granted?"

"I don't know," said Lanser. "Such orders will have to come from home. Do you want to get home for Christmas?"

"Well, I'd kind of like to."

"Maybe you will," said Lanser, "maybe you will."

Lieutenant Tonder said, "We won't drop out of this occupation, will we, sir, after the war is over?"

"I don't know," said the colonel. "Why?"

"Well," said Tonder, "it's a nice country, nice people. Our men—some of them—might even settle here."

Lanser said jokingly, "You've seen some place you like, perhaps?"

"Well," said Tonder, "there are some beautiful farms here. If four or five of them were thrown together, it would be a nice place to settle, I think."

"You have no family land, then?" Lanser asked.

"No, sir, not any more. Inflation took it away."

Lanser was tired now of talking to children. He said, "Ah, well, we still have a war to fight. We still have coal to take out. Do you suppose we can wait until it is over before we build up these estates? Such orders will come from above. Captain Loft can tell you that." His manner changed. He said, "Hunter, your steel will be in tomorrow. You can get your tracks started this week."

There was a knock at the door and a sentry put his head in. He said, "Mr. Corell wishes to see you, sir."

"Send him in," said the colonel. And he said to the others, "This is the man who did the preliminary work here. We might have some trouble with him."

"Did he do a good job?" Tonder asked.

"Yes, he did, and he won't be popular with the people here. I wonder whether he will be popular with us."

"He deserves credit, certainly," Tonder said.

"Yes," Lanser said, "and don't think he won't claim it."

Corell came in, rubbing his hands. He radiated good-will and good-fellowship. He was dressed still in his black business suit, but on his head there was a patch of white bandage, stuck to his hair with a cross of adhesive tape. He advanced to the center of the room and said, "Good morning, Colonel. I should have called yesterday after the trouble downstairs, but I knew how busy you would be."

The colonel said, "Good morning." Then with a circular gesture of his hand. "This is my staff, Mr. Corell."

"Fine boys," said Corell. "They did a good job. Well, I tried to prepare for them well."

Hunter looked down at his board and he took out an inking-pen and dipped it and began to ink in his drawing.

Lanser said, "You did very well. I wish you hadn't killed those six men, though. I wish their soldiers hadn't come back."

Corell spread his hands and said comfortably, "Six men is a small loss for a town of this size, with a coal mine, too."

Lanser said sternly, "I am not averse to killing people if that finishes it. But sometimes it is better not to."

Corell had been studying the officers. He looked sideways at the lieutenants, and he said, "Could we—perhaps—talk alone, Colonel?"

"Yes, if you wish. Lieutenant Prackle and Lieutenant Tonder, will you go to your room, please?" And the colonel said to Corell, "Major Hunter is working. He doesn't hear anything when he's working." Hunter looked up from his board and smiled quietly and looked down again. The young lieutenants left the room, and when they were gone Lanser said, "Well, here we are. Won't you sit down?"

"Thank you, sir," and Corell sat down behind the table.

Lanser looked at the bandage on Corell's head. He said bluntly, "Have they tried to kill you already?"

Corell felt the bandage with his fingers. "This? Oh, this was a stone that fell from a cliff in the hills this morning."

"You're sure it wasn't thrown?"

"What do you mean?" Corell asked. "These aren't fierce people. They haven't had a war for a hundred years. They've forgotten about fighting."

"Well, you've lived among them," said the colonel. "You ought to know." He stepped close to Corell. "But if you are safe, these people are different from any in the world. I've helped to occupy countries before. I was in Belgium twenty years ago and in France." He shook his head a little as though to clear it, and he said gruffly, "You did a good job. We should thank you. I mentioned your work in my report."

"Thank you, sir," said Corell. "I did my best."

Lanser said, a little wearily, "Well, sir, now what shall we do? Would you like to go back to the capital? We can put you on a coal barge if you're in a hurry, or on a destroyer if you want to wait."

Corell said, "But I don't want to go back. I'll stay here."

Lanser studied this for a moment and he said, "You know, I haven't a great many men. I can't give you a very adequate bodyguard."

"But I don't need a bodyguard. I tell you these aren't violent people."

Lanser looked at the bandage for a moment. Hunter glanced up from his board and remarked, "You'd better start wearing a helmet." He looked down at his work again.

Now Corell moved forward in his chair. "I wanted particularly to talk to you, Colonel. I thought I might help with the civil administration."

Lanser turned on his heel and walked to the window and looked out, and then he swung around and said quietly, "What have you in mind?"

"Well, you must have a civil authority you can trust. I thought perhaps that Mayor Orden might step down now and—well, if I were to take over his office, it and the military would work very nicely together."

Lanser's eyes seemed to grow large and bright. He came close to Corell and he spoke sharply. "Have you mentioned this in your report?"

Corell said, "Well, yes, naturally—in my analysis."

Lanser interrupted. "Have you talked to any of the town people since we arrived—outside of the Mayor, that is?"

"Well, no. You see, they are still a bit startled. They didn't expect it." He chuckled. "No, sir, they certainly didn't expect it."

But Lanser pressed his point. "So you don't really know what's going on in their minds?"

"Why, they're startled," said Corell. "They're—well, they're almost dreaming."

"You don't know what they think of you?" Lanser asked.

"I have many friends here. I know everyone."

"Did anyone buy anything in your store this morning?"

"Well, of course, business is at a standstill," Corell answered. "No one's buying anything."

Lanser relaxed suddenly. He went to a chair and sat down and crossed his legs. He said quietly, "Yours is a difficult and brave branch of the service. It should be greatly rewarded."

"Thank you, sir."

"You will have their hatred in time," said the colonel.

"I can stand that, sir. They are the enemy."

Now Lanser hesitated a long moment before he spoke, and then he said softly, "You will not even have *our* respect."

Corell jumped to his feet excitedly. "This is contrary to the Leader's words!" he said. "The Leader has said that all branches are equally honorable."

Lanser went on very quietly, "I hope the Leader knows. I hope he can read the minds of soldiers." And then almost compassionately he said, "You should be greatly rewarded." For a moment he sat quietly and then he pulled himself together and said, "Now we must come to exactness. I am in charge here. My job is to get coal out. To do that I must maintain order and discipline, and to do that I must know what is in the minds of these people. I must anticipate revolt. Do you understand that?"

"Well, I can find out what you wish to know, sir. As Mayor here, I will be very effective," said Corell.

Lanser shook his head. "I have no orders about this. I must use my own judgment. I think you will never again know what is going on here. I think no one will speak to you; no one will be near to you except those people who will live on money, who can live on money. I think without a guard you will be in great danger. It will please me if you go back to the capital, there to be rewarded for your fine work."

"But my place is here, sir," said Corell. "I have made my place. It is all in my report."

Lanser went on as though he had not heard. "Mayor Orden is more than a mayor," he said. "He is his people. He knows what they are doing, thinking, without asking, because he will think what they think. By watching him I will know them. He must stay. That is my judgment."

Corell said, "My work, sir, merits better treatment than being sent away."

"Yes, it does," Lanser said slowly. "But to the larger work I think you are only a detriment now. If you are not hated yet, you will be. In any little revolt you will be the first to be killed. I think I will suggest that you go back."

Corell said stiffly, "You will, of course, permit me to wait for a reply to my report to the capital?"

"Yes, of course. But I shall recommend that you go back for your own safety. Frankly, Mr. Corell, you have no value here. But—well, there must be other plans and other countries. Perhaps you will go now to some new town in some new country. You will win new confidence in a new field. You may be given a larger town, even a city, a greater responsibility. I think I will recommend you highly for your work here."

Corell's eyes were shining with gratification. "Thank you, sir," he said. "I've worked hard. Perhaps you are right. But you must permit me to wait for the reply from the capital."

Lanser's voice was tight. His eyes were slitted. He said harshly, "Wear a helmet, keep indoors, do not go out at night, and, above all, do not drink. Trust no woman nor any man. Do you understand that?"

Corell looked pityingly at the colonel. "I don't think you understand. I have a little house. A pleasant country girl waits on me. I even think she's a little fond of me. These are simple, peaceful people. I know them."

Lanser said, "There are no peaceful people. When will you learn it? There are no friendly people. Can't you understand that? We have invaded this country—you, by what they call treachery, prepared for us." His face grew red and his voice rose. "Can't you understand that we are at war with these people?"

Corell said, a little smugly, "We have defeated them."

The colonel stood up and swung his arms helplessly, and Hunter looked up from his board and put his hand out to protect his board from being jiggled. Hunter said, "Careful now, sir. I'm inking in. I wouldn't want to do it all over again."

Lanser looked down at him and said, "Sorry," and went on as though he were instructing a class. He said, "Defeat is a momentary thing. A defeat doesn't last. We were defeated and now we attack. Defeat means nothing. Can't you understand that? Do you know what they are whispering behind doors?"

Corell asked, "Do you?"

"No, but I suspect."

Then Corell said insinuatingly, "Are you afraid, Colonel? Should the commander of this occupation be afraid?"

Lanser sat down heavily and said, "Maybe that's it." And he said disgustedly, "I'm tired of people who have not been at war who know all about it." He held his chin in his hand and said, "I remember a little old woman in Brussels—sweet face, white hair; she was only four feet eleven; delicate old hands. You could see the veins almost black against her skin. And her black shawl and her blue-white hair. She used to sing our national songs to us in a quivering, sweet voice. She always knew where to find a cigarette or a virgin." He dropped his hand from his chin, and he caught himself as though he had been asleep. "We didn't know her son had been executed," he said. "When we finally shot her, she had killed twelve men with a long, black hatpin. I have it yet at home. It has an enamel button with a bird over it, red and blue."

Corell said, "But you shot her?"

"Of course we shot her."

"And the murders stopped?" asked Corell.

"No, the murders did not stop. And when we finally retreated, the people cut off stragglers and they burned some and they gouged the eyes from some, and some they even crucified."

Corell said loudly, "These are not good things to say, Colonel."

"They are not good things to remember," said Lanser.

Corell said, "You should not be in command if you are afraid."

And Lanser answered softly, "I know how to fight, you see. If you know, at least you do not make silly errors."

"Do you talk this way to the young officers?"

Lanser shook his head. "No, they wouldn't believe me."

"Why do you tell me, then?"

"Because, Mr. Corell, your work is done. I remember one time—" and as he spoke there was a tumble of feet on the stairs and the door burst open. A sentry looked in and Captain Loft brushed past him. Loft was rigid and cold and military; he said, "There's trouble, sir."

"Trouble?"

"I have to report, sir, that Captain Bentick has been killed."

Lanser said, "Oh—yes—Bentick!"

There was the sound of a number of footsteps on the stairs and two stretcher-bearers came in, carrying a figure covered with blankets.

Lanser said, "Are you sure he's dead?"

"Quite sure," Loft said stiffly.

The lieutenants came in from the bedroom, their mouths a little open, and they looked frightened. Lanser said, "Put him down there," and he pointed to the wall beside the windows. When the bearers had gone, Lanser knelt and lifted a corner of the blanket and then quickly put it down again. And still kneeling, he looked at Loft and said, "Who did this?"

"A miner," said Loft.

"Why?"

"I was there, sir."

"Well, make your report, then! Make your report, damn it, man!"

Loft drew himself up and said formally, "I had just relieved Captain Bentick, as the colonel ordered. Captain Bentick was about to leave to come here when I had some trouble about a recalcitrant miner who wanted to quit work. He shouted something about being a free man. When I ordered him to work, he rushed at me with his pick. Captain Bentick tried to interfere." He gestured slightly toward the body.

Lanser, still kneeling, nodded slowly. "Bentick was a curious man," he said. "He loved the English. He loved everything about them. I don't think he liked to fight very much. . . . You captured the man?"

"Yes, sir," Loft said.

Lanser stood up slowly and spoke as though to himself. "So it starts again. We will shoot this man and make twenty new enemies. It's the only thing we know, the only thing we know."

Prackle said, "What do you say, sir?"

Lanser answered, "Nothing, nothing at all. I was just thinking." He turned to Loft and said, "Please give my compliments to Mayor Orden and my request that he see me immediately. It is very important."

Major Hunter looked up, dried his inking-pen carefully, and put it away in a velvet-lined box.

CHAPTER THREE

In the town the people moved sullenly through the streets. Some of the light of astonishment was gone from their eyes, but still a light of anger had not taken its place. In the coal shaft the workingmen pushed the coal cars sullenly. The small tradesmen stood behind their counters and served the people, but no one communicated with them. The people spoke to one another in monosyllables, and everyone was thinking of the war, thinking of himself, thinking of the past and how it had suddenly been changed.

In the drawing-room of the palace of Mayor Orden a small fire burned and the lights were on, for it was a gray day outside and there was frost in the air. The room was itself undergoing a change. The tapestry-covered chairs were pushed back, the little tables out of the way, and through the doorway to the right Joseph and Annie were struggling to bring in a large, square dining-table. They had it on its side. Joseph was in the drawing-room and Annie's red face showed through the door. Joseph maneuvered the legs around sideways, and he cried, "Don't push, Annie! Now!"

"I am 'now-ing,'" said Annie the red-nosed, the red-eyed, the angry. Annie was always a little angry and these soldiers, this occupation, did not improve her temper. Indeed, what for years had been considered simply a bad disposition was suddenly become a patriotic emotion. Annie had gained some little reputation as an exponent of liberty by throwing hot water on the soldiers. She would have thrown it on anyone who cluttered up her porch, but it just happened that she had become a heroine; and since anger had been the beginning of her success, Annie went on to new successes by whipping herself into increased and constant anger.

"Don't scuff the bottom," Joseph said. The table wedged in the doorway. "Steady!" Joseph warned.

"I am steady," said Annie.

Joseph stood off and studied the table, and Annie crossed her arms and glared at him. He tested a leg. "Don't push," he said. "Don't push so hard." And by himself he got the table through while Annie followed with crossed arms. "Now, up she goes," said Joseph, and at last Annie helped him settle it on four legs and move it to the center of the room. "There," Annie said. "If His Excellency hadn't told me to, I wouldn't have done it. What right have they got moving tables around?"

"What right coming in at all?" said Joseph.

"None," said Annie.

"None," repeated Joseph. "I see it like they have no right at all, but they do it, with their guns and their parachutes; they do it, Annie."

"They got no right," said Annie. "What do they want with a table in here, anyway? This isn't a dining-room."

Joseph moved a chair up to the table and he set it carefully at the right distance from the table, and he adjusted it. "They're going to hold a trial," he said. "They're going to try Alexander Morden."

"Molly Morden's husband?"

"Molly Morden's husband."

"For bashing that fellow with a pick?"

"That's right," said Joseph.

"But he's a nice man," Annie said. "They've got no right to try him. He gave Molly a big red dress for her birthday. What right have they got to try Alex?"

"Well," Joseph explained, "he killed this fellow."

"Suppose he did; the fellow ordered Alex around. I heard about it. Alex doesn't like to be ordered. Alex's been an alderman in his time, and his father, too. And Molly Morden makes a nice cake," Annie said charitably. "But her frosting gets too hard. What'll they do with Alex?"

"Shoot him," Joseph said gloomily.

"They can't do that."

"Bring up the chairs, Annie. Yes, they can. They'll just do it."

Annie shook a very rigid finger in his face. "You remember my words," she said angrily. "People aren't going to like it if they hurt Alex. People like Alex. Did he ever hurt anybody before? Answer me that!"

"No," said Joseph.

"Well, there, you see! If they hurt Alex, people are going to be mad and I'm going to be mad. I won't stand for it!"

"What will you do?" Joseph asked her.

"Why, I'll kill some of them myself," said Annie.

"And then they'll shoot you," said Joseph.

"Let them! I tell you, Joseph, things can go too far —tramping in and out all hours of the night, shooting people."

Joseph adjusted a chair at the head of the table, and he became in some curious way a conspirator. He said softly, "Annie."

She paused and, sensing his tone, walked nearer to him. He said, "Can you keep a secret?"

She looked at him with a little admiration, for he had never had a secret before. "Yes. What is it?"

"Well, William Deal and Walter Doggel got away last night."

"Got away? Where?"

"They got away to England, in a boat."

Annie sighed with pleasure and anticipation. "Does everybody know it?"

"Well, not everybody," said Joseph. "Everybody

but—" and he pointed a quick thumb toward the ceiling.

"When did they go? Why didn't I hear about it?"

"You were busy." Joseph's voice and face were cold. "You know that Corell?"

"Yes."

Joseph came close to her. "I don't think he's going to live long."

"What do you mean?" Annie asked.

"Well, people are talking."

Annie sighed with tension. "Ah-h-h!!"

Joseph at last had opinions. "People are getting together," he said. "They don't like to be conquered. Things are going to happen. You keep your eyes peeled, Annie. There're going to be things for you to do."

Annie asked, "How about His Excellency? What's he going to do? How does His Excellency stand?"

"Nobody knows," said Joseph. "He doesn't say anything."

"He wouldn't be against us," Annie said.

"He doesn't say," said Joseph.

The knob turned on the left-hand door, and Mayor

Orden came in slowly. He looked tired and old. Behind him Doctor Winter walked. Orden said, "That's good, Joseph. Thank you, Annie. It looks very well."

They went out and Joseph looked back through the door for a moment before he closed it.

Mayor Orden walked to the fire and turned to warm his back. Doctor Winter pulled out the chair at the head of the table and sat down. "I wonder how much longer I can hold this position?" Orden said. "The people don't quite trust me and neither does the enemy. I wonder whether this is a good thing."

"I don't know;" said Winter. "You trust yourself, don't you? There's no doubt in your own mind?"

"Doubt? No. I am the Mayor. I don't understand many things." He pointed to the table. "I don't know why they have to hold this trial in here. They're going to try Alex Morden here for murder. You remember Alex? He has that pretty little wife, Molly."

"I remember," said Winter. "She used to teach in the grammar school. Yes, I remember. She's so pretty, she hated to get glasses when she needed them. Well, I guess Alex killed an officer, all right. Nobody's questioned that."

Mayor Orden said bitterly, "Nobody questions it. But why do they try him? Why don't they shoot him? This is not a matter of doubt or certainty, justice or injustice. There's none of that here. Why must they try him—and in my house?"

Winter said, "I would guess it is for the show. There's an idea about it: if you go through the form of a thing, you have it, and sometimes people are satisfied with the form of a thing. We had an army—soldiers with guns—but it wasn't an army, you see. The invaders will have a trial and hope to convince the people that there is justice involved. Alex did kill the captain, you know."

"Yes, I see that," Orden said.

And Winter went on, "If it comes from your house, where the people expect justice——"

He was interrupted by the opening of the door to the right. A young woman entered. She was about thirty and quite pretty. She carried her glasses in her hand. She was dressed simply and neatly and she was very excited. She said quickly, "Annie told me to come right in, sir."

"Why, of course," said the Mayor. "You're Molly Morden."

"Yes, sir, I am. They say that Alex is to be tried and shot."

Orden looked down at the floor for a moment, and Molly went on, "They say you will sentence him. It will be your words that send him out."

Orden looked up, startled. "What's this? Who says this?"

"The people in the town." She held herself very straight and she asked, half pleadingly, half demandingly, "You wouldn't do that, would you, sir?"

"How could the people know what I don't know?" he said.

"That is a great mystery," said Doctor Winter. "That is a mystery that has disturbed rulers all over the world—how the people know. It disturbs the invaders now, I am told, how news runs through censorships, how the truth of things fights free of control. It is a great mystery."

The girl looked up, for the room had suddenly darkened, and she seemed to be afraid. "It's a cloud," she said. "There's word snow is on the way, and it's early, too." Doctor Winter went to the window and squinted up at the sky, and he said, "Yes, it's a big cloud; maybe it will pass over."

Mayor Orden switched on a lamp that made only a little circle of light. He switched it off again and said, "A light in the daytime is a lonely thing."

Now Molly came near to him again. "Alex is not a murdering man," she said. "He's a quick-tempered man, but he's never broken a law. He's a respected man."

Orden rested his hand on her shoulder and he said, "I have known Alex since he was a little boy. I knew his father and his grandfather. His grandfather was a bear-hunter in the old days. Did you know that?"

Molly ignored him. "You wouldn't sentence Alex?"

"No," he said. "How could I sentence him?"

"The people said you would, for the sake of order."

Mayor Orden stood behind a chair and gripped its back with his hands. "Do the people want order, Molly?"

"I don't know," she said. "They want to be free."

"Well, do they know how to go about it? Do they know what method to use against an armed enemy?"

"No," Molly said, "I don't think so."

"You are a bright girl, Molly; do you know?"

"No, sir, but I think the people feel that they are beaten if they are docile. They want to show these soldiers they're unbeaten."

"They've had no chance to fight. It's no fight to go against machine guns," Doctor Winter said.

Orden said, "When you know what they want to do, will you tell me, Molly?"

She looked at him suspiciously. "Yes—" she said.

"You mean 'no.' You don't trust me."

"But how about Alex?" she questioned.

"I'll not sentence him. He has committed no crime against our people," said the Mayor.

Molly was hesitant now. She said, "Will they—will they kill Alex?"

Orden stared at her and he said, "Dear child, my dear child."

She held herself rigid. "Thank you."

Orden came close to her and she said weakly, "Don't touch me. Please don't touch me. Please don't touch me." And his hand dropped. For a moment she stood still, then she turned stiffly and went out of the door.

She had just closed the door when Joseph entered. "Excuse me, sir, the colonel wants to see you. I said you were busy. I knew she was here. And Madame wants to see you, too."

Orden said, "Ask Madame to come in."

Joseph went out and Madame came in immediately. "I don't know how I can run a house," she began; "it's more people than the house can stand. Annie's angry all the time."

"Hush!" Orden said.

Madame looked at him in amazement. "I don't know what—"

"Hush!" he said. "Sarah, I want you to go to Alex Morden's house. Do you understand? I want you to stay with Molly Morden while she needs you. Don't talk, just stay with her."

Madame said, "I've a hundred things—"

"Sarah, I want you to stay with Molly Morden. Don't leave her alone. Go now."

She comprehended slowly. "Yes," she said. "Yes, I will. When will it be over?"

"I don't know," he said. "I'll send Annie when it's time."

She kissed him lightly on the cheek and went out. Orden walked to the door and called, "Joseph, I'll see the colonel now."

Lanser came in. He had on a new pressed uniform with a little ornamental dagger at the belt. He said, "Good morning, Your Excellency. I wish to speak to you informally." He glanced at Doctor Winter. "I should like to speak to you alone."

Winter went slowly to the door and as he reached it Orden said, "Doctor!"

Winter turned. "Yes?"

"Will you come back this evening?"

"You will have work for me?" the doctor asked.

"No–no. I just won't like to be alone."

"I will be here," said the doctor.

"And, Doctor, do you think Molly looked all right?"

"Oh, I think so. Close to hysteria, I guess. But she's good stock. She's good, strong stock. She is a Kenderly, you know."

"I'd forgotten," Orden said. "Yes, she is a Kenderly, isn't she?"

Doctor Winter went out and shut the door gently behind him.

Lanser had waited courteously. He watched the door close. He looked at the table and the chairs about it. "I will not tell you, sir, how sorry I am about this. I wish it had not happened."

Mayor Orden bowed, and Lanser went on, "I like you, sir, and I respect you, but I have a job to do. You surely recognize that."

Orden did not answer. He looked straight into Lanser's eyes.

"We do not act alone or on our own judgment."

Between sentences Lanser waited for an answer but he received none.

"There are rules laid down for us, rules made in the capital. This man has killed an officer."

At last Orden answered, "Why didn't you shoot him then? That was the time to do it."

Lanser shook his head. "If I agreed with you, it would make no difference. You know as well as I that punishment is largely for the purpose of deterring the potential criminal. Thus, since punishment is for others than the punished, it must be publicized. It must even be dramatized." He thrust a finger in back of his belt and flipped his little dagger.

Orden turned away and looked out of the window at the dark sky. "It will snow tonight," he said.

"Mayor Orden, you know our orders are inexorable. We must get the coal. If your people are not orderly, we will have to restore that order by force." His voice grew stern. "We must shoot people if it is necessary. If you wish to save your people from hurt, you must help us to keep order. Now, it is considered wise by my government that punishment emanate from the local authority. It makes for a more orderly situation."

Orden said softly, "So the people did know. That is a mystery." And louder he said, "You wish me to pass sentence of death on Alexander Morden after a trial here?"

"Yes, and you will prevent much bloodshed later if you will do it."

Orden went to the table and pulled out the big chair at its head and sat down. And suddenly he seemed to be the judge, with Lanser the culprit. He drummed with his fingers on the table. He said, "You and your government do not understand. In all the world yours is the only government and people with a record of defeat after defeat for centuries and every time because you did not understand people." He paused. "This principle does not work. First, I am the Mayor. I have no right to pass sentence of death. There is no one in this community with that right. If I should do it, I would be breaking the law as much as you."

"Breaking the law?" said Lanser.

"You killed six men when you came in. Under our law you are guilty of murder, all of you. Why do you go into this nonsense of law, Colonel? There is no law between you and us. This is war. Don't you know you will have to kill all of us or we in time will kill all of you? You destroyed the law when you came in, and a new law took its place. Don't you know that?"

Lanser said, "May I sit down?"

"Why do you ask? That is another lie. You could make me stand if you wished."

Lanser said, "No; it is true whether you believe it or not: personally, I have respect for you and your office, and"—he put his forehead in his hand for a moment—"you see, what I think, sir, I, a man of a certain age and certain memories, is of no importance. I might agree with you, but that would change nothing. The military, the political pattern I work in has certain tendencies and practices which are invariable."

Orden said, "And these tendencies and practices have been proven wrong in every single case since the beginning of the world."

Lanser laughed bitterly. "I, an individual man with certain memories, might agree with you, might even add that one of the tendencies of the military mind and pattern is an inability to learn, an inability to see beyond the killing which is its job. But I am not a man subject to memories. The coal miner must be shot publicly, because the theory is that others will then restrain themselves from killing our men."

Orden said, "We need not talk any more, then."

"Yes, we must talk. We want you to help."

Orden sat quietly for a while and then he said, "I'll tell you what I'll do. How many men were on the machine guns which killed our soldiers?"

"Oh, not more than twenty, I guess," said Lanser.

"Very well. If you will shoot them, I will condemn Morden."

"You're not serious!" said the colonel.

"But I am serious."

"This can't be done. You know it."

"I know it," said Orden. "And what you ask cannot be done."

Lanser said, "I suppose I knew. Corell will have to be Mayor after all." He looked up quickly. "You will stay for the trial?"

"Yes, I'll stay. Then Alex won't be so lonely."

Lanser looked at him and smiled a little sadly. "We have taken on a job, haven't we?"

"Yes," said the Mayor, "the one impossible job in the world, the one thing that can't be done."

"And that is?"

"To break man's spirit permanently."

Orden's head sank a little toward the table, and he said, without looking up, "It's started to snow. It didn't wait for night. I like the sweet, cool smell of the snow."

CHAPTER FOUR

By eleven o'clock the snow was falling heavily in big, soft puffs and the sky was not visible at all. People were scurrying through the falling snow, and snow piled up in the doorways and it piled up on the statue in the public square and on the rails from the mine to the harbor. Snow piled up and the little cartwheels skidded as they were pushed along. And over the town there hung a blackness that was deeper than the cloud, and over the town there hung a sullenness and a dry, growing hatred. The people did not stand in the streets long, but they entered the doors and the doors closed and there seemed to be eyes looking from behind the curtains, and when the military went through the street or when the patrol walked down the main street, the eyes were on the patrol, cold and sullen. And in the shops people came to buy little things for lunch and they asked for the goods and got it and paid for it and exchanged no good-day with the seller.

In the little palace drawing-room the lights were on and the lights shone on the falling snow outside the window. The court was in session. Lanser sat at the head of the table with Hunter on his right, then Tonder, and, at the lower end, Captain Loft with a little pile of papers in front of him. On the opposite side, Mayor Orden sat on the colonel's left and Prackle was next to him—Prackle, who scribbled on his pad of paper. Beside the table two guards stood with bayonets fixed, with helmets on their heads, and they were little wooden images. Between them was Alex Morden, a big young man with a wide, low forehead, with deep-set eyes and a long, sharp nose. His chin was firm and his mouth sensual and wide. He was wide of shoulder, narrow of hip, and in front of him his manacled hands clasped and unclasped. He was dressed in black trousers, a blue shirt open at the neck, and a dark coat shiny from wear.

Captain Loft read from the paper in front of him, " 'When ordered back to work, he refused to go, and when the order was repeated, the prisoner attacked Captain Loft with the pick-ax he carried. Captain Bentick interposed his body—' "

Mayor Orden coughed and, when Loft stopped reading, said, "Sit down, Alex. One of you guards get him a chair." The guard turned and pulled up a chair unquestioningly.

Loft said, "It is customary for the prisoner to stand."

"Let him sit down," Orden said. "Only we will know. You can report that he stood."

"It is not customary to falsify reports," said Loft.

"Sit down, Alex," Orden repeated.

And the big young man sat down and his manacled hands were restless in his lap.

Loft began, "This is contrary to all—"

The colonel said, "Let him be seated."

Captain Loft cleared his throat. " 'Captain Bentick interposed his body and received a blow on the head which crushed his skull.' A medical report is appended. Do you wish me to read it?"

"No need," said Lanser. "Make it as quick as you can."

" 'These facts have been witnessed by several of our soldiers, whose statements are attached. This military court finds that the prisoner is guilty of murder and recommends a death sentence.' Do you wish me to read the statements of the soldiers?"

Lanser sighed. "No." He turned to Alex. "You don't deny that you killed the captain, do you?"

Alex smiled sadly. "I hit him," he said. "I don't know that I killed him."

Orden said, "Good work, Alex!" And the two looked at each other as friends.

Loft said, "Do you mean to imply that he was killed by someone else?"

"I don't know," said Alex. "I only hit him, and then somebody hit me."

Colonel Lanser said, "Do you want to offer any explanation? I can't think of anything that will change the sentence, but we will listen."

Loft said, "I respectfully submit that the colonel should not have said that. It indicates that the court is not impartial."

Orden laughed dryly. The colonel looked at him and smiled a little. "Have you any explanation?" he repeated.

Alex lifted a hand to gesture and the other came with it. He looked embarrassed and put them in his lap again. "I was mad," he said. "I have a pretty bad temper. He said I must work. I am a free man. I got mad and I hit him. I guess I hit him hard. It was the wrong man." He pointed at Loft. "That's the man I wanted to hit, that one."

Lanser said, "It doesn't matter whom you wanted to hit. Anybody would have been the same. Are you sorry you did it?" He said aside to the table, "It would look well in the record if he were sorry."

"Sorry?" Alex asked. "I'm not sorry. He told me to go to work—me, a free man! I used to be alderman. He said I had to work."

"But if the sentence is death, won't you be sorry then?"

Alex sank his head and really tried to think honestly. "No," he said. "You mean, would I do it again?"

"That's what I mean."

"No," Alex said thoughtfully, "I don't think I'm sorry."

Lanser said, "Put in the record that the prisoner was overcome with remorse. Sentence is automatic. Do you understand?" he said to Alex. "The court has no leeway. The court finds you guilty and sentences you to be shot immediately. I do not see any reason to torture you with this any more. Captain Loft, is there anything I have forgotten?"

"You've forgotten me," said Orden. He stood up and pushed back his chair and stepped over to Alex. And Alex, from long habit, stood up respectfully. "Alexander, I am the elected Mayor."

"I know it, sir."

"Alex, these men are invaders. They have taken our country by surprise and treachery and force."

Captain Loft said, "Sir, this should not be permitted."

Lanser said, "Hush! Is it better to hear it, or would you rather it were whispered?"

Orden went on as though he had not been interrupted. "When they came, the people were confused and I was confused. We did not know what to do or think. Yours was the first clear act. Your private anger was the beginning of a public anger. I know it is said in town that I am acting with these men. I can show the town, but you—you are going to die. I want you to know."

Alex dropped his head and then raised it. "I know, sir."

Lanser said, "Is the squad ready?"

"Outside, sir."

"Who is commanding?"

"Lieutenant Tonder, sir."

Tonder raised his head and his chin was hard and he held his breath.

Orden said softly, "Are you afraid, Alex?"

And Alex said, "Yes, sir."

"I can't tell you not to be. I would be, too, and so would these young—gods of war."

Lanser said, "Call your squad." Tonder got up quickly and went to the door. "They're here, sir." He opened the door wide and the helmeted men could be seen.

Orden said, "Alex, go, knowing that these men will have no rest, no rest at all until they are gone, or dead. You will make the people one. It's a sad knowledge and little enough gift to you, but it is so. No rest at all."

Alex shut his eyes tightly. Mayor Orden leaned close and kissed him on the cheek. "Good-by, Alex," he said.

The guard took Alex by the arm and the young man kept his eyes tightly closed, and they guided him through the door. The squad faced about, and their feet marched away down out of the house and into the snow, and the snow muffled their footsteps.

The men about the table were silent. Orden looked toward the window and saw a little round spot being rubbed clear of snow by a quick hand. He stared at it, fascinated, and then he looked quickly away. He said to the colonel, "I hope you know what you are doing."

Captain Loft gathered his papers and Lanser asked, "In the square, Captain?"

"Yes, in the square. It must be public," Loft said.

And Orden said, "I hope you know."

"Man," said the colonel, "whether we know or not, it is what must be done."

Silence fell on the room and each man listened. And it was not long. From the distance there came a crash of firing. Lanser sighed deeply. Orden put his hand to his forehead and filled his lungs deeply. Then there was a shout outside. The glass of the window crashed inward and Lieutenant Prackle wheeled about. He brought his hand up to his shoulder and stared at it.

Lanser leaped up, crying, "So, it starts! Are you badly hurt, Lieutenant?"

"My shoulder," said Prackle.

Lanser took command. "Captain Loft, there will be tracks in the snow. Now, I want every house searched for firearms. I want every man who has one taken hostage. You, sir," he said to the Mayor, "are placed in protective custody. And understand this, please: we will shoot, five, ten, a hundred for one."

Orden said quietly, "A man of certain memories."

Lanser stopped in the middle of an order. He looked over slowly at the Mayor and for a moment they understood each other. And then Lanser straightened his shoulders. "A man of no memories!" he said sharply. And then, "I want every weapon in town gathered.

Bring in everyone who resists. Hurry, before their tracks are filled."

The staff found their helmets and loosed their pistols and started out. And Orden went to the broken window. He said sadly, "The sweet, cool smell of the snow."

CHAPTER FIVE

THE DAYS and the weeks dragged on, and the months dragged on. The snow fell and melted and fell and melted and finally fell and stuck. The dark buildings of the little town wore bells and hats and eyebrows of white and there were trenches through the snow to the doorways. In the harbor the coal barges came empty and went away loaded, but the coal did not come out of the ground easily. The good miners made mistakes. They were clumsy and slow. Machinery broke and took a long time to fix. The people of the conquered country settled in a slow, silent, waiting revenge. The men who had been traitors, who had helped the invaders—and many of them believed it was for a better state and an ideal way of life—found that the control they took was insecure, that the people they had known looked at them coldly and never spoke.

And there was death in the air, hovering and waiting. Accidents happened on the railroad, which clung to the mountains and connected the little town with the rest of the nation. Avalanches poured down on the tracks and rails were spread. No train could move unless the tracks were first inspected. People were shot in reprisal and it made no difference. Now and then a group of young men escaped and went to England. And the English bombed the coal mine and did some damage and killed some of both their friends and their enemies. And it did no good. The cold hatred grew with the winter, the silent, sullen hatred, the waiting hatred. The food supply was controlled–issued to the obedient and withheld from the disobedient–so that the whole population turned coldly obedient. There was a point where food could not be withheld, for a starving man cannot mine coal, cannot lift and carry. And the hatred was deep in the eyes of the people, beneath the surface.

Now it was that the conqueror was surrounded, the

men of the battalion alone among silent enemies, and no man might relax his guard for even a moment. If he did, he disappeared, and some snowdrift received his body. If he went alone to a woman, he disappeared and some snowdrift received his body. If he drank, he disappeared. The men of the battalion could sing only together, could dance only together, and dancing gradually stopped and the singing expressed a longing for home. Their talk was of friends and relatives who loved them and their longings were for warmth and love, because a man can be a soldier for only so many hours a day and for only so many months in a year, and then he wants to be a man again, wants girls and drinks and music and laughter and ease, and when these are cut off, they become irresistibly desirable.

And the men thought always of home. The men of the battalion came to detest the place they had conquered, and they were curt with the people and the people were curt with them, and gradually a little fear began to grow in the conquerors, a fear that it would never be over, that they could never relax or go home, a fear that one day they would crack and be hunted through the mountains like rabbits, for the conquered never relaxed their hatred. The patrols, seeing lights, hearing laughter, would be drawn as to a fire, and when they came near, the laughter stopped, the warmth went out, and the people were cold and obedient. And the soldiers, smelling warm food from the little restaurants, went in and ordered the warm food and found that it was oversalted or overpeppered.

Then the soldiers read the news from home and from the other conquered countries, and the news was always good, and for a little while they believed it, and then after a while they did not believe it any more. And every man carried in his heart the terror. "If home crumbled, they would not tell us, and then it would be too late. These people will not spare us. They will kill us all." They remembered stories of their men retreating through Belgium and retreating out of Russia. And the more literate remembered the frantic, tragic retreat from Moscow, when every peasant's pitchfork tasted blood and the snow was rotten with bodies.

And they knew when they cracked, or relaxed, or slept too long, it would be the same here, and their sleep was restless and their days were nervous. They asked questions their officers could not answer because they did not know. They were not told, either. They did not believe the reports from home, either.

Thus it came about that the conquerors grew afraid of the conquered and their nerves wore thin and they shot at shadows in the night. The cold, sullen silence was with them always. Then three soldiers went insane in a week and cried all night and all day until they were sent away home. And others might have gone insane if they had not heard that mercy deaths awaited the insane at home, and a mercy death is a terrible thing to think of. Fear crept in on the men in their billets and it made them sad, and it crept into the patrols and it made them cruel.

The year turned and the nights grew long. It was dark at three o'clock in the afternoon and not light again until nine in the morning. The jolly lights did not shine out on the snow, for by law every window must be black against the bombers. And yet when the English bombers came over, some light always appeared near the coal mine. Sometimes the sentries shot a man with a lantern and once a girl with a flashlight.

And it did no good. Nothing was cured by the shooting.

And the officers were a reflection of their men, more restrained because their training was more complete, more resourceful because they had more responsibility, but the same fears were a little deeper buried in them, the same longings were more tightly locked in their hearts. And they were under a double strain, for the conquered people watched them for mistakes and their own men watched them for weakness, so that their spirits were taut to the breaking-point. The conquerors were under a terrible spiritual siege and everyone knew, conquered and conquerors, what would happen when the first crack appeared.

From the upstairs room of the Mayor's palace the comfort seemed to have gone. Over the windows black paper was tacked tightly and there were little piles of precious equipment about the room—the instruments and equipment that could not be jeopardized, the glasses and masks and helmets. And discipline here at least was laxer, as though these officers knew there must be some laxness somewhere or the machine would break. On the table were two gasoline lanterns which threw a hard, brilliant light and they made great shadows on the walls, and their hissing was an undercurrent in the room.

Major Hunter went on with his work. His drawing-board was permanently ready now, for the bombs tore out his work nearly as fast as he put it in. And he had little sorrow, for to Major Hunter building was life and here he had more building than he could project or accomplish. He sat at his drawing-board with a light behind him and his T-square moved up and down the board and his pencil was busy.

Lieutenant Prackle, his arm still in a sling, sat in a straight chair behind the center table, reading an illustrated paper. At the end of the table Lieutenant Tonder was writing a letter. He held his pen pinched high and occasionally he looked up from his letter and gazed at the ceiling, to find words to put in his letter.

Prackle turned a page of the illustrated paper and he said, "I can close my eyes and see every shop on this street here." And Hunter went on with his work and Tonder wrote a few more words. Prackle continued, "There is a restaurant right behind here. You can't see it in the picture. It's called Burden's."

Hunter did not look up. He said, "I know the place. They had good scallops."

"Sure they did," Prackle said. "Everything was good there. Not a single bad thing did they serve. And their coffee——"

Tonder looked up from his letter and said, "They won't be serving coffee now—or scallops."

"Well, I don't know about that," said Prackle. "They did and they will again. And there was a waitress there." He described her figure with his hand, with the good hand. "Blonde, so and so." He looked down at the magazine. "She had the strangest eyes—has, I mean—always kind of moist-looking as though she had just been laughing or crying." He glanced at the ceiling and he spoke softly. "I was out with her. She was lovely. I wonder why I didn't go back oftener. I wonder if she's still there."

Tonder said gloomily, "Probably not. Working in a factory, maybe."

Prackle laughed. "I hope they aren't rationing girls at home."

"Why not?" said Tonder.

Prackle said playfully, "You don't care much for girls, do you? Not much, you don't!"

Tonder said, "I like them for what girls are for. I don't let them crawl around my other life."

And Prackle said tauntingly, "It seems to me that they crawl all over you all the time."

Tonder tried to change the subject. He said, "I hate these damn lanterns. Major, when are you going to get that dynamo fixed?"

Major Hunter looked up slowly from his board and said, "It should be done by now. I've got good men working on it. I'll double the guard on it from now on, I guess."

"Did you get the fellow that wrecked it?" Prackle asked.

And Hunter said grimly, "It might be any one of five men. I got all five." He went on musingly, "It's so easy to wreck a dynamo if you know how. Just short it and it wrecks itself." He said, "The light ought to be on any time now."

Prackle still looked at his magazine. "I wonder when we will be relieved. I wonder when we will go home for a while. Major, wouldn't you like to go home for a rest?"

Hunter looked up from his work and his face was hopeless for a moment. "Yes, of course." He recovered himself. "I've built this siding four times. I don't know why a bomb always knocks out this particular siding. I'm getting tired of this piece of track. I have to change the route every time because of the craters. There's no time to fill them in. The ground is frozen too hard. It seems to be too much work."

Suddenly the electric lights came on and Tonder automatically reached out and turned off the two gasoline lanterns. The hissing was gone from the room.

Tonder said, "Thank God for that! That hissing gets on my nerves. It makes me think there's whispering." He folded the letter he had been writing and he said, "It's strange more letters don't come through. I've only had one in two weeks."

Prackle said, "Maybe nobody writes to you."

"Maybe," said Tonder. He turned to the major. "If anything happened—at home, I mean—do you think they would let us know—anything bad, I mean, any deaths or anything like that?"

Hunter said, "I don't know."

"Well," Tonder went on, "I would like to get out of this god-forsaken hole!"

Prackle broke in, "I thought you were going to live here after the war?" And he imitated Tonder's voice. "Put four or five farms together. Make a nice place, a kind of family seat. Wasn't that it? Going to be a little lord of the valley, weren't you? Nice, pleasant people, beautiful lawns and deer and little children. Isn't that the way it was, Tonder?"

As Prackle spoke, Tonder's hand dropped. Then he clasped his temples with his hands and he spoke with emotion. "Be still! Don't talk like that! These people! These horrible people! These cold people! They never look at you." He shivered. "They never speak. They answer like dead men. They obey, these horrible people. And the girls are frozen!"

There was a light tap on the door and Joseph came in with a scuttle of coal. He moved silently through the room and set the scuttle down so softly that he made no noise, and he turned without looking up at anyone and went toward the door again. Prackle said loudly, "Joseph!" And Joseph turned without replying, without looking up, and he bowed very slightly. And Prackle said still loudly, "Joseph, is there any wine or any brandy?" Joseph shook his head.

Tonder started up from the table, his face wild with anger, and he shouted, "Answer, you swine! Answer in words!"

Joseph did not look up. He spoke tonelessly. "No, sir; no, sir, there is no wine."

And Tonder said furiously, "And no brandy?"

Joseph looked down and spoke tonelessly again. "There is no brandy, sir." He stood perfectly still.

"What do you want?" Tonder said.

"I want to go, sir."

"Then go, goddamn it!"

Joseph turned and went silently out of the room and Tonder took a handkerchief out of his pocket and wiped his face. Hunter looked up at him and said, "You shouldn't let him beat you so easily."

Tonder sat down in his chair and put his hands to his temples and he said brokenly, "I want a girl. I want to go home. I want a girl. There's a girl in this town, a pretty girl. I see her all the time. She has blond hair. She lives beside the old-iron store. I want that girl."

Prackle said, "Watch yourself. Watch your nerves."

At that moment the lights went out again and the room was in darkness. Hunter spoke while the matches were being struck and an attempt was being made to light the lanterns; he said, "I thought I had all of them. I must have missed one. But I can't be running down there all the time. I've got good men down there."

Tonder lighted the first lantern and then he lighted the other, and Hunter spoke sternly to Tonder. "Lieutenant, do your talking to us if you have to talk. Don't let the enemy hear you talk this way. There's nothing these people would like better than to know your nerves are getting thin. Don't let the enemy hear you."

Tonder sat down again. The light was sharp on his face and the hissing filled the room. He said, "That's it! The enemy's everywhere! Every man, every woman, even children! The enemy's everywhere! Their faces look out of doorways. The white faces behind the curtains, listening. We have beaten them, we have won everywhere, and they wait and obey, and they wait. Half the world is ours. Is it the same in other places, Major?"

And Hunter said, "I don't know."

"That's it," Tonder said. "We don't know. The reports—everything in hand. Conquered countries cheer our soldiers, cheer the new order." His voice changed and grew soft and still softer. "What do the reports say about us? Do they say we are cheered, loved, flowers in our paths? Oh, these horrible people waiting in the snow!"

And Hunter said, "Now that's off your chest, do you feel better?"

Prackle had been beating the table softly with his good fist, and he said, "He shouldn't talk that way. He should keep things to himself. He's a soldier, isn't he? Then let him be a soldier."

The door opened quietly and Captain Loft came in and there was snow on his helmet and snow on his shoulders. His nose was pinched and red and his overcoat collar was high about his ears. He took off his helmet and the snow fell to the floor and he brushed his shoulders. "What a job!" he said.

"More trouble?" Hunter asked.

"Always trouble. I see they've got your dynamo again. Well, I think I fixed the mine for a while."

"What's your trouble?" Hunter asked.

"Oh, the usual thing with me—the slow-down and a wrecked dump car. I saw the wrecker, though. I shot him. I think I have a cure for it, Major, now. I just thought it up. I'll make each man take out a certain amount of coal. I can't starve the men or they can't work, but I've really got the answer. If the coal doesn't come out, no food for the families. We'll have the men eat at the mine, so there's no dividing at home. That ought to cure it. They work or their kids don't eat. I told them just now."

"What did they say?"

Loft's eyes narrowed fiercely. "Say? What do they ever say? Nothing! Nothing at all! But we'll see whether the coal comes out now." He took off his coat and shook it, and his eyes fell on the entrance door and he saw that it was open a crack. He moved silently to the door, jerked it open, then closed it. "I thought I had closed that door tight," he said.

"You did," said Hunter.

Prackle still turned the pages of his illustrated paper. His voice was normal again. "Those are monster guns we're using in the east. I never saw one of them. Did you, Captain?"

"Oh, yes," said Captain Loft. "I've seen them fired. They're wonderful. Nothing can stand up against them."

Tonder said, "Captain, do you get much news from home?"

"A certain amount," said Loft.

"Is everything well there?"

"Wonderful!" said Loft. "The armies move ahead everywhere."

"The British aren't defeated yet?"

"They are defeated in every engagement."

"But they fight on?"

"A few air raids, no more."

"And the Russians?"

"It's all over."

Tonder said insistently, "But they fight on?"

"A little skirmishing, no more."

"Then we have just about won, haven't we, Captain?" Tonder asked.

"Yes, we have."

Tonder looked closely at him and said, "You believe this, don't you, Captain?"

Prackle broke in, "Don't let him start that again!"

Loft scowled at Tonder. "I don't know what you mean."

Tonder said, "I mean this: we'll be going home before long, won't we?"

"Well, the reorganization will take some time," Hunter said. "The new order can't be put into effect in a day, can it?"

Tonder said, "All our lives, perhaps?"

And Prackle said, "Don't let him start it again!"

Loft came very close to Tonder and he said, "Lieutenant, I don't like the tone of your questions. I don't like the tone of doubt."

Hunter looked up and said, "Don't be hard on him, Loft. He's tired. We're all tired."

"Well, I'm tired, too," said Loft, "but I don't let treasonable doubts get in."

Hunter said, "Don't bedevil him, I tell you! Where's the colonel, do you know?"

"He's making out his report. He's asking for reinforcements," said Loft. "It's a bigger job than we thought."

Prackle asked excitedly, "Will he get them—the reinforcements?"

"How would I know?"

Tonder smiled. "Reinforcements!" he said softly. "Or maybe replacements. Maybe we could go home for a while." And he said, smiling, "Maybe I could walk down the street and people would say, 'Hello,' and they'd say, 'There goes a soldier,' and they'd be glad for me and they'd be glad of me. And there'd be friends about, and I could turn my back to a man without being afraid."

Prackle said, "Don't start that again! Don't let him get out of hand again!"

And Loft said disgustedly, "We have enough trouble now without having the staff go crazy."

But Tonder went on, "You really think replacements will come, Captain?"

"I didn't say so."

"But you said they might."

"I said I didn't know. Look, Lieutenant, we've conquered half the world. We must police it for a while. You know that."

"But the other half?" Tonder asked.

"They will fight on hopelessly for a while," said Loft.

"Then we must be spread out all over."

"For a while," said Loft.

Prackle said nervously, "I wish you'd make him shut up. I wish you would shut him up. Make him stop it."

Tonder got out his handkerchief and blew his nose, and he spoke a little like a man out of his head. He laughed embarrassedly. He said, "I had a funny dream. I guess it was a dream. Maybe it was a thought. Maybe a thought or a dream."

Prackle said, "Make him stop, Captain!"

Tonder said, "Captain, is this place conquered?"

"Of course," said Loft.

A little note of hysteria crept into Tonder's laughter. He said, "Conquered and we're afraid; conquered and we're surrounded." His laughter grew shrill. "I had a dream—or a thought—out in the snow with the black shadows and the faces in the doorways, the cold faces behind curtains. I had a thought or a dream."

Prackle said, "Make him stop!"

Tonder said, "I dreamed the Leader was crazy."

And Loft and Hunter laughed together and Loft said, "The enemy have found out how crazy. I'll have to write that one home. The papers would print that one. The enemy have learned how crazy the Leader is."

And Tonder went on laughing. "Conquest after conquest, deeper and deeper into molasses." His laughter choked him and he coughed into his handkerchief. "Maybe the Leader is crazy. Flies conquer the flypaper. Flies capture two hundred miles of new flypaper!" His laughter was growing more hysterical now.

Prackle leaned over and shook him with his good hand, "Stop it! You stop it! You have no right!"

And gradually Loft recognized that the laughter was hysterical and he stepped close to Tonder and slapped him in the face. He said, "Lieutenant, stop it!"

Tonder's laughter went on and Loft slapped him again in the face and he said, "Stop it, Lieutenant! Do you hear me?"

Suddenly Tonder's laughter stopped and the room was quiet except for the hissing of the lanterns. Tonder looked in amazement at his hand and he felt his bruised face with his hand and he looked at his hand again and his head sank down toward the table. "I want to go home," he said.

CHAPTER SIX

THERE was a little street not far from the town square where small peaked roofs and little shops were mixed up together. The snow was beaten down on the walks and in the street, but it piled high on the fences and it puffed on the roof peaks. It drifted against the shuttered windows of the little houses. And into the yards paths were shoveled. The night was dark and cold and no light showed from the windows to attract the bombers. And no one walked in the streets, for the curfew was strict. The houses were dark lumps against the snow. Every little while the patrol of six men walked down the street, peering about, and each man carried a long flashlight. The hushed tramp of their feet sounded in the street, the squeaks of their boots on the packed snow. They were muffled figures deep in thick coats; under their helmets were knitted caps which came down over their ears and covered their chins and mouths. A little snow fell, only a little, like rice.

The patrol talked as they walked, and they talked of things that they longed for—of meat and of hot soup and of the richness of butter, of the prettiness of girls and of their smiles and of their lips and their eyes. They talked of these things and sometimes they talked of their hatred of what they were doing and of their loneliness.

A small, peak-roofed house beside the iron shop was shaped like the others and wore its snow cap like the others. No light came from its shuttered windows and its storm doors were tightly closed. But inside a lamp burned in the small living-room and the door to the bedroom was open and the door to the kitchen was open. An iron stove was against the back wall with a little coal fire burning in it. It was a warm, poor, comfortable room, the floor covered with worn carpet, the walls papered in warm brown with an old-fashioned fleur-de-lis figure in gold. And on the back wall were two pictures, one of fish lying dead on a plate of ferns and the other of grouse lying dead on a fir bough. On the right wall there was a picture of Christ walking on the waves toward the despairing fishermen. Two straight chairs were in the room and a couch covered with a bright blanket. There was a little round table in the middle of the room, on which stood a kerosene lamp with a round flowered shade on it, and the light in the room was warm and soft.

The inner door, which led to the passage, which in turn led to the storm door, was beside the stove.

In a cushioned old rocking-chair beside the table Molly Morden sat alone. She was unraveling the wool from an old blue sweater and winding the yarn on a ball. She had quite a large ball of it. And on the table beside her was her knitting with the needles sticking in it, and a large pair of scissors. Her glasses lay on the table beside her, for she did not need them for knitting. She was pretty and young and neat. Her golden hair was done up on the top of her head and a blue bow was in her hair. Her hands worked quickly with the raveling. As she worked, she glanced now and then at the door to the passage. The wind whistled in the chimney softly, but it was a quiet night, muffled with snow.

Suddenly she stopped her work. Her hands were still. She looked toward the door and listened. The tramping feet of the patrol went by in the street and the sound of their voices could be heard faintly. The sound faded away. Molly ripped out new yarn and wound it on the ball. And again she stopped. There was a rustle at the door and then three short knocks. Molly put down her work and went to the door.

"Yes?" she called.

She unlocked the door and opened it and a heavily cloaked figure came in. It was Annie, the cook, red-eyed and wrapped in mufflers. She slipped in quickly, as though practiced at getting speedily through doors and getting them closed again behind her. She stood there red-nosed, sniffling and glancing quickly around the room.

Molly said, "Good evening, Annie. I didn't expect you tonight. Take your things off and get warm. It's cold out."

Annie said, "The soldiers brought winter early. My father always said a war brought bad weather, or bad weather brought a war. I don't remember which."

"Take off your things and come to the stove."

"I can't," said Annie importantly. "They're coming."

"Who are coming?" Molly said.

"His Excellency," said Annie, "and the doctor and the two Anders boys."

"Here?" Molly asked. "What for?"

Annie held out her hand and there was a little package in it. "Take it," she said. "I stole it from the colonel's plate. It's meat."

And Molly unwrapped the little cake of meat and put it in her mouth and she spoke around her chewing. "Did you get some?"

Annie said, "I cook it, don't I? I always get some."

"When are they coming?"

Annie sniffled. "The Anders boys are sailing for England. They've got to. They're hiding now."

"Are they?" Molly asked. "What for?"

"Well, it was their brother, Jack, was shot today for wrecking that little car. The soldiers are looking for the rest of the family. You know how they do."

"Yes," Molly said, "I know how they do. Sit down, Annie."

"No time," said Annie. "I've got to get back and tell His Excellency it's all right here."

Molly said, "Did anybody see you come?"

Annie smiled proudly. "No, I'm awful good at sneaking."

"How will the Mayor get out?"

Annie laughed. "Joseph is going to be in his bed in case they look in, right in his nightshirt, right next to Madame!" And she laughed again. She said, "Joseph better lie pretty quiet."

Molly said, "It's an awful night to be sailing."

"It's better than being shot."

"Yes, so it is. Why is the Mayor coming here?"

"I don't know. He wants to talk to the Anders boys. I've got to go now, but I came to tell you."

Molly said, "How soon are they coming?"

"Oh, maybe half, maybe three-quarters of an hour," Annie said. "I'll come in first. Nobody bothers with old cooks." She started for the door and she turned midway, and as though accusing Molly of saying the last words she said truculently, "I'm not so old!" And she slipped out of the door and closed it behind her.

Molly went on knitting for a moment and then she got up and went to the stove and lifted the lid. The glow of the fire lighted her face. She stirred the fire and added a few lumps of coal and closed the stove again. Before she could get to her chair, there was a knocking on the outer door. She crossed the room and said to herself, "I wonder what she forgot." She went into the passage and she said, "What do you want?"

A man's voice answered her. She opened the door and a man's voice said, "I don't mean any harm. I don't mean any harm."

Molly backed into the room and Lieutenant Tonder followed her in. Molly said, "Who are you? What do you want? You can't come in here. What do you want?"

Lieutenant Tonder was dressed in his great gray overcoat. He entered the room and took off his helmet and he spoke pleadingly. "I don't mean any harm. Please let me come in."

Molly said, "What do you want?"

She shut the door behind him and he said, "Miss, I

only want to talk, that's all. I want to hear you talk. That's all I want."

"Are you forcing yourself on me?" Molly asked.

"No, miss, just let me stay a little while and then I'll go."

"What is it you want?"

Tonder tried to explain. "Can you understand this—can you believe this? Just for a little while, can't we forget this war? Just for a little while. Just for a little while, can't we talk together like people—together?"

Molly looked at him for a long time and then a smile came to her lips. "You don't know who I am, do you?"

Tonder said, "I've seen you in the town. I know you're lovely. I know I want to talk to you."

And Molly still smiled. She said softly, "You don't know who I am." She sat in her chair and Tonder stood like a child, looking very clumsy. Molly continued, speaking quietly, "Why, you're lonely. It's as simple as that, isn't it?"

Tonder licked his lips and he spoke eagerly. "That's it," he said. "You understand. I knew you would. I knew you'd have to." His words came tumbling out.

"I'm lonely to the point of illness. I'm lonely in the quiet and the hatred." And he said pleadingly, "Can't we talk, just a little bit?"

Molly picked up her knitting. She looked quickly at the front door. "You can stay not more than fifteen minutes. Sit down a little, Lieutenant."

She looked at the door again. The house creaked. Tonder became tense and he said, "Is someone here?"

"No, the snow is heavy on the roof. I have no man any more to push it down."

Tonder said gently, "Who did it? Was it something we did?"

And Molly nodded, looking far off. "Yes."

He sat down. "I'm sorry." After a moment he said, "I wish I could do something. I'll have the snow pushed off the roof."

"No," said Molly, "no."

"Why not?"

"Because the people would think I had joined with you. They would expel me. I don't want to be expelled."

Tonder said, "Yes, I see how that would be. You all hate us. But I'll take care of you if you'll let me."

Now Molly knew she was in control, and her eyes narrowed a little cruelly and she said, "Why do you ask? You are the conqueror. Your men don't have to ask. They take what they want."

"That's not what I want," Tonder said. "That's not the way I want it."

And Molly laughed, still a little cruelly. "You want me to like you, don't you, Lieutenant?"

He said simply, "Yes," and he raised his head and he said, "You are so beautiful, so warm. Your hair is bright. Oh, I've seen no kindness in a woman's face for so long!"

"Do you see any in mine?" she asked.

He looked closely at her. "I want to."

She dropped her eyes at last. "You're making love to me, aren't you, Lieutenant?"

And he said clumsily, "I want you to like me. Surely I want you to like me. Surely I want to see that in your eyes. I have seen you in the streets. I have watched you pass by. I've given orders that you mustn't be molested. Have you been molested?"

And Molly said quietly, "Thank you; no, I've not been molested."

His words rushed on. "Why, I've even written a poem for you. Would you like to see my poem?"

And she said sardonically, "Is it a long poem? You have to go very soon."

He said, "No, it's a little tiny poem. It's a little bit of a poem." He reached inside his tunic and brought out a folded paper and handed it to her. She leaned close to the lamp and put on her glasses and she read quietly.

Your eyes in their deep heavens
Possess me and will not depart;
A sea of blue thoughts rushing
And pouring over my heart.

She folded the paper and put it in her lap. "Did you write this, Lieutenant?"

"Yes."

She said a little tauntingly, "To me?"

And Tonder answered uneasily, "Yes."

She looked at him steadily, smiling. "You didn't write it, Lieutenant, did you?"

He smiled back like a child caught in a lie. "No."

Molly asked him, "Do you know who did?"

Tonder said, "Yes, Heine wrote it. It's '*Mit deinen*

blauen Augen.' I've always loved it." He laughed embarrassedly and Molly laughed with him, and suddenly they were laughing together. He stopped laughing just as suddenly and a bleakness came into his eyes. "I haven't laughed like that since forever." He said, "They told us the people would like us, would admire us. They do not. They only hate us." And then he changed the subject as though he worked against time. "You are so beautiful. You are as beautiful as the laughter."

Molly said, "You're beginning to make love to me, Lieutenant. You must go in a moment."

And Tonder said, "Maybe I want to make love to you. A man needs love. A man dies without love. His insides shrivel and his chest feels like a dry chip. I'm lonely."

Molly got up from her chair. She looked nervously at the door and she walked to the stove and, coming back, her face grew hard and her eyes grew punishing and she said, "Do you want to go to bed with me, Lieutenant?"

"I didn't say that! Why do you talk that way?"

Molly said cruelly, "Maybe I'm trying to disgust

you. I was married once. My husband is dead. You see, I'm not a virgin." Her voice was bitter.

Tonder said, "I only want you to like me."

And Molly said, "I know. You are a civilized man. You know that love-making is more full and whole and delightful if there is liking, too."

Tonder said, "Don't talk that way! Please don't talk that way!"

Molly glanced quickly at the door. She said, "We are a conquered people, Lieutenant. You have taken the food away. I'm hungry. I'll like you better if you feed me."

Tonder said, "What are you saying?"

"Do I disgust you, Lieutenant? Maybe I'm trying to. My price is two sausages."

Tonder said, "You can't talk this way!"

"What about your own girls, Lieutenant, after the last war? A man could choose among your girls for an egg or a slice of bread. Do you want me for nothing, Lieutenant? Is the price too high?"

He said, "You fooled me for a moment. But you hate me, too, don't you? I thought maybe you wouldn't."

"No, I don't hate you," she said, "I'm hungry and—I hate you!"

Tonder said, "I'll give you anything you need, but——"

And she interrupted him. "You want to call it something else? You don't want a whore. Is that what you mean?"

Tonder said, "I don't know what I mean. You make it sound full of hatred."

Molly laughed. She said, "It's not nice to be hungry. Two sausages, two fine, fat sausages can be the most precious things in the world."

"Don't say those things," he said. "Please don't!"

"Why not? They're true."

"They aren't true! This can't be true!"

She looked at him for a moment and then she sat down and her eyes fell to her lap and she said, "No, it's not true. I don't hate you. I'm lonely, too. And the snow is heavy on the roof."

Tonder got up and moved near to her. He took one of her hands in both of his and he said softly, "Please don't hate me. I'm only a lieutenant. I didn't ask to come here. You didn't ask to be my enemy. I'm only a man, not a conquering man."

Molly's fingers encircled his hand for a moment and she said softly, "I know; yes, I know."

And Tonder said, "We have some little right to life in all this death."

She put her hand to his cheek for a moment and she said, "Yes."

"I'll take care of you," he said. "We have some right to life in all the killing." His hand rested on her shoulder. Suddenly she grew rigid and her eyes were wide and staring as though she saw a vision. His hand released her and he asked, "What's the matter? What is it?" Her eyes stared straight ahead and he repeated, "What is it?"

Molly spoke in a haunted voice. "I dressed him like a little boy for his first day in school. And he was afraid. I buttoned his shirt and tried to comfort him, but he was beyond comfort. And he was afraid."

Tonder said, "What are you saying?"

And Molly seemed to see what she described. "I don't know why they let him come home. He was confused. He didn't know what was happening. He didn't even kiss me when he went away. He was afraid, and very brave, like a little boy on his first day of school."

Tonder stood up. "That was your husband."

Molly said, "Yes, my husband. I went to the Mayor, but he was helpless. And then he marched away—not very well nor steadily—and you took him out and you shot him. It was more strange than terrible then. I didn't quite believe it then."

Tonder said, "Your husband!"

"Yes; and now in the quiet house, I believe it. Now with the heavy snow on the roof, I believe it. And in the loneliness before daybreak, in the half-warmed bed, I know it then."

Tonder stood in front of her. His face was full of misery. "Good night," he said. "God keep you. May I come back?"

And Molly looked at the wall and at the memory. "I don't know," she said.

"I'll come back."

"I don't know."

He looked at her and then he quietly went out of the door, and Molly still stared at the wall. "God keep me!" She stayed for a moment staring at the wall. The door opened silently and Annie came in. Molly did not even see her.

Annie said disapprovingly, "The door was open."

Molly looked slowly toward her, her eyes still wide open. "Yes. Oh, yes, Annie."

"The door was open. There was a man came out. I saw him. He looked like a soldier."

And Molly said, "Yes, Annie."

"Was it a soldier here?"

"Yes, it was a soldier."

And Annie asked suspiciously, "What was he doing here?"

"He came to make love to me."

Annie said, "Miss, what are you doing? You haven't joined them, have you? You aren't with them, like that Corell?"

"No, I'm not with them, Annie."

Annie said, "If the Mayor's here and they come back, it'll be your fault if anything happens; it'll be your fault!"

"He won't come back. I won't let him come back."

But the suspicion stayed with Annie. She said, "Shall I tell them to come in now? Do you say it's safe?"

"Yes, it's safe. Where are they?"

"They're out behind the fence," said Annie.

"Tell them to come in."

And while Annie went out, Molly got up and smoothed her hair and she shook her head, trying to be alive again. There was a little sound in the passage. Two tall, blond young men entered. They were dressed in pea-jackets and dark turtle-neck sweaters. They wore stocking caps perched on their heads. They were wind-burned and strong and they looked almost like twins, Will Anders and Tom Anders, the fishermen.

"Good evening, Molly. You've heard?"

"Annie told me. It's a bad night to go."

Tom said, "It's better than a clear night. The planes see you on a clear night. What's the Mayor want, Molly?"

"I don't know. I heard about your brother. I'm sorry."

The two were silent and they looked embarrassed. Tom said, "You know how it is, better than most."

"Yes; yes, I know."

Annie came in the door again and she said in a hoarse whisper, "They're here!" And Mayor Orden and Doctor Winter came in. They took off their coats and caps and laid them on the couch. Orden went to Molly and kissed her on the forehead.

"Good evening, dear."

He turned to Annie. "Stand in the passage, Annie. Give us one knock for the patrol, one when it's gone, and two for danger. You can leave the outer door open a crack so you can hear if anyone comes."

Annie said, "Yes, sir." She went into the passage and shut the door behind her.

Doctor Winter was at the stove, warming his hands. "We got word you boys were going tonight."

"We've got to go," Tom said.

Orden nodded. "Yes, I know. We heard you were going to take Mr. Corell with you."

Tom laughed bitterly. "We thought it would be only right. We're taking his boat. We can't leave him around. It isn't good to see him in the streets."

Orden said sadly, "I wish he had gone away. It's just a danger to you, taking him."

"It isn't good to see him in the streets," Will echoed his brother. "It isn't good for the people to see him here."

Winter asked, "Can you take him? Isn't he cautious at all?"

"Oh, yes, he's cautious, in a way. At twelve o'clock, though, he walks to his house usually. We'll be behind the wall. I think we can get him through his lower garden to the water. His boat's tied up there. We were on her today getting her ready."

Orden repeated, "I wish you didn't have to. It's just an added danger. If he makes a noise, the patrol might come."

Tom said, "He won't make a noise, and it's better if he disappears at sea. Some of the town people might get him and then there would be too much killing. No, it's better if he goes to sea."

Molly took up her knitting again. She said, "Will you throw him overboard?"

Will blushed. "He'll go to sea, ma'am." He turned to the Mayor. "You wanted to see us, sir?"

"Why, yes, I want to talk to you. Doctor Winter and I have tried to think—there's so much talk about justice, injustice, conquest. Our people are invaded, but I don't think they're conquered."

There was a sharp knock on the door and the room

was silent. Molly's needles stopped, and the Mayor's outstretched hand remained in the air. Tom, scratching his ear, left his hand there and stopped scratching. Everyone in the room was motionless. Every eye was turned toward the door. Then, first faintly and then growing louder, there came the tramp of the patrol, the squeak of their boots in the snow, and the sound of their talking as they went by. They passed the door and their footsteps disappeared in the distance. There was a second tap on the door. And in the room the people relaxed.

Orden said, "It must be cold out there for Annie." He took up his coat from the couch and opened the inner door and handed his coat through. "Put this around your shoulders, Annie," he said and closed the door.

"I don't know what I'd do without her," he said, "She gets everywhere, she sees and hears everything."

Tom said, "We should be going pretty soon, sir."

And Winter said, "I wish you'd forget about Mr. Corell."

"We can't. It isn't good to see him in the streets." He looked inquiringly at Mayor Orden.

Orden began slowly. "I want to speak simply. This is a little town. Justice and injustice are in terms of little things. Your brother's shot and Alex Morden's shot. Revenge against a traitor. The people are angry and they have no way to fight back. But it's all in little terms. It's people against people, not idea against idea."

Winter said, "It's funny for a doctor to think of destruction, but I think all invaded people want to resist. We are disarmed; our spirits and bodies aren't enough. The spirit of a disarmed man sinks."

Will Anders asked, "What's all this for, sir? What do you want of us?"

"We want to fight them and we can't," Orden said. "They're using hunger on the people now. Hunger brings weakness. You boys are sailing for England. Maybe nobody will listen to you, but tell them from us—from a small town—to give us weapons."

Tom asked, "You want guns?"

Again there was a quick knock on the door and the people froze where they were, and from outside there came the sound of the patrol, but at double step, running. Will moved quickly toward the door. The running steps came abreast of the house. There were muffled orders and the patrol ran by, and there was a second tap at the door.

Molly said, "They must be after somebody. I wonder who this time."

"We should be going," Tom said uneasily. "Do you want guns, sir? Shall we ask for guns?"

"No, tell them how it is. We are watched. Any move we make calls for reprisal. If we could have simple, secret weapons, weapons of stealth, explosives, dynamite to blow up rails, grenades, if possible, even poison." He spoke angrily. "This is no honorable war. This is a war of treachery and murder. Let us use the methods that have been used on us! Let the British bombers drop their big bombs on the works, but let them also drop us little bombs to use, to hide, to slip under the rails, under tanks. Then we will be armed, secretly armed. Then the invader will never know which of us is armed. Let the bombers bring us simple weapons. We will know how to use them!"

Winter broke in. "They'll never know where it will strike. The soldiers, the patrol, will never know which of us is armed."

Tom wiped his forehead. "If we get through, we'll tell them, sir, but—well, I've heard it said that in England there are still men in power who do not dare to put weapons in the hands of common people."

Orden stared at him. "Oh! I hadn't thought of that. Well, we can only see. If such people still govern England and America, the world is lost, anyway. Tell them what we say, if they will listen. We must have help, but if we get it"—his face grew very hard—"if we get it, we will help ourselves."

Winter said, "If they will even give us dynamite to hide, to bury in the ground to be ready against need, then the invader can never rest again, never! We will blow up his supplies."

The room grew excited. Molly said fiercely, "Yes, we could fight his rest, then. We could fight his sleep. We could fight his nerves and his certainties."

Will asked quietly, "Is that all, sir?"

"Yes." Orden nodded. "That's the core of it."

"What if they won't listen?"

"You can only try, as you are trying the sea tonight."

"Is that all, sir?"

The door opened and Annie came quietly in. Orden went on, "That's all. If you have to go now, let me send Annie out to see that the way is clear." He looked up and saw that Annie had come in. Annie said, "There's a soldier coming up the path. He looks like the soldier that was here before. There was a soldier here with Molly before."

The others looked at Molly. Annie said, "I locked the door."

"What does he want?" Molly asked. "Why does he come back?"

There was a gentle knocking at the outside door. Orden went to Molly. "What is this, Molly? Are you in trouble?"

"No," she said, "no! Go out the back way. You can get out through the back. Hurry, hurry out!"

The knocking continued on the front door. A man's voice called softly. Molly opened the door to the kitchen. She said, "Hurry, hurry!"

The Mayor stood in front of her. "Are you in trouble, Molly? You haven't done anything?"

Annie said coldly, "It looks like the same soldier. There was a soldier here before."

"Yes," Molly said to the Mayor. "Yes, there was a soldier here before."

The Mayor said, "What did he want?"

"He wanted to make love to me."

"But he didn't?" Orden said.

"No," she said, "he didn't. Go now, and I'll take care."

Orden said, "Molly, if you're in trouble, let us help you."

"The trouble I'm in no one can help me with," she said. "Go now," and she pushed them out of the door.

Annie remained behind. She looked at Molly. "Miss, what does this soldier want?"

"I don't know what he wants."

"Are you going to tell him anything?"

"No." Wonderingly, Molly repeated, "No." And then sharply she said, "No, Annie, I'm not!"

Annie scowled at her. "Miss, you'd better not tell him anything!" And she went out and closed the door behind her.

The tapping continued on the front door and a man's voice could be heard through the door.

Molly went to the center lamp, and her burden was

heavy on her. She looked down at the lamp. She looked at the table, and she saw the big scissors lying beside her knitting. She picked them up wonderingly by the blades. The blades slipped through her fingers until she held the long shears and she was holding them like a knife, and her eyes were horrified. She looked down into the lamp and the light flooded up in her face. Slowly she raised the shears and placed them inside her dress.

The tapping continued on the door. She heard the voice calling to her. She leaned over the lamp for a moment and then suddenly she blew out the light. The room was dark except for a spot of red that came from the coal stove. She opened the door. Her voice was strained and sweet. She called, "I'm coming, Lieutenant, I'm coming!"

CHAPTER SEVEN

In the dark, clear night a white, half-withered moon brought little light. The wind was dry and singing over the snow, a quiet wind that blew steadily, evenly from the cold point of the Pole. Over the land the snow lay very deep and dry as sand. The houses snuggled down in the hollows of banked snow, and their windows were dark and shuttered against the cold, and only a little smoke rose from the banked fires.

In the town the footpaths were frozen hard and packed hard. And the streets were silent, too, except when the miserable, cold patrol came by. The houses were dark against the night, and a little lingering warmth remained in the houses against the morning. Near the mine entrance the guards watched the sky and trained their instruments on the sky and turned their listening-instruments against the sky, for it was a clear night for bombing. On nights like this the feathered steel spindles came whistling down and roared to splinters. The land would be visible from the sky tonight, even though the moon seemed to throw little light.

Down toward one end of the village, among the small houses, a dog complained about the cold and the loneliness. He raised his nose to his god and gave a long and fulsome account of the state of the world as it applied to him. He was a practiced singer with a full bell throat and great versatility of range and control. The six men of the patrol slogging dejectedly up and down the streets heard the singing of the dog, and one of the muffled soldiers said, "Seems to me he's getting worse every night. I suppose we ought to shoot him."

And another answered, "Why? Let him howl. He sounds good to me. I used to have a dog at home that howled. I never could break him. Yellow dog. I don't mind the howl. They took my dog when they took the others," he said factually, in a dull voice.

And the corporal said, "Couldn't have dogs eating up food that was needed."

"Oh, I'm not complaining. I know it was necessary. I can't plan the way the leaders do. It seems funny to me, though, that some people here have dogs, and they don't have even as much food as we have. They're pretty gaunt, though, dogs and people."

"They're fools," said the corporal. "That's why they lost so quickly. They can't plan the way we can."

"I wonder if we'll have dogs again after it's over," said the soldier. "I suppose we could get them from America or some place and start the breeds again. What kind of dogs do you suppose they have in America?"

"I don't know," said the corporal. "Probably dogs as crazy as everything else they have." And he went on, "Maybe dogs are no good, anyway. It might be just as well if we never bothered with them, except for police work."

"It might be," said the soldier. "I've heard the Leader doesn't like dogs. I've heard they make him itch and sneeze."

"You hear all kinds of things," the corporal said.

"Listen!" The patrol stopped and from a great distance came the bee hum of planes.

"There they come," the corporal said. "Well, there aren't any lights. It's been two weeks, hasn't it, since they came before?"

"Twelve days," said the soldier.

The guards at the mine heard the high drone of the planes. "They're flying high," a sergeant said. And Captain Loft tilted his head back so that he could see under the rim of his helmet. "I judge over 20,000 feet," he said. "Maybe they're going on over."

"Aren't very many." The sergeant listened. "I don't think there are more than three of them. Shall I call the battery?"

"Just see they're alert, and then call Colonel Lanser—no, don't call him. Maybe they aren't coming here. They're nearly over and they haven't started to dive yet."

"Sounds to me like they're circling. I don't think there are more than two," the sergeant said.

In their beds the people heard the planes and they squirmed deep into their featherbeds and listened. In the palace of the Mayor the little sound awakened

Colonel Lanser, and he turned over on his back and looked at the dark ceiling with wide-open eyes, and he held his breath to listen better and then his heart beat so that he could not hear as well as he could when he was breathing. Mayor Orden heard the planes in his sleep and they made a dream for him and he moved and whispered in his sleep.

High in the air the two bombers circled, mud-colored planes. They cut their throttles and soared, circling. And from the belly of each one tiny little objects dropped, hundreds of them, one after another. They plummeted a few feet and then little parachutes opened and drifted small packages silently and slowly downward toward the earth, and the planes raised their throttles and gained altitude, and then cut their throttles and circled again, and more of the little objects plummeted down, and then the planes turned and flew back in the direction from which they had come.

The tiny parachutes floated like thistledown and the breeze spread them out and distributed them as seeds on the ends of thistledown are distributed. They drifted so slowly and landed so gently that sometimes the ten-inch packages of dynamite stood upright in the snow, and the little parachutes folded gently down around them. They looked black against the snow. They landed in the white fields and among the woods of the hills and they landed in trees and hung down from the branches. Some of them landed on the house-tops of the little town, some in the small front yards, and one landed and stood upright in the snow crown on top of the head of the village statue of St. Albert the Missionary.

One of the little parachutes came down in the street ahead of the patrol and the sergeant said, "Careful! It's a time bomb."

"It ain't big enough," a soldier said.

"Well, don't go near it." The sergeant had his flash-light out and he turned it on the object, a little para-chute no bigger than a handkerchief, colored light blue, and hanging from it a package wrapped in blue paper.

"Now don't anybody touch it," the sergeant said. "Harry, you go down to the mine and get the captain. We'll keep an eye on this damn thing."

The late dawn came and the people moving out of

their houses in the country saw the spots of blue against the snow. They went to them and picked them up. They unwrapped the paper and read the printed words. They saw the gift and suddenly each finder grew furtive, and he concealed the long tube under his coat and went to some secret place and hid the tube.

And word got to the children about the gift and they combed the countryside in a terrible Easter egg hunt, and when some lucky child saw the blue color, he rushed to the prize and opened it and then he hid the tube and told his parents about it. There were some people who were frightened, who turned the tubes over to the military, but they were not very many. And the soldiers scurried about the town in another Easter egg hunt, but they were not so good at it as the children were.

In the drawing-room of the palace of the Mayor the dining-table remained with the chairs about as it had been placed the day Alex Morden was shot. The room had not the grace it had when it was still the palace of the Mayor. The walls, bare of standing chairs, looked very blank. The table with a few papers scattered about on it made the room look like a business office.

The clock on the mantel struck nine. It was a dark day now, overcast with clouds, for the dawn had brought the heavy snow clouds.

Annie came out of the Mayor's room; she swooped by the table and glanced at the papers that lay there. Captain Loft came in. He stopped in the doorway, seeing Annie.

"What are you doing here?" he demanded.

And Annie said sullenly, "Yes, sir."

"I said, what are you doing here?"

"I thought to clean up, sir."

"Let things alone, and go along."

And Annie said, "Yes, sir," and she waited until he was clear of the door, and she scuttled out.

Captain Loft turned back through the doorway and he said, "All right, bring it in." A soldier came through the door behind him, his rifle hung over his shoulder by a strap, and in his arms he held a number of the blue packages, and from the ends of the packages there dangled the little strings and pieces of blue cloth.

Loft said, "Put them on the table." The soldier gingerly laid the packages down. "Now go upstairs and report to Colonel Lanser that I'm here with the—

things," and the soldier wheeled about and left the room.

Loft went to the table and picked up one of the packages, and his face wore a look of distaste. He held up the little blue cloth parachute, held it above his head and dropped it, and the cloth opened and the package floated to the floor. He picked up the package again and examined it.

Now Colonel Lanser came quickly into the room, followed by Major Hunter. Hunter was carrying a square of yellow paper in his hand. Lanser said, "Good morning, Captain," and he went to the head of the table and sat down. For a moment he looked at the little pile of tubes, and then he picked one up and held it in his hand. "Sit down, Hunter," he said. "Have you examined these?"

Hunter pulled out a chair and sat down. He looked at the yellow paper in his hand. "Not very carefully," he said. "There are three breaks in the railroad all within ten miles."

"Well, take a look at them and see what you think," Lanser said.

Hunter reached for a tube and stripped off the outer

covering, and inside was a small package next to the tube. Hunter took out a knife and cut into the tube. Captain Loft looked over his shoulder. Then Hunter smelled the cut and rubbed his fingers together, and he said, "It's silly. It's commercial dynamite. I don't know what per cent of nitroglycerin until I test it." He looked at the end. "It has a regular dynamite cap, fulminate of mercury, and a fuse—about a minute, I suppose." He tossed the tube back onto the table. "It's very cheap and very simple," he said.

The colonel looked at Loft. "How many do you think were dropped?"

"I don't know, sir," said Loft. "We picked up about fifty of them, and about ninety parachutes they came in. For some reason the people leave the parachutes when they take the tubes, and then there are probably a lot we haven't found yet."

Lanser waved his hand. "It doesn't really matter," he said. "They can drop as many as they want. We can't stop it, and we can't use it against them, either. They haven't conquered anybody."

Loft said fiercely, "We can beat them off the face of the earth!"

Hunter was prying the copper cap out of the top of one of the sticks, and Lanser said, "Yes—we can do that. Have you looked at this wrapper, Hunter?"

"Not yet, I haven't had time."

"It's kind of devilish, this thing," said Colonel Lanser. "The wrapper is blue, so that it's easy to see. Unwrap the outer paper and here"—he picked up the small package—"here is a piece of chocolate. Everybody will be looking for it. I'll bet our own soldiers steal the chocolate. Why, the kids will be looking for them, like Easter eggs."

A soldier came in and laid a square of yellow paper in front of the colonel and retired, and Lanser glanced at it and laughed harshly. "Here's something for you, Hunter. Two more breaks in your line."

Hunter looked up from the copper cap he was examining, and he asked, "How general is this? Did they drop them everywhere?"

Lanser was puzzled. "Now, that's the funny thing. I've talked to the capital. This is the only place they've dropped them."

"What do you make of that?" Hunter asked.

"Well, it's hard to say. I think this is a test place. I

suppose if it works here they'll use it all over, and if it doesn't work here they won't bother."

"What are you going to do?" Hunter asked.

"The capital orders me to stamp this out so ruthlessly that they won't drop it any place else."

Hunter said plaintively, "How am I going to mend five breaks in the railroad? I haven't rails right now for five breaks."

"You'll have to rip out some of the old sidings, I guess," said Lanser.

Hunter said, "That'll make a hell of a roadbed."

"Well, anyway, it will make a roadbed."

Major Hunter tossed the tube he had torn apart onto the pile, and Loft broke in, "We must stop this thing at once, sir. We must arrest and punish people who pick these things up, before they use them. We have to get busy so these people won't think we are weak."

Lanser was smiling at him, and he said, "Take it easy, Captain. Let's see what we have first, and then we'll think of remedies."

He took a new package from the pile and unwrapped it. He took the little piece of chocolate, tasted it, and he said, "This is a devilish thing. It's good chocolate, too. I can't even resist it myself. The prize in the grab-bag." Then he picked up the dynamite. "What do you think of this really, Hunter?"

"What I told you. It's very cheap and very effective for small jobs, dynamite with a cap and a one-minute fuse. It's good if you know how to use it. It's no good if you don't."

Lanser studied the print on the inside of the wrapper. "Have you read this?"

"Glanced at it," said Hunter.

"Well, I have read it, and I want you to listen to it carefully," said Lanser. He read from the paper, " 'To the unconquered people: Hide this. Do not expose yourself. You will need this later. It is a present from your friends to you and from you to the invader of your country. Do not try to do large things with it.' " He began to skip through the bill. "Now here, 'rails in the country.' And, 'work at night.' And, 'tie up transportation.' Now here, 'Instructions: rails. Place stick under rail close to the joint, and tight against a tie. Pack mud or hard-beaten snow around it so that it is firm. When the fuse is lighted you have a slow count of sixty before it explodes.' "

He looked up at Hunter and Hunter said simply, "It works." Lanser looked back at his paper and he skipped through. " 'Bridges: Weaken, do not destroy.' And here, 'transmission poles,' and here, 'culverts, trucks.' " He laid the blue handbill down. "Well, there it is."

Loft said angrily, "We must do something! There must be a way to control this. What does headquarters say?"

Lanser pursed his lips and his fingers played with one of the tubes. "I could have told you what they'd say before they said it. I have the orders. 'Set booby traps and poison the chocolate.' " He paused for a moment and then he said, "Hunter, I'm a good, loyal man, but sometimes when I hear the brilliant ideas of headquarters, I wish I were a civilian, an old, crippled civilian. They always think they are dealing with stupid people. I don't say that this is a measure of their intelligence, do I?"

Hunter looked amused. "Do you?"

Lanser said sharply, "No, I don't. But what will happen? One man will pick up one of these and get blown to bits by our booby trap. One kid will eat chocolate and die of strychnine poisoning. And then?" He looked down at his hands. "They will poke them with poles, or lasso them, before they touch them. They will try the chocolate on the cat. Goddamn it, Major, these are intelligent people. Stupid traps won't catch them twice."

Loft cleared his throat. "Sir, this is defeatist talk," he said. "We must do something. Why do you suppose it was only dropped here, sir?"

And Lanser said, "For one of two reasons: either this town was picked at random or else there is communication between this town and the outside. We know that some of the young men have got away."

Loft repeated dully, "We must do something, sir."

Now Lanser turned on him. "Loft, I think I'll recommend you for the General Staff. You want to get to work before you even know what the problem is. This is a new kind of conquest. Always before, it was possible to disarm a people and keep them in ignorance. Now they listen to their radios and we can't stop them. We can't even find their radios."

A soldier looked in through the doorway. "Mr. Corell to see you, sir."

Lanser replied, "Tell him to wait." He continued to talk to Loft. "They read the handbills; weapons drop from the sky for them. Now it's dynamite, Captain. Pretty soon it may be grenades, and then poison."

Loft said anxiously, "They haven't dropped poison yet."

"No, but they will. Can you think what will happen to the morale of our men or even to you if the people had some of those little game darts, you know, those silly little things you throw at a target, the points coated perhaps with cyanide, silent, deadly little things that you couldn't hear coming, that would pierce the uniform and make no noise? And what if our men knew that arsenic was about? Would you or they drink or eat comfortably?"

Hunter said dryly, "Are you writing the enemy's campaign, Colonel?"

"No, I'm trying to anticipate it."

Loft said, "Sir, we sit here talking when we should be searching for this dynamite. If there is organization among these people, we have to find it, we have to stamp it out."

"Yes," said Lanser, "we have to stamp it out, ferociously, I suppose. You take a detail, Loft. Get Prackle to take one. I wish we had more junior officers. Tonder's getting killed didn't help us a bit. Why couldn't he let women alone?"

Loft said, "I don't like the way Lieutenant Prackle is acting, sir."

"What's he doing?"

"He isn't doing anything, but he's jumpy and he's gloomy."

"Yes," Lanser said, "I know. It's a thing I've talked about so much. You know," he said, "I might be a major-general if I hadn't talked about it so much. We trained our young men for victory and you've got to admit they're glorious in victory, but they don't quite know how to act in defeat. We told them they were brighter and braver than other young men. It was a kind of shock to them to find out that they aren't a bit braver or brighter than other young men."

Loft said harshly, "What do you mean by defeat? We are not defeated."

And Lanser looked coldly up at him for a long moment and did not speak, and finally Loft's eyes wavered, and he said, "Sir."

"Thank you," said Lanser.

"You don't demand it of the others, sir."

"They don't think about it, so it isn't an insult. When you leave it out, it's insulting."

"Yes, sir," said Loft.

"Go on, now, try to keep Prackle in hand. Start your search. I don't want any shooting unless there's an overt act, do you understand?"

"Yes, sir," said Loft, and he saluted formally and went out of the room.

Hunter regarded Colonel Lanser amusedly. "Weren't you rough on him?"

"I had to be. He's frightened. I know his kind. He has to be disciplined when he's afraid or he'll go to pieces. He relies on discipline the way other men rely on sympathy. I suppose you'd better get to your rails. You might as well expect that tonight is the time when they'll really blow them, though."

Hunter stood up and he said, "Yes. I suppose the orders are coming in from the capital?"

"Yes."

"Are they——"

"You know what they are," Lanser interrupted. "You

know what they'd have to be. Take the leaders, shoot the leaders, take hostages, shoot the hostages, take more hostages, shoot them"—his voice had risen but now it sank almost to a whisper—"and the hatred growing and the hurt between us deeper and deeper."

Hunter hesitated. "Have they condemned any from the list of names?" and he motioned slightly toward the Mayor's bedroom.

Lanser shook his head. "No, not yet. They are just arrested so far."

Hunter said quietly, "Colonel, do you want me to recommend—maybe you're overtired, Colonel? Could I—you know—could I report that you're overtired?"

For a moment Lanser covered his eyes with his hand, and then his shoulders straightened and his face grew hard. "I'm not a civilian, Hunter. We're short enough of officers already. You know that. Get to your work, Major. I have to see Corell."

Hunter smiled. He went to the door and opened it, and he said out of the door, "Yes, he's here," and over his shoulder he said to Lanser, "It's Prackle. He wants to see you."

"Send him in," said Lanser.

Prackle came in, his face sullen, belligerent. "Colonel Lanser, sir, I wish to—"

"Sit down," said Lanser. "Sit down and rest a moment. Be a good soldier, Lieutenant."

The stiffness went out of Prackle quickly. He sat down beside the table and rested his elbows on it. "I wish—"

And Lanser said, "Don't talk for a moment. I know what it is. You didn't think it would be this way, did you? You thought it would be rather nice."

"They hate us," Prackle said. "They hate us so much."

Lanser smiled. "I wonder if I know what it is. It takes young men to make good soldiers, and young men need young women, is that it?"

"Yes, that's it."

"Well," Lanser said kindly, "does she hate you?"

Prackle looked at him in amazement. "I don't know, sir. Sometimes I think she's only sorry."

"And you're pretty miserable?"

"I don't like it here, sir."

"No, you thought it would be fun, didn't you? Lieutenant Tonder went to pieces and then he went out and they got a knife in him. I could send you home.

Do you want to be sent home, knowing we need you here?"

Prackle said uneasily, "No, sir, I don't."

"Good. Now I'll tell you, and I hope you'll understand it. You're not a man any more. You are a soldier. Your comfort is of no importance and, Lieutenant, your life isn't of much importance. If you live, you will have memories. That's about all you will have. Meanwhile you must take orders and carry them out. Most of the orders will be unpleasant, but that's not your business. I will not lie to you, Lieutenant. They should have trained you for this, and not for flower-strewn streets. They should have built your soul with truth, not led it along with lies." His voice grew hard. "But you took the job, Lieutenant. Will you stay with it or quit it? We can't take care of your soul."

Prackle stood up. "Thank you, sir."

"And the girl," Lanser continued, "the girl, Lieutenant, you may rape her, or protect her, or marry her—that is of no importance so long as you shoot her when it is ordered."

Prackle said wearily, "Yes, sir, thank you, sir."

"I assure you it is better to know. I assure you of

that. It is better to know. Go now, Lieutenant, and if Corell is still waiting, send him in." And he watched Lieutenant Prackle out of the doorway.

When Mr. Corell came in, he was a changed man. His left arm was in a cast, and he was no longer the jovial, friendly, smiling Corell. His face was sharp and bitter, and his eyes squinted down like little dead pig's eyes.

"I should have come before, Colonel," he said, "but your lack of co-operation made me hesitant."

Lanser said, "You were waiting for a reply to your report, I remember."

"I was waiting for much more than that. You refused me a position of authority. You said I was valueless. You did not realize that I was in this town long before you were. You left the Mayor in his office, contrary to my advice."

Lanser said, "Without him here we might have had more disorder than we have."

"That is a matter of opinion," Corell said. "This man is a leader of a rebellious people."

"Nonsense," said Lanser; "he's just a simple man."

With his good hand Corell took a black notebook

from his right pocket and opened it with his fingers. "You forgot, Colonel, that I had my sources, that I had been here a long time before you. I have to report to you that Mayor Orden has been in constant contact with every happening in this community. On the night when Lieutenant Tonder was murdered, he was in the house where the murder was committed. When the girl escaped to the hills, she stayed with one of his relatives. I traced her there, but she was gone. Whenever men have escaped, Orden has known about it and has helped them. And I even strongly suspect that he is somewhere in the picture of these little parachutes."

Lanser said eagerly, "But you can't prove it."

"No," Corell said, "I can't prove it. The first thing I know; the last I only suspect. Perhaps now you will be willing to listen to me."

Lanser said quietly, "What do you suggest?"

"These suggestions, Colonel, are a little stronger than suggestions. Orden must now be a hostage and his life must depend on the peacefulness of this community. His life must depend on the lighting of one single fuse on one single stick of dynamite."

He reached into his pocket again and brought out a little folding book, and he flipped it open and laid it in front of the colonel. "This, sir, was the answer to my report from headquarters. You will notice that it gives me certain authority."

Lanser looked at the little book and he spoke quietly. "You really did go over my head, didn't you?" He looked up at Corell with frank dislike in his eyes. "I heard you'd been injured. How did it happen?"

Corell said, "On the night when your lieutenant was murdered I was waylaid. The patrol saved me. Some of the townsmen escaped in my boat that night. Now, Colonel, must I express more strongly than I have that Mayor Orden must be held hostage?"

Lanser said, "He is here, he hasn't escaped. How can we hold him more hostage than we are?"

Suddenly in the distance there was a sound of an explosion, and both men looked around in the direction from which it came. Corell said, "There it is, Colonel, and you know perfectly well that if this experiment succeeds there will be dynamite in every invaded country."

Lanser repeated quietly, "What do you suggest?"

"Just what I have said. Orden must be held against rebellion."

"And if they rebel and we shoot Orden?"

"Then that little doctor is next; although he holds no position, he's next in authority in the town."

"But he holds no office."

"He has the confidence of the people."

"And when we shoot him, what then?"

"Then we have authority. Then rebellion will be broken. When we have killed the leaders, the rebellion will be broken."

Lanser asked quizzically, "Do you really think so?"

"It must be so."

Lanser shook his head slowly and then he called, "Sentry!" The door opened and a soldier appeared in the doorway. "Sergeant," said Lanser, "I have placed Mayor Orden under arrest, and I have placed Doctor Winter under arrest. You will see to it that Orden is guarded and you will bring Winter here immediately."

The sentry said, "Yes, sir."

Lanser looked up at Corell and he said, "You know, I hope you know what you're doing. I do hope you know what you're doing."

CHAPTER EIGHT

IN THE little town the news ran quickly. It was communicated by whispers in doorways, by quick, meaningful looks—"The Mayor's been arrested"—and through the town a little quiet jubilance ran, a fierce little jubilance, and people talked quietly together and went apart, and people going in to buy food leaned close to the clerks for a moment and a word passed between them.

The people went into the country, into the woods, searching for dynamite. And children playing in the snow found the dynamite, and by now even the children had their instructions. They opened the packages and ate the chocolate, and then they buried the dynamite in the snow and told their parents where it was.

Far out in the country a man picked up a tube and read the instructions and he said to himself, "I wonder if this works." He stood the tube up in the snow and lighted the fuse, and he ran back from it and counted, but his count was fast. It was sixty-eight before the dynamite exploded. He said, "It does work," and he went hurriedly about looking for more tubes.

Almost as though at a signal the people went into their houses and the doors were closed, the streets were quiet. At the mine the soldiers carefully searched every miner who went into the shaft, searched and re-searched, and the soldiers were nervous and rough and they spoke harshly to the miners. The miners looked coldly at them, and behind their eyes was a little fierce jubilance.

In the drawing-room of the palace of the Mayor the table had been cleaned up, and a soldier stood guard at Mayor Orden's bedroom door. Annie was on her knees in front of the coal grate, putting little pieces of coal on the fire. She looked up at the sentry standing in front of Mayor Orden's door and she said truculently, "Well, what are you going to do to him?" The soldier did not answer.

The outside door opened and another soldier came in, holding Doctor Winter by the arm. He closed the door behind Doctor Winter and stood against the door inside the room. Doctor Winter said, "Hello, Annie, how's His Excellency?"

And Annie pointed at the bedroom and said, "He's in there."

"He isn't ill?" Doctor Winter said.

"No, he didn't seem to be," said Annie. "I'll see if I can tell him you're here." She went to the sentry and spoke imperiously. "Tell His Excellency that Doctor Winter is here, do you hear me?"

The sentry did not answer and did not move, but behind him the door opened and Mayor Orden stood in the doorway. He ignored the sentry and brushed past him and stepped into the room. For a moment the sentry considered taking him back, and then he returned to his place beside the door. Orden said, "Thank you, Annie. Don't go too far away, will you? I might need you."

Annie said, "No, sir, I won't. Is Madame all right?"

"She's doing her hair. Do you want to see her, Annie?"

"Yes, sir," said Annie, and she brushed past the sentry, too, and went into the bedroom and shut the door.

Orden said, "Is there something you want, Doctor?"

Winter grinned sardonically and pointed over his shoulder to his guard. "Well, I guess I'm under arrest. My friend here brought me."

Orden said, "I suppose it was bound to come. What will they do now, I wonder?" And the two men looked at each other for a long time and each one knew what the other one was thinking.

And then Orden continued as though he had been talking. "You know, I couldn't stop it if I wanted to."

"I know," said Winter, "but they don't know." And he went on with a thought he had been having. "A time-minded people," he said, "and the time is nearly up. They think that just because they have only one leader and one head, we are all like that. They know that ten heads lopped off will destroy them, but we are a free people; we have as many heads as we have people, and in a time of need leaders pop up among us like mushrooms."

Orden put his hand on Winter's shoulder and he

said, "Thank you. I knew it, but it's good to hear you say it. The little people won't go under, will they?" He searched Winter's face anxiously.

And the doctor reassured him, "Why, no, they won't. As a matter of fact, they will grow stronger with outside help."

The room was silent for a moment. The sentry shifted his position a little and his rifle clinked on a button.

Orden said, "I can talk to you, Doctor, and I probably won't be able to talk again. There are little shameful things in my mind." He coughed and glanced at the rigid soldier, but the soldier gave no sign of having heard. "I have been thinking of my own death. If they follow the usual course, they must kill me, and then they must kill you." And when Winter was silent, he said, "Mustn't they?"

"Yes, I guess so." Winter walked to one of the gilt chairs, and as he was about to sit down he noticed that its tapestry was torn, and he petted the seat with his fingers as though that would mend it. And he sat down gently because it was torn.

And Orden went on, "You know, I'm afraid, I have

been thinking of ways to escape, to get out of it. I have been thinking of running away. I have been thinking of pleading for my life, and it makes me ashamed."

And Winter, looking up, said, "But you haven't done it."

"No, I haven't."

"And you won't do it."

Orden hesitated. "No, I won't. But I have thought of it."

And Winter said, gently, "How do you know everyone doesn't think of it? How do you know I haven't thought of it?"

"I wonder why they arrested you, too," Orden said. "I guess they will have to kill you, too."

"I guess so," said Winter. He rolled his thumbs and watched them tumble over and over.

"You know so." Orden was silent for a moment and then he said, "You know, Doctor, I am a little man and this is a little town, but there must be a spark in little men that can burst into flame. I am afraid, I am terribly afraid, and I thought of all the things I might do to save my own life, and then that went away, and sometimes now I feel a kind of exultation, as though I were bigger and better than I am, and do you know what I have been thinking, Doctor?" He smiled, remembering. "Do you remember in school, in the *Apology*? Do you remember Socrates says, 'Someone will say, "And are you not ashamed, Socrates, of a course of life which is likely to bring you to an untimely end?" To him I may fairly answer, "There you are mistaken: a man who is good for anything ought not to calculate the chance of living or dying; he ought only to consider whether he is doing right or wrong."'" Orden paused, trying to remember.

Doctor Winter sat tensely forward now, and he went on with it, "'Acting the part of a good man or of a bad.' I don't think you have it quite right. You never were a good scholar. You were wrong in the denunciation, too."

Orden chuckled. "Do you remember that?"

"Yes," said Winter, eagerly, "I remember it well. You forgot a line or a word. It was graduation, and you were so excited you forgot to tuck in your shirt-tail and your shirt-tail was out. You wondered why they laughed."

Orden smiled to himself, and his hand went secretly behind him and patrolled for a loose shirt-tail. "I was Socrates," he said, "and I denounced the School Board. How I denounced them! I bellowed it, and I could see them grow red."

Winter said, "They were holding their breaths to keep from laughing. Your shirt-tail was out."

Mayor Orden laughed. "How long ago? Forty years."

"Forty-six."

The sentry by the bedroom door moved quietly over to the sentry by the outside door. They spoke softly out of the corners of their mouths like children whispering in school. "How long you been on duty?"

"All night. Can't hardly keep my eyes open."

"Me too. Hear from your wife on the boat yesterday?"

"Yes! She said say hello to you. Said she heard you was wounded. She don't write much."

"Tell her I'm all right."

"Sure—when I write."

The Mayor raised his head and looked at the ceiling and he muttered, "Um—um—um. I wonder if I can remember—how does it go?"

And Winter prompted him, "'And now, O men——'"

And Orden said softly, "'And now, O men who have condemned me——'"

Colonel Lanser came quietly into the room; the sentries stiffened. Hearing the words, the colonel stopped and listened.

Orden looked at the ceiling, lost in trying to remember the old words. "'And now, O men who have condemned me,'" he said, "'I would fain prophesy to you—for I am about to die—and—in the hour of death—men are gifted with prophetic power. And I—prophesy to you who are my murderers—that immediately after my—my death——'"

And Winter stood up, saying, "Departure."

Orden looked at him. "What?"

And Winter said, "The word is 'departure,' not 'death.' You made the same mistake before. You made that mistake forty-six years ago."

"No, it is death. It is death." Orden looked around

and saw Colonel Lanser watching him. He asked, "Isn't it 'death'?"

Colonel Lanser said, "'Departure.' It is 'immediately after my departure.'"

Doctor Winter insisted, "You see, that's two against one. 'Departure' is the word. It is the same mistake you made before."

Then Orden looked straight ahead and his eyes were in his memory, seeing nothing outward. And he went on, "'I prophesy to you who are my murderers that immediately after my—departure punishment far heavier than you have inflicted on me will surely await you.'"

Winter nodded encouragingly, and Colonel Lanser nodded, and they seemed to be trying to help him to remember. And Orden went on, "'Me you have killed because you wanted to escape the accuser, and not to give an account of your lives—!'"

Lieutenant Prackle entered excitedly, crying, "Colonel Lanser!"

Colonel Lanser said, "Shh—" and he held out his hand to restrain him.

And Orden went on softly, "'But that will not be as you suppose; far otherwise.'" His voice grew stronger. " 'For I say that there will be more accusers of you than there are now' "—he made a little gesture with his hand, a speech-making gesture—" 'accusers whom hitherto I have restrained; and as they are younger they will be more inconsiderate with you, and you will be more offended at them.' " He frowned, trying to remember.

And Lieutenant Prackle said, "Colonel Lanser, we have found some men with dynamite."

And Lanser said, "Hush."

Orden continued. " 'If you think that by killing men you can prevent someone from censuring your evil lives, you are mistaken.' " He frowned and thought and he looked at the ceiling, and he smiled embarrassedly and he said, "That's all I can remember. It is gone away from me."

And Doctor Winter said, "It's very good after forty-six years, and you weren't very good at it forty-six years ago."

Lieutenant Prackle broke in, "The men have dynamite, Colonel Lanser."

"Did you arrest them?"

"Yes, sir. Captain Loft and—"

Lanser said, "Tell Captain Loft to guard them." He recaptured himself and he advanced into the room and he said, "Orden, these things must stop."

And the Mayor smiled helplessly at him. "They cannot stop, sir."

Colonel Lanser said harshly, "I arrested you as a hostage for the good behavior of your people. Those are my orders."

"But that won't stop it," Orden said simply. "You don't understand. When I have become a hindrance to the people, they will do without me."

Lanser said, "Tell me truly what you think. If the people know you will be shot if they light another fuse, what will they do?"

The Mayor looked helplessly at Doctor Winter. And then the bedroom door opened and Madame came out, carrying the Mayor's chain of office in her hand. She said, "You forgot this."

Orden said, "What? Oh, yes," and he stooped his head and Madame slipped the chain of office over his head, and he said, "Thank you, dear."

Madame complained, "You always forget it. You forget it all the time."

The Mayor looked at the end of the chain he held in his hand—the gold medallion with the insignia of his office carved on it. Lanser pressed him. "What will they do?"

"I don't know," said the Mayor. "I think they will light the fuse."

"Suppose you ask them not to?"

Winter said, "Colonel, this morning I saw a little boy building a snow man, while three grown soldiers watched to see that he did not caricature your leader. He made a pretty good likeness, too, before they destroyed it."

Lanser ignored the doctor. "Suppose you ask them not to?" he repeated.

Orden seemed half asleep; his eyes were drooped, and he tried to think. He said, "I am not a very brave man, sir. I think they will light it, anyway." He struggled with his speech. "I hope they will, but if I ask them not to, they will be sorry."

Madame said, "What is this all about?"

"Be quiet a moment, dear," the Mayor said.

"But you think they will light it?" Lanser insisted.

The Mayor spoke proudly. "Yes, they will light it.

I have no choice of living or dying, you see, sir, but—I do have a choice of how I do it. If I tell them not to fight, they will be sorry, but they will fight. If I tell them to fight, they will be glad, and I who am not a very brave man will have made them a little braver." He smiled apologetically. "You see, it is an easy thing to do, since the end for me is the same."

Lanser said, "If you say yes, we can tell them you said no. We can tell them you begged for your life."

And Winter broke in angrily, "They would know. You do not keep secrets. One of your men got out of hand one night and he said the flies had conquered the flypaper, and now the whole nation knows his words. They have made a song of it. The flies have conquered the flypaper. You do not keep secrets, Colonel."

From the direction of the mine a whistle tooted shrilly. And a quick gust of wind sifted dry snow against the windows.

Orden fingered his gold medallion. He said quietly, "You see, sir, nothing can change it. You will be destroyed and driven out." His voice was very soft. "The people don't like to be conquered, sir, and so they will not be. Free men cannot start a war, but once it is started, they can fight on in defeat. Herd men, followers of a leader, cannot do that, and so it is always the herd men who win battles and the free men who win wars. You will find that is so, sir."

Lanser was erect and stiff. "My orders are clear. Eleven o'clock was the deadline. I have taken hostages. If there is violence, the hostages will be executed."

And Doctor Winter said to the colonel, "Will you carry out the orders, knowing they will fail?"

Lanser's face was tight. "I will carry out my orders no matter what they are, but I do think, sir, a proclamation from you might save many lives."

Madame broke in plaintively, "I wish you would tell me what all this nonsense is."

"It is nonsense, dear."

"But they can't arrest the Mayor," she explained to him.

Orden smiled at her. "No," he said, "they can't arrest the Mayor. The Mayor is an idea conceived by free men. It will escape arrest."

From the distance there was a sound of an explosion. And the echo of it rolled to the hills and back again. The whistle at the coal mine tooted a shrill, sharp warning. Orden stood very tensely for a moment and then he smiled. A second explosion roared—nearer this time and heavier—and its echo rolled back from the mountains. Orden looked at his watch and then he took his watch and chain and put them in Doctor Winter's hand. "How did it go about the flies?" he asked.

"The flies have conquered the flypaper," Winter said.

Orden called, "Annie!" The bedroom door opened instantly and the Mayor said, "Were you listening?"

"Yes, sir." Annie was embarrassed.

And now an explosion roared near by and there was a sound of splintering wood and breaking glass, and the door behind the sentries puffed open. And Orden said, "Annie, I want you to stay with Madame as long as she needs you. Don't leave her alone." He put his arm around Madame and he kissed her on the forehead and then he moved slowly toward the door where Lieutenant Prackle stood. In the doorway he turned back to Doctor Winter. "Crito, I owe a cock to Asclepius," he said tenderly. "Will you remember to pay the debt?"

Winter closed his eyes for a moment before he answered, "The debt shall be paid."

Orden chuckled then. "I remembered that one. I didn't forget that one." He put his hand on Prackle's arm, and the lieutenant flinched away from him.

And Winter nodded slowly. "Yes, you remembered. The debt shall be paid."

THE LONG VALLEY

The Long Valley

John Steinbeck

P. F. COLLIER & SON CORPORATION
NEW YORK

TC

MANUFACTURED IN THE UNITED STATES OF AMERICA

CONTENTS

THE CHRYSANTHEMUMS

THE CHRYSANTHEMUMS

THE high grey-flannel fog of winter closed off the Salinas Valley from the sky and from all the rest of the world. On every side it sat like a lid on the mountains and made of the great valley a closed pot. On the broad, level land floor the gang plows bit deep and left the black earth shining like metal where the shares had cut. On the foot-hill ranches across the Salinas River, the yellow stubble fields seemed to be bathed in pale cold sunshine, but there was no sunshine in the valley now in December. The thick willow scrub along the river flamed with sharp and positive yellow leaves.

It was a time of quiet and of waiting. The air was cold and tender. A light wind blew up from the southwest so that the farmers were mildly hopeful of a good rain before long; but fog and rain do not go together.

Across the river, on Henry Allen's foothill ranch there was little work to be done, for the hay was cut and stored and the orchards were plowed up to receive the rain deeply when it should come. The cattle on the higher slopes were becoming shaggy and rough-coated.

Elisa Allen, working in her flower garden, looked down across the yard and saw Henry, her husband, talking to two men in business suits. The three of them stood by the tractor shed, each man with one foot on the side of the little Fordson. They smoked cigarettes and studied the machine as they talked.

Elisa watched them for a moment and then went back to her work. She was thirty-five. Her face was lean and strong and her eyes were as clear as water. Her figure looked blocked and heavy in her gardening costume, a man's black hat pulled low down over her eyes, clod-hopper shoes, a figured print dress almost completely covered by a big corduroy apron with four big pockets to hold the snips, the trowel and scratcher, the seeds and the knife she worked with. She wore heavy leather gloves to protect her hands while she worked.

She was cutting down the old year's chrysanthemum stalks with a pair of short and powerful scissors. She looked down toward the men by the tractor shed now and then. Her face was eager and mature and handsome; even her work with the scissors was over-eager, over-powerful. The chrysanthemum stems seemed too small and easy for her energy.

She brushed a cloud of hair out of her eyes with the back of her glove, and left a smudge of earth on her cheek in doing it. Behind her stood the neat white farm house with red geraniums close-banked around it as high as the windows. It was a hard-swept looking little house, with hard-polished windows, and a clean mud-mat on the front steps.

Elisa cast another glance toward the tractor shed. The strangers were getting into their Ford coupe. She took off a glove and put her strong fingers down into the forest of new green chrysanthemum sprouts that were growing around the old roots. She spread the leaves and looked down among the close-growing stems. No aphids were there, no sowbugs or snails or cutworms. Her terrier fingers destroyed such pests before they could get started.

Elisa started at the sound of her husband's voice. He had come near quietly, and he leaned over the wire fence that protected her flower garden from cattle and dogs and chickens.

"At it again," he said. "You've got a strong new crop coming."

Elisa straightened her back and pulled on the gardening glove again. "Yes. They'll be strong this coming year." In her tone and on her face there was a little smugness.

"You've got a gift with things," Henry observed. "Some of those yellow chrysanthemums you had this year were ten inches across. I wish you'd work out in the orchard and raise some apples that big."

Her eyes sharpened. "Maybe I could do it, too. I've a gift with things, all right. My mother had it. She could stick anything in the ground and make it grow. She said it was having planters' hands that knew how to do it."

"Well, it sure works with flowers," he said.

"Henry, who were those men you were talking to?"

"Why, sure, that's what I came to tell you. They were from the Western Meat Company. I sold those thirty head of three-year-old steers. Got nearly my own price, too."

"Good," she said. "Good for you."

"And I thought," he continued, "I thought how it's Saturday afternoon, and we might go into Salinas for dinner at a restaurant, and then to a picture show—to celebrate, you see."

"Good," she repeated. "Oh, yes. That will be good."

Henry put on his joking tone. "There's fights tonight. How'd you like to go to the fights?"

"Oh, no," she said breathlessly. "No, I wouldn't like fights."

"Just fooling, Elisa. We'll go to a movie. Let's see. It's two now. I'm going to take Scotty and bring down those steers from the hill. It'll take us maybe two hours. We'll go in town about five and have dinner at the Cominos Hotel. Like that?"

"Of course I'll like it. It's good to eat away from home."

"All right, then. I'll go get up a couple of horses."

She said, "I'll have plenty of time to transplant some of these sets, I guess."

She heard her husband calling Scotty down by the barn. And a little later she saw the two men ride up the pale yellow hillside in search of the steers.

There was a little square sandy bed kept for rooting the chrysanthemums. With her trowel she turned the soil over and over, and smoothed it and patted it firm. Then she dug ten parallel trenches to receive the sets. Back at the chysanthemum bed she pulled out the little crisp shoots, trimmed off the leaves of each one with her scissors and laid it on a small orderly pile.

A squeak of wheels and plod of hoofs came from the road. Elisa looked up. The country road ran along the dense bank of willows and cottonwoods that bordered the river, and up this road came a curious vehicle, curiously drawn. It was an old spring-wagon, with a round canvas top on it like the cover of a prairie schooner. It was drawn by an old bay horse and a little grey-and-white burro. A big stubble-bearded man sat between the cover flaps and drove the crawling team. Underneath the wagon, between the hind wheels, a lean and rangy mongrel dog walked sedately. Words were painted on the canvas, in clumsy, crooked letters. "Pots, pans, knives, sisors, lawn mores, Fixed." Two rows of articles, and the triumphantly definitive "Fixed" below. The black paint had run down in little sharp points beneath each letter.

Elisa, squatting on the ground, watched to see the crazy, loose-jointed wagon pass by. But it didn't pass. It turned into the farm road in front of her house, crooked old wheels skirling and squeaking. The rangy dog darted from between the wheels and ran ahead. Instantly the two ranch shepherds flew out at him. Then all three stopped, and with stiff and quivering tails, with taut straight legs, with ambassadorial dignity, they slowly circled, sniffing daintily. The caravan pulled up to Elisa's wire fence and stopped. Now the newcomer dog, feeling out-numbered, lowered his tail and retired under the wagon with raised hackles and bared teeth.

The man on the wagon seat called out, "That's a bad dog in a fight when he gets started."

Elisa laughed. "I see he is. How soon does he generally get started?"

The man caught up her laughter and echoed it heartily. "Sometimes not for weeks and weeks," he said. He climbed stiffly down, over the wheel. The horse and the donkey drooped like unwatered flowers.

Elisa saw that he was a very big man. Although his hair and beard were greying, he did not look old. His worn black suit was wrinkled and spotted with grease. The laughter had disappeared from his face and eyes the moment his laughing voice ceased. His eyes were dark, and they were full of the brooding that gets in the eyes of teamsters and of sailors. The calloused hands he rested on the wire fence were cracked, and every crack was a black line. He took off his battered hat.

"I'm off my general road, ma'am," he said. "Does this dirt road cut over across the river to the Los Angeles highway?"

Elisa stood up and shoved the thick scissors in her apron pocket. "Well, yes, it does, but it winds around and then fords the river. I don't think your team could pull through the sand."

He replied with some asperity, "It might surprise you what them beasts can pull through."

"When they get started?" she asked.

He smiled for a second. "Yes. When they get started."

"Well," said Elisa, "I think you'll save time if you go back to the Salinas road and pick up the highway there."

He drew a big finger down the chicken wire and made it sing. "I ain't in any hurry, ma'am. I go from Seattle to San Diego and back every year. Takes all my time. About six months each way. I aim to follow nice weather."

Elisa took off her gloves and stuffed them in the apron pocket with the scissors. She touched the under edge of her man's hat, searching for fugitive hairs. "That sounds like a nice kind of a way to live," she said.

He leaned confidentially over the fence. "Maybe you noticed the writing on my wagon. I mend pots and sharpen knives and scissors. You got any of them things to do?"

"Oh, no," she said quickly. "Nothing like that." Her eyes hardened with resistance.

"Scissors is the worst thing," he explained. "Most people just ruin scissors trying to sharpen 'em, but I know how. I got a special tool. It's a little bobbit kind of thing, and patented. But it sure does the trick."

"No. My scissors are all sharp."

"All right, then. Take a pot," he continued earnestly, "a bent pot, or a pot with a hole. I can make it like new so you don't have to buy no new ones. That's a saving for you."

"No," she said shortly. "I tell you I have nothing like that for you to do."

His face fell to an exaggerated sadness. His voice took on a whining undertone. "I ain't had a thing to do today. Maybe I won't have no supper tonight. You see I'm off my regular road. I know folks on the highway clear from Seattle to San Diego. They save their things for me to sharpen up because they know I do it so good and save them money."

"I'm sorry," Elisa said irritably. "I haven't anything for you to do."

His eyes left her face and fell to searching the ground. They roamed about until they came to the chrysanthemum bed where she had been working. "What's them plants, ma'am?"

The irritation and resistance melted from Elisa's face. "Oh, those are chrysanthemums, giant whites and yellows. I raise them every year, bigger than anybody around here."

"Kind of a long-stemmed flower? Looks like a quick puff of colored smoke?" he asked.

"That's it. What a nice way to describe them."

"They smell kind of nasty till you get used to them," he said.

"It's a good bitter smell," she retorted, "not nasty at all."

He changed his tone quickly. "I like the smell myself."

"I had ten-inch blooms this year," she said.

The man leaned farther over the fence. "Look. I know a lady down the road a piece, has got the nicest garden you ever seen. Got nearly every kind of flower but no chrysantheums. Last time I was mending a copper-bottom washtub for her (that's a hard job but I do it good), she said to me, 'If you ever run acrost some nice chrysantheums I wish you'd try to get me a few seeds.' That's what she told me."

Elisa's eyes grew alert and eager. "She couldn't have known much about chrysanthemums. You *can* raise them from seed, but it's much easier to root the little sprouts you see there."

"Oh," he said. "I s'pose I can't take none to her, then."

"Why yes you can," Elisa cried. "I can put some in damp sand, and you can carry them right along with you. They'll take root in the pot if you keep them damp. And then she can transplant them."

"She'd sure like to have some, ma'am. You say they're nice ones?"

"Beautiful," she said. "Oh, beautiful." Her eyes shone. She tore off the battered hat and shook out her dark pretty hair. "I'll put them in a flower pot, and you can take them right with you. Come into the yard."

While the man came through the picket gate Elisa ran excitedly along the geranium-bordered path to the back of the house. And she returned carrying a big red flower pot. The gloves were forgotten now. She kneeled on the ground by the starting bed and dug up the sandy soil with her fingers and scooped it into the bright new flower pot. Then she picked up the little pile of shoots she had prepared. With her strong fingers she pressed them into the sand and tamped around them with her knuckles. The man stood over her. "I'll tell you what to do," she said. "You remember so you can tell the lady."

"Yes, I'll try to remember."

"Well, look. These will take root in about a month. Then she must set them out, about a foot apart in good rich earth like this, see?" She lifted a handful of dark soil for him to look at. "They'll grow fast and tall. Now remember this: In July tell her to cut them down, about eight inches from the ground."

"Before they bloom?" he asked.

"Yes, before they bloom." Her face was tight with eagerness. "They'll grow right up again. About the last of September the buds will start."

She stopped and seemed perplexed. "It's the budding that takes the most care," she said hesitantly. "I don't know how to tell you." She looked deep into his eyes, searchingly. Her mouth opened a little, and she seemed to be listening. "I'll try to tell you," she said. "Did you ever hear of planting hands?"

"Can't say I have, ma'am."

"Well, I can only tell you what it feels like. It's when you're picking off the buds you don't want. Everything goes right down into your fingertips. You watch your fingers work. They do it themselves. You can feel how it is. They pick and pick the buds. They never make a mistake. They're with the plant. Do you see? Your fingers and the plant. You can feel that, right up your arm. They know. They never make a mistake. You can feel it.

When you're like that you can't do anything wrong. Do you see that? Can you understand that?"

She was kneeling on the ground looking up at him. Her breast swelled passionately.

The man's eyes narrowed. He looked away self-consciously. "Maybe I know," he said. "Sometimes in the night in the wagon there——"

Elisa's voice grew husky. She broke in on him, "I've never lived as you do, but I know what you mean. When the night is dark—why, the stars are sharp-pointed, and there's quiet. Why, you rise up and up! Every pointed star gets driven into your body. It's like that. Hot and sharp and—lovely."

Kneeling there, her hand went out toward his legs in the greasy black trousers. Her hesitant fingers almost touched the cloth. Then her hand dropped to the ground. She crouched low like a fawning dog.

He said, "It's nice, just like you say. Only when you don't have no dinner, it ain't."

She stood up then, very straight, and her face was ashamed. She held the flower pot out to him and placed it gently in his arms. "Here. Put it in your wagon, on the seat, where you can watch it. Maybe I can find something for you to do."

At the back cf the house she dug in the can pile and found two old and battered aluminum saucepans. She carried them back and gave them to him. "Here, maybe you can fix these."

His manner changed. He became professional. "Good as new I can fix them." At the back of his wagon he set a little anvil, and out of an oily tool box dug a small machine hammer. Elisa came through the gate to watch him while he pounded out the dents in the kettles. His mouth grew sure and knowing. At a difficult part of the work he sucked his under-lip.

"You sleep right in the wagon?" Elisa asked.

"Right in the wagon, ma'am. Rain or shine I'm dry as a cow in there."

"It must be nice," she said. "It must be very nice. I wish women could do such things."

"It ain't the right kind of a life for a woman."

Her upper lip raised a little, showing her teeth. "How do you know? How can you tell?" she said.

"I don't know, ma'am," he protested. "Of course I don't know. Now here's your kettles, done. You don't have to buy no new ones."

"How much?"

"Oh, fifty cents'll do. I keep my prices down and my work good. That's why I have all them satisfied customers up and down the highway."

Elisa brought him a fifty-cent piece from the house and dropped it in his hand. "You might be surprised to have a rival some time. I can sharpen scissors, too. And I can beat the dents out of little pots. I could show you what a woman might do."

He put his hammer back in the oily box and shoved the little anvil out of sight. "It would be a lonely life for a woman, ma'am, and a scarey life, too, with animals creeping under the wagon all night." He climbed over the singletree, steadying himself with a hand on the burro's white rump. He settled himself in the seat, picked up the lines. "Thank you kindly, ma'am," he said. "I'll do like you told me; I'll go back and catch the Salinas road."

"Mind," she called, "if you're long in getting there, keep the sand damp."

"Sand, ma'am? . . . Sand? Oh, sure. You mean around the chrysantheums. Sure I will." He clucked his tongue. The beasts leaned luxuriously into their collars. The mongrel dog took his place between the back wheels. The wagon turned and crawled out the entrance road and back the way it had come, along the river.

Elisa stood in front of her wire fence watching the slow progress of the caravan. Her shoulders were straight, her head thrown back, her eyes half-closed, so that the scene came vaguely into them. Her lips moved silently, forming the words "Good-bye—good-bye." Then she whispered, "That's a bright direction. There's a glowing there." The sound of her whisper startled her. She shook herself free and looked about to see whether anyone had been listening. Only the dogs had heard. They lifted their heads toward her from their sleeping in the dust, and then stretched out their chins and settled asleep again. Elisa turned and ran hurriedly into the house.

In the kitchen she reached behind the stove and felt the water tank. It was full of hot water from the noonday cooking. In the bathroom she tore off her soiled clothes and flung them into the corner. And then she scrubbed herself with a little block of pumice, legs and thighs, loins and chest and arms, until her skin was scratched and red. When she had dried herself she stood in front of a mirror in her bedroom and looked at her body. She tightened her stomach and threw out her chest. She turned and looked over her shoulder at her back.

After a while she began to dress, slowly. She put on her newest underclothing and her nicest stockings and the dress which was the symbol of her prettiness. She worked carefully on her hair, penciled her eyebrows and rouged her lips.

Before she was finished she heard the little thunder of hoofs and the shouts of Henry and his helper as they drove the red steers into the corral. She heard the gate bang shut and set herself for Henry's arrival.

His step sounded on the porch. He entered the house calling, "Elisa, where are you?"

"In my room, dressing. I'm not ready. There's hot water for your bath. Hurry up. It's getting late."

When she heard him splashing in the tub, Elisa laid his dark suit on the bed, and shirt and socks and tie beside it. She stood his polished shoes on the floor beside the bed. Then she went to the porch and sat primly and stiffly down. She looked toward the river road where the willow-line was still yellow with frosted leaves so that under the high grey fog they seemed a thin band of sunshine. This was the only color in the grey afternoon. She sat unmoving for a long time. Her eyes blinked rarely.

Henry came banging out of the door, shoving his tie inside his vest as he came. Elisa stiffened and her face grew tight. Henry stopped short and looked at her. "Why —why, Elisa. You look so nice!"

"Nice? You think I look nice? What do you mean by 'nice'?"

Henry blundered on. "I don't know. I mean you look different, strong and happy."

"I am strong? Yes, strong. What do you mean 'strong'?"

He looked bewildered. "You're playing some kind of a game," he said helplessly. "It's a kind of a play. You look strong enough to break a calf over your knee, happy enough to eat it like a watermelon."

For a second she lost her rigidity. "Henry! Don't talk like that. You didn't know what you said." She grew complete again. "I'm strong," she boasted. "I never knew before how strong."

Henry looked down toward the tractor shed, and when he brought his eyes back to her, they were his own again. "I'll get out the car. You can put on your coat while I'm starting."

Elisa went into the house. She heard him drive to the gate and idle down his motor, and then she took a long time to put on her hat. She pulled it here and pressed it there. When Henry turned the motor off she slipped into her coat and went out.

The little roadster bounced along on the dirt road by the river, raising the birds and driving the rabbits into the brush. Two cranes flapped heavily over the willow-line and dropped into the river-bed.

Far ahead on the road Elisa saw a dark speck. She knew.

She tried not to look as they passed it, but her eyes would not obey. She whispered to herself sadly, "He might have thrown them off the road. That wouldn't have been much trouble, not very much. But he kept the pot," she explained. "He had to keep the pot. That's why he couldn't get them off the road."

The roadster turned a bend and she saw the caravan ahead. She swung full around toward her husband so she could not see the little covered wagon and the mismatched team as the car passed them.

In a moment it was over. The thing was done. She did not look back.

She said loudly, to be heard above the motor, "It will be good, tonight, a good dinner."

"Now you're changed again," Henry complained. He took one hand from the wheel and patted her knee. "I ought to take you in to dinner oftener. It would be good for both of us. We get so heavy out on the ranch."

"Henry," she asked, "could we have wine at dinner?"

"Sure we could. Say! That will be fine."

She was silent for a while; then she said, "Henry, at those prize fights, do the men hurt each other very much?"

"Sometimes a little, not often. Why?"

"Well, I've read how they break noses, and blood runs down their chests. I've read how the fighting gloves get heavy and soggy with blood."

He looked around at her. "What's the matter, Elisa? I didn't know you read things like that." He brought the car to a stop, then turned to the right over the Salinas River bridge.

"Do any women ever go to the fights?" she asked.

"Oh, sure, some. What's the matter, Elisa? Do you want to go? I don't think you'd like it, but I'll take you if you really want to go."

She relaxed limply in the seat. "Oh, no. No. I don't want to go. I'm sure I don't." Her face was turned away from him. "It will be enough if we can have wine. It will be plenty." She turned up her coat collar so he could not see that she was crying weakly—like an old woman.

For a moment it was over. The thing was done. She did not look back.

She said loudly, to be heard above the motor, "It will be good, tonight, a good dinner."

"Now you're changed again," Henry complained. He took one hand from the wheel and patted her knee. "I ought to take you in to dinner oftener. It would be good for both of us. We get so heavy out on the ranch."

"Henry," she asked, "could we have wine at dinner?"

"Sure we could. Say! That will be fine."

She was silent for a while; then she said, "Henry, at those prize fights, do the men hurt each other very much?"

"Sometimes a little, not often. Why?"

"Well, I've read how they break noses, and blood runs down their chests. I've read how the fighting gloves get heavy and soggy with blood."

He looked around at her. "What's the matter, Elisa? I didn't know you read things like that." He brought the car to a stop, then turned to the right over the Salinas River bridge.

"Do any women ever go to the fights?" she asked.

"Oh, sure, some. What's the matter, Elisa? Do you want to go? I don't think you'd like it, but I'll take you if you really want to go."

She relaxed limply in the seat. "Oh, no. No. I don't want to go. I'm sure I don't." Her face was turned away from him. "It will be enough if we can have wine. It will be plenty." She turned up her coat collar so he could not see that she was crying weakly—like an old woman.

THE WHITE QUAIL

THE WHITE QUAIL

THE WALL opposite the fireplace in the living-room was a big dormer window stretching from the cushioned window seats almost to the ceiling—small diamond panes set in lead. From the window, preferably if you were sitting on the window seat, you could look across the garden and up the hill. There was a stretch of shady lawn under the garden oaks—around each oak there was a circle of carefully tended earth in which grew cinerarias, big ones with loads of flowers so heavy they bent the stems over, and ranging in color from scarlet to ultramarine. At the edge of the lawn, a line of fuchsias grew like little symbolic trees. In front of the fuchsias lay a shallow garden pool, the coping flush with the lawn for a very good reason.

Right at the edge of the garden, the hill started up, wild with cascara bushes and poison oak, with dry grass and live oak, very wild. If you didn't go around to the front of the house you couldn't tell it was on the very edge of the town.

Mary Teller, Mrs. Harry E. Teller, that is, knew the window and the garden were Right and she had a very good reason for knowing. Hadn't she picked out the place where the house and the garden would be years ago? Hadn't she seen the house and the garden a thousand times while the place was still a dry flat against the shoulder of a hill? For that matter, hadn't she, during five years, looked at every attentive man and wondered whether he and that garden would go together? She didn't think so much, "Would this man like such a garden?" but, "Would the garden like such a man?" For the garden was herself, and after all she had to marry some one she liked.

When she met Harry Teller, the garden seemed to like him. It may have surprised him a little when, after he had proposed and was waiting sulkily for his answer, as men do, Mary broke into a description of a big dormer window and a garden with a lawn and oak trees and cinerarias and then a wild hill.

He said, "Of course," rather perfunctorily.

Mary asked, "Do you think it's silly?"

He was waiting a little sullenly. "Of course not."

And then she remembered that he had proposed to her, and she accepted him, and let him kiss her. She said, "There will be a little cement pool flush with the lawn. Do you know why? Well, there are more birds on that hill than you'd ever think, yellowhammers and wild canaries and red-wing blackbirds, and of course sparrows and linnets, and lots of quail. Of course they'll be coming down to drink there, won't they?"

She was very pretty. He wanted to kiss her over and over, and she let him. "And fuchsias," she said. "Don't forget fuchsias. They're like little tropical Christmas trees. We'll have to have the lawn raked every day to keep the oak leaves clear."

He laughed at her. "You're a funny little bug. The lot isn't bought, and the house isn't built, and the garden isn't planted; and already you're worrying about oak leaves on the lawn. You're so pretty. You make me kind of—hungry."

That startled her a little. A little expression of annoyance crossed her face. But nevertheless she let him kiss her again, and then sent him home and went to her room, where she had a little blue writing desk and on it a copy-book to write things in. She took up a pen, of which the handle was a peacock feather, and she wrote, "Mary Teller" over and over again. Once or twice she wrote, "Mrs. Harry E. Teller."

II

The lot was bought and the house was built, and they were married. Mary drew a careful plan of the garden, and when the workmen were putting it in she didn't leave them alone for a moment. She knew to an inch where everything should be. And she drew the shape of the shallow pool for the cement workers, a kind of heart-shaped pool with no point at the bottom, with gradually sloping edges so the birds could drink easily.

Harry watched her with admiration. "Who could tell that such a pretty girl could have so much efficiency," he said.

That pleased her, too; and she was very happy, so that she said, "You can plant some of the things you like in the garden, if you want."

"No, Mary, I like too much to see your own mind coming out in the garden. You do it all your own way."

She loved him for that; but after all, it was her garden. She had invented it, and willed it, and she had worked out the colors too, so carefully. It really wouldn't have been nice if, for instance, Harry had wanted some flowers that didn't go with the garden.

At last the green lawn was up, and the cinerarias around the oak trees bloomed in sunken pots. The little fuchsia trees had been moved in so carefully that not a leaf wilted. The window seats behind the dormer windows were piled with cushions covered with bright, fadeless fabrics, for the sun shone in that window a good part of the day.

Mary waited until it was all done, all finished exactly as her mind had seen it; and then one evening when Harry came home from the office, she led him to the window seat. "You see," she said softly. "There it is, just the way I wanted it."

"It's beautiful," said Harry, "very beautiful."

"In a way I'm sad that it's done," she said. "But mostly I'm glad. We won't ever change it, will we, Harry? If a bush dies, we'll put another one just like it in the same place."

"Curious little bug," he said.

"Well, you see I've thought about it so long that it's part of me. If anything should be changed it would be like part of me being torn out."

He put out his hand to touch her, and then withdrew it. "I love you so much," he said, and then paused. "But I'm afraid of you, too."

She smiled quietly. "You? Afraid of me? What's there about me you can be afraid of?"

"Well, you're kind of untouchable. There's an inscrutability about you. Probably you don't even know it yourself. You're kind of like your own garden—fixed, and just so. I'm afraid to move around. I might disturb some of your plants."

Mary was pleased. "Dear," she said. "You let me do it. You made it my garden. Yes, you are dear." And she let him kiss her.

III

He was proud of her when people came in to dinner. She was so pretty, so cool and perfect. Her bowls of flowers were exquisite, and she talked about the garden modestly, hesitantly, almost as though she were talking about herself. Sometimes she took her guests into the garden. She pointed to a fuchsia tree. "I didn't know whether he would succeed," she said, just as though the plant were a person. "He ate a lot of plant food before he decided to come around." She smiled quietly to herself.

She was delightful when she worked in the garden. She wore a bright print dress, quite long in the skirt, and sleeveless. Somewhere she had found an old-fashioned sunbonnet. She wore good sturdy gloves to protect her hands. Harry liked to watch her going about with a bag and a big spoon, putting plant food about the roots of her flowers. He liked it, too, when they went out at night to kill slugs and snails. Mary held the flashlight while Harry did the actual killing, crushing the slugs and snails into oozy, bubbling masses. He knew it must be a disgusting business to her, but the light never wavered. "Brave girl," he thought. "She has a sturdiness in back of that fragile beauty." She made the hunts exciting too. "There's a big one, creeping and creeping," she would say. "He's after that big bloom. Kill him! Kill him quickly!" They came into the house after the hunts laughing happily.

Mary was worried about the birds. "They don't come down to drink," she complained. "Not many of them. I wonder what's keeping them away."

"Maybe they aren't used to it yet. They'll come later. Maybe there's a cat around."

Her face flushed and she breathed deeply. Her pretty lips tightened away from her teeth. "If there's a cat, I'll put out poisoned fish," she cried. "I won't have a cat after my birds!"

Harry had to soothe her. "I'll tell you what I'll do. I'll buy an air gun. Then if a cat comes, we can shoot it, and it won't kill the cat, but it'll hurt, and the cat won't come back."

"Yes," she said more calmly. "That might be better."

The living-room was very pleasant at night. The fire burned up in a sheet of flame. If there was a moon, Mary turned off the lights and then they sat looking through the window at the cool blue garden and the dark oak trees.

It was utterly calm and eternal out there. And then the garden ended and the dark thickets of the hill began.

"That's the enemy," Mary said one time. "That's the world that wants to get in, all rough and tangled and unkempt. But it can't get in because the fuchsias won't let it. That's what the fuchsias are there for, and they know it. The birds can get in. They live out in the wild, but they come to my garden for peace and for water." She laughed softly. "There's something profound in all that, Harry. I don't know quite what it is. The quail are beginning to come down now. At least a dozen were at the pool this evening."

He said, "I wish I could see the inside of your mind. It seems to flutter around, but it's a cool, collected mind. It's so—sure of itself."

Mary went to sit on his lap for a moment. "Not so awfully sure. You don't know, and I'm glad you don't."

IV

One night when Harry was reading his paper under the lamp, Mary jumped up. "I left my garden scissors outside," she said. "The dew will rust them."

Harry looked over his paper. "Can't I get them for you?"

"No, I'll go. You couldn't find them." She went out into the garden and found the shears, and then she looked in the window, into the living room. Harry was still reading his paper. The room was clear, like a picture, like the set of a play that was about to start. A curtain of fire waved up in the fireplace. Mary stood still and looked. There was the big, deep chair she had been sitting in a minute ago. What would she be doing if she hadn't come outside? Suppose only essence, only mind and sight had come, leaving Mary in the chair? She could almost see herself sitting there. Her round arms and long fingers were resting on the chair. Her delicate, sensitive face was in profile, looking reflectively into the firelight. "What is she thinking about?" Mary whispered. "I wonder what's going on in her mind. Will she get up? No, she's just sitting there. The neck of that dress is too wide, see how it slips sideways over the shoulder. But that's rather pretty. It looks careless, but neat and pretty. Now—she's smiling. She must be thinking something nice."

Suddenly Mary came to herself and realized what she had been doing. She was delighted. "There were two me's," she thought. "It was like having two lives, being able to see myself. That's wonderful. I wonder whether I can see it whenever I want to. I saw just what other people see when they look at me. I must tell Harry about that." But then a new picture formed; she saw herself explaining, trying to describe what had happened. She saw him looking over his paper with an intent, puzzled, almost pained look in his eyes. He tried so hard to understand when she told him things. He wanted to understand, and he never quite succeeded. If she told him about this vision tonight, he would ask questions. He would turn the thing over and over, trying to understand it, until finally he ruined it. He didn't want to spoil the things she told him, but he just couldn't help it. He needed too much light on things that light shriveled. No, she wouldn't tell him. She would want to come out and do it again, and she couldn't if he spoiled it for her.

Through the window she saw Harry put his paper down on his knee and look up at the door. She hurried in, showing him the shears to prove what she had gone for. "See, the rust was forming already. They'd've been all brown and nasty by morning."

He nodded and smiled at her. "It says in the paper we're going to have more trouble with that new loan bill. They put a lot of difficulties in our way. Somebody has to loan money when people want to borrow."

"I don't understand loans," she said. "Somebody told me your company had title to nearly every automobile in town."

He laughed. "Well, not all, but a good many of them, anyway. When times are a little bit hard, we make money."

"It sounds terrible," she observed. "It sounds like taking unfair advantage."

He folded the paper and put it on the table beside his chair. "No, I don't think it's unfair," he said. "The people must have the money, and we supply it. The law regulates the interest rate. We haven't anything to do with that."

She stretched her pretty arms and fingers on the chair, as she had seen them through the window. "I suppose it really isn't unfair," she said. "It just sounds as though you took advantage of people when they were down."

Harry looked seriously into the fire for a long time. Mary could see him, and she knew he was worrying about what she said. Well, it would do him no harm to see what business really was like. Things seemed righter when you did them than when you thought about them. A little mental housecleaning mightn't be a bad thing for Harry.

After a little, he looked over at her. "Dear, you don't think it's unfair practice, do you?"

"Why, I don't know anything about loans. How can I tell what is fair?"

Harry insisted, "But do you *feel* it's unfair? Are you ashamed of my business? I wouldn't like it if you were."

Suddenly Mary felt very glad and pleased. "I'm not ashamed, silly. Every one has a right to make a living. You do what you do well."

"You're sure, now?"

"Of course I'm sure, silly."

After she was in bed in her own little bedroom she heard a faint click and saw the door knob turn, and then turn slowly back. The door was locked. It was a signal;

there were things Mary didn't like to talk about. The lock was an answer to a question, a clean, quick, decisive answer. It was peculiar about Harry, though. He always tried the door silently. It seemed as though he didn't want her to know he had tried it. But she always did know. He was sweet and gentle. It seemed to make him ashamed when he turned the knob and found the door locked.

Mary pulled the light chain, and when her eyes had become accustomed to the dark, she looked out the window at her garden in the half moonlight. Harry was sweet, and understanding, too. That time about the dog. He had come running into the house, really running. His face was so red and excited that Mary had a nasty shock. She thought there had been an accident. Later in the evening she had a headache from the shock. Harry had shouted, "Joe Adams—his Irish Terrier bitch had puppies. He's going to give me one! Thoroughbred stock, red as strawberries!" He had really wanted one of the pups. It hurt Mary that he couldn't have one. But she was proud of his quick understanding of the situation. When she explained how a dog would—do things on the plants of her garden, or even dig in her flower beds, how, worst of all, a dog would keep the birds away from the pool, Harry understood. He might have trouble with complicated things, like that vision from the garden, but he understood about the dog. Later in the evening, when her head ached, he soothed her and patted Florida Water on her head. That was the curse of imagination. Mary had seen, actually seen the dog in her garden, and the dug holes, and ruined plants. It was almost as bad as though it actually happened. Harry was ashamed, but really he couldn't help it if she had such an imagination. Mary couldn't blame him, how could he have known?

V

Late in the afternoon, when the sun had gone behind the hill, there was a time Mary called the really-garden-time. Then the high school girl was in from school and had taken charge of the kitchen. It was almost a sacred time. Mary walked out into the garden and across the lawn to a folding chair half behind one of the lawn oaks. She could watch the birds drinking in the pool from there. She could really *feel* the garden. When Harry came home from the office, he stayed in the house and read his paper until she came in from the garden, star-eyed. It made her unhappy to be disturbed.

The summer was just breaking. Mary looked into the kitchen and saw that everything was all right there. She went through the living room and lighted the laid fire, and then she was ready for the garden. The sun had just dropped behind the hill, and the blue gauze of the evening had settled among the oaks.

Mary thought, "It's like millions of not quite invisible fairies coming into my garden. You can't see one of them, but the millions change the color of the air." She smiled to herself at the nice thought. The clipped lawn was damp and fresh with watering. The brilliant cinerarias threw little haloes of color into the air. The fuchsia trees were loaded with blooms. The buds, like little red Christmas tree ornaments, and the open blooms like ballet-skirted ladies. They were so *right*, the fuchsias, so absolutely right. And they discouraged the enemy on the other side, the brush and scrubby, untrimmed trees.

Mary walked across the lawn in the evening to her chair, and sat down. She could hear the birds gathering to come down to the pool. "Making up parties," she thought, "coming to my garden in the evening. How they must love it! How I would like to come to my garden for the first time. If I could be two people— 'Good evening, come into the garden, Mary.' 'Oh, isn't it lovely.' 'Yes, I like it, especially at this time. Quiet, now, Mary. Don't frighten the birds.'" She sat as still as a mouse. Her lips were parted with expectancy. In the brush the quail twittered sharply. A yellowhammer dropped to the edge of the pool. Two little flycatchers flickered out over the water and stood still in the air, beating their wings. And then the quail ran out, with funny little steps. They stopped and cocked their heads, to see whether it was safe. Their leader, a big fellow with a crest like a black question mark, sounded the bugle-like "All clear" call, and the band came down to drink.

And then it happened, the wonderful thing. Out of the brush ran a white quail. Mary froze. Yes, it was a quail, no doubt of it, and white as snow. Oh, this was wonderful! A shiver of pleasure, a bursting of pleasure swelled in Mary's breast. She held her breath. The dainty little white hen quail went to the other side of the pool, away from the ordinary quail. She paused and looked around, and then dipped her beak in the water.

"Why," Mary cried to herself, "she's like me!" A powerful ecstasy quivered in her body. "She's like the essence of me, an essence boiled down to utter purity. She must be the queen of the quail. She makes every lovely thing that ever happened to me one thing."

The white quail dipped her beak again and threw back her head to swallow.

The memories welled in Mary and filled her chest. Something sad, always something sad. The packages that came; untying the string was the ecstasy. The thing in the package was never quite——

The marvelous candy from Italy. "Don't eat it, dear. It's prettier than it's good." Mary never ate it, but looking at it was an ecstasy like this.

"What a pretty girl Mary is. She's like a gentian, so quiet." The hearing was an ecstasy like this.

"Mary dear, be very brave now. Your father has—passed away." The first moment of loss was an ecstasy like this.

The white quail stretched a wing backward and smoothed down the feathers with her beak. "This is the me that was everything beautiful. This is the center of me, my heart."

VI

The blue air became purple in the garden. The fuchsia buds blazed like little candles. And then a gray shadow moved out of the brush. Mary's mouth dropped open. She sat paralyzed with fear. A gray cat crept like death out of the brush, crept toward the pool and the drinking birds. Mary stared in horror. Her hand rose up to her tight throat. Then she broke the paralysis. She screamed terribly. The quail flew away on muttering wings. The cat bounded back into the brush. Still Mary screamed and screamed. Harry ran out of the house crying, "Mary! What is it, Mary?"

She shuddered when he touched her. She began to cry hysterically. He took her up in his arms and carried her into the house, and into her own room. She lay quivering on the bed. "What was it, dear? What frightened you?"

"It was a cat," she moaned. "It was creeping up on the birds." She sat up; her eyes blazed. "Harry, you must put out poison. Tonight you simply must put out some poison for that cat."

"Lie back, dear. You've had a shock."

"Promise me you'll put out poison." She looked closely at him and saw a rebellious light come into his eyes. "Promise."

"Dear," he apologized, "some dog might get it. Animals suffer terribly when they get poison."

"I don't care," she cried. "I don't want any animals in my garden, any kind."

"No," he said. "I won't do that. No, I can't do that. But I'll get up early in the morning. I'll take the new air gun and I'll shoot that cat so he'll never come back. The air gun shoots hard. It'll make a hurt the cat won't forget."

It was the first thing he had ever refused. She didn't know how to combat it; but her head ached, terribly. When it ached its worst he tried to make it up to her for refusing the poison. He kept a little pad soaked with Florida Water, and he patted it on her forehead. She wondered whether she should tell him about the white quail. He wouldn't believe it. But maybe if he knew how important it was, he might poison the cat. She waited until her nerves were calm before she told him. "Dear, there was a white quail in the garden."

"A white quail? Are you sure it wasn't a pigeon?"

There it was. Right from the first he spoiled it. "I

know quail," she cried. "It was quite close to me. A white hen quail."

"That would be a thing to see," he said. "I never heard of one."

"But I tell you I saw it."

He dabbed at her forehead. "Well, I suppose it was an albino. No pigment in the feathers, something like that."

She was growing hysterical again. "You don't understand. That white quail was me, the secret me that no one can ever get at, the me that's way inside." Harry's face was contorted with the struggle to understand. "Can't you see, dear? The cat was after me. It was going to kill me. That's why I want to poison it." She studied his face. No, he didn't understand, he couldn't. Why had she told him? If she hadn't been so upset she never would have told him.

"I'll set my alarm clock," he assured her. "Tomorrow morning I'll give that cat something to remember."

At ten o'clock he left her alone. And when he had gone Mary got up and locked the door.

His alarm-clock bell awakened Mary in the morning. It was still dark in her room, but she could see the gray light of morning through the window. She heard Harry dressing quietly. He tiptoed past her door and went outside, closing the door silently for fear of awakening her. He carried the new shining air gun in his hand. The fresh gray morning air made him throw back his shoulders and step lightly over the damp lawn. He walked to the corner of the garden and lay down on his stomach in the wet grass.

The garden grew lighter. Already the quail were twittering metallically. The little brown band came to the edge of the brush and cocked their heads. Then the big leader called, "All's well," and his charges ran with quick steps to the pool. A moment later the white quail followed them. She went to the other side of the pool and dipped her beak and threw back her head. Harry raised the gun. The white quail tipped her head and looked toward him. The air gun spat with a vicious whisper. The quail flew off into the brush. But the white quail fell over and shuddered a moment, and lay still on the lawn.

Harry walked slowly over to her and picked her up. "I didn't mean to kill it," he said to himself. "I just wanted to scare it away." He looked at the white bird in his hand. Right in the head, right under the eye the BB shot had gone. Harry stepped to the line of fuchsias and threw the quail up into the brush. The next moment he put down the gun and crashed up through the undergrowth. He found the white quail, carried her far up the hill and buried her under a pile of leaves.

Mary heard him pass her door. "Harry, did you shoot the cat?"

"It won't ever come back," he said through the door.

"Well, I hope you killed it, but I don't want to hear the details."

Harry walked on into the living-room and sat down in a big chair. The room was still dusky, but through the big dormer window the garden glowed and the tops of the lawn oaks were afire with sunshine.

"What a skunk I am," Harry said to himself. "What a dirty skunk, to kill a thing she loved so much." He dropped his head and looked at the floor. "I'm lonely," he said. "Oh, Lord, I'm so lonely!"

FLIGHT

FLIGHT

ABOUT fifteen miles below Monterey, on the wild coast, the Torres family had their farm, a few sloping acres above a cliff that dropped to the brown reefs and to the hissing white waters of the ocean. Behind the farm the stone mountains stood up against the sky. The farm buildings huddled like little clinging aphids on the mountain skirts, crouched low to the ground as though the wind might blow them into the sea. The little shack, the rattling, rotting barn were grey-bitten with sea salt, beaten by the damp wind until they had taken on the color of the granite hills. Two horses, a red cow and a red calf, half a dozen pigs and a flock of lean, multi-colored chickens stocked the place. A little corn was raised on the sterile slope, and it grew short and thick under the wind, and all the cobs formed on the landward sides of the stalks.

Mama Torres, a lean, dry woman with ancient eyes, had ruled the farm for ten years, ever since her husband tripped over a stone in the field one day and fell full length on a rattlesnake. When one is bitten on the chest there is not much that can be done.

Mama Torres had three children, two undersized black ones of twelve and fourteen, Emilio and Rosy, whom Mama kept fishing on the rocks below the farm when the sea was kind and when the truant officer was in some distant part of Monterey County. And there was Pepé, the tall smiling son of nineteen, a gentle, affectionate boy, but very lazy. Pepé had a tall head, pointed at the top, and from its peak, coarse black hair grew down like a thatch all around. Over his smiling little eyes Mama cut a straight bang so he could see. Pepé had sharp Indian cheek bones and an eagle nose, but his mouth was as sweet and shapely as a girl's mouth, and his chin was fragile and chiseled. He was loose and gangling, all legs and feet and wrists, and he was very lazy. Mama thought him fine and brave, but she never told him so. She said, "Some lazy cow must have got into thy father's family, else how could I have a son like thee." And she said, "When I carried thee, a sneaking lazy coyote came out of the brush and looked at me one day. That must have made thee so."

Pepé smiled sheepishly and stabbed at the ground with his knife to keep the blade sharp and free from rust. It was his inheritance, that knife, his father's knife. The long heavy blade folded back into the black handle. There was a button on the handle. When Pepé pressed the button, the blade leaped out ready for use. The knife was with Pepé always, for it had been his father's knife.

One sunny morning when the sea below the cliff was glinting and blue and the white surf creamed on the reef, when even the stone mountains looked kindly, Mama Torres called out the door of the shack, "Pepé, I have a labor for thee."

There was no answer. Mama listened. From behind the

barn she heard a burst of laughter. She lifted her full long skirt and walked in the direction of the noise.

Pepé was sitting on the ground with his back against a box. His white teeth glistened. On either side of him stood the two black ones, tense and expectant. Fifteen feet away a redwood post was set in the ground. Pepé's right hand lay limply in his lap, and in the palm the big black knife rested. The blade was closed back into the handle. Pepé looked smiling at the sky.

Suddenly Emilio cried, "Ya!"

Pepé's wrist flicked like the head of a snake. The blade seemed to fly open in mid-air, and with a thump the point dug into the redwood post, and the black handle quivered. The three burst into excited laughter. Rosy ran to the post and pulled out the knife and brought it back to Pepé. He closed the blade and settled the knife carefully in his listless palm again. He grinned self-consciously at the sky.

"Ya!"

The heavy knife lanced out and sunk into the post again. Mama moved forward like a ship and scattered the play.

"All day you do foolish things with the knife, like a toy-baby," she stormed. "Get up on thy huge feet that eat up shoes. Get up!" She took him by one loose shoulder and hoisted at him. Pepé grinned sheepishly and came half-heartedly to his feet. "Look!" Mama cried. "Big lazy, you must catch the horse and put on him thy father's saddle. You must ride to Monterey. The medicine bottle is empty. There is no salt. Go thou now, Peanut! Catch the horse."

A revolution took place in the relaxed figure of Pepé. "To Monterey, me? Alone? *Sí*, Mama."

She scowled at him. "Do not think, big sheep, that you will buy candy. No, I will give you only enough for the medicine and the salt."

Pepé smiled. "Mama, you will put the hatband on the hat?"

She relented then. "Yes, Pepé. You may wear the hatband."

His voice grew insinuating, "And the green handkerchief, Mama?"

"Yes, if you go quickly and return with no trouble, the silk green handkerchief will go. If you make sure to take off the handkerchief when you eat so no spot may fall on it. . . ."

'*Sí*, Mama. I will be careful. I am a man."

"Thou? A man? Thou art a peanut."

He went into the rickety barn and brought out a rope, and he walked agilely enough up the hill to catch the horse.

When he was ready and mounted before the door, mounted on his father's saddle that was so old that the oaken frame showed through torn leather in many places, then Mama brought out the round black hat with the tooled leather band, and she reached up and knotted the green silk handkerchief about his neck. Pepé's blue denin coat was much darker than his jeans, for it had been washed much less often.

Mama handed up the big medicine bottle and the silver coins. "That for the medicine," she said, "and that for the salt. That for a candle to burn for the papa. That for *dulces* for the little ones. Our friend Mrs. Rodriguez will give you dinner and maybe a bed for the night When you go to the church say only ten Paternosters and only twenty-five Ave Marias. Oh! I know, big coyote. You would sit there flapping your mouth over Aves all day while you looked at the candles and the holy pictures. That is not good devotion to stare at the pretty things."

The black hat, covering the high pointed head and black thatched hair of Pepé, gave him dignity and age. He sat the rangy horse well. Mama thought how handsome he was, dark and lean and tall. "I would not send thee now alone, thou little one, except for the medicine," she said softly. "It is not good to have no medicine, for who knows when the toothache will come, or the sadness of the stomach. These things are."

"Adios, Mama," Pepé cried. "I will come back soon. You may send me often alone. I am a man."

"Thou art a foolish chicken."

He straightened his shoulders, flipped the reins against the horse's shoulder and rode away. He turned once and saw that they still watched him, Emilio and Rosy and Mama. Pepé grinned with pride and gladness and lifted the tough buckskin horse to a trot.

When he had dropped out of sight over a little dip in the road, Mama turned to the black ones, but she spoke to herself. "He is nearly a man now," she said. "It will be a nice thing to have a man in the house again." Her eyes sharpened on the children. "Go to the rocks now. The tide is going out. There will be abalones to be found." She put the iron hooks into their hands and saw them down the steep trail to the reefs. She brought the smooth stone *metate* to the doorway and sat grinding her corn to flour and looking occasionally at the road over which Pepé had gone. The noonday came and then the afternoon, when the little ones beat the abalones on a rock to make them tender and Mama patted the tortillas to make them thin. They ate their dinner as the red sun was plunging down toward the ocean. They sat on the doorsteps and watched the big white moon come over the mountain tops.

Mama said, "He is now at the house of our friend Mrs. Rodriguez. She will give him nice things to eat and maybe a present."

Emilio said, "Some day I too will ride to Monterey for medicine. Did Pepé come to be a man today?"

Mama said wisely, "A boy gets to be a man when a man is needed. Remember this thing. I have known boys forty years old because there was no need for a man."

Soon afterwards they retired, Mama in her big oak bed on one side of the room, Emilio and Rosy in their boxes full of straw and sheepskins on the other side of the room.

The moon went over the sky and the surf roared on the rocks. The roosters crowed the first call. The surf subsided to a whispering surge against the reef. The moon dropped toward the sea. The roosters crowed again.

The moon was near down to the water when Pepé rode on a winded horse to his home flat. His dog bounced out and circled the horse yelping with pleasure. Pepé slid off the saddle to the ground. The weathered little shack was silver in the moonlight and the square shadow of it was black to the north and east. Against the east the piling mountains were misty with light; their tops melted into the sky.

Pepé walked wearily up the three steps and into the house. It was dark inside. There was a rustle in the corner.

Mama cried out from her bed. "Who comes? Pepé, is it thou?"

"Sí, Mama."

"Did you get the medicine?"

"Sí, Mama."

"Well, go to sleep, then. I thought you would be sleeping at the house of Mrs. Rodriguez." Pepé stood silently in the dark room. "Why do you stand there, Pepé? Did you drink wine?"

"Sí, Mama."

"Well, go to bed then and sleep out the wine."

His voice was tired and patient, but very firm. "Light the candle, Mama. I must go away into the mountains."

"What is this, Pepé? You are crazy." Mama struck a sulphur match and held the little blue burr until the flame spread up the stick. She set light to the candle on the floor beside her bed. "Now, Pepé, what is this you say?" She looked anxiously into his face.

He was changed. The fragile quality seemed to have gone from his chin. His mouth was less full than it had been, the lines of the lips were straighter, but in his eyes the greatest change had taken place. There was no laughter in them any more, nor any bashfulness. They were sharp and bright and purposeful.

He told her in a tired monotone, told her everything just as it had happened. A few people came into the kitchen of Mrs. Rodriguez. There was wine to drink. Pepé drank wine. The little quarrel—the man started toward Pepé and then the knife—it went almost by itself.

it flew, it darted before Pepé knew it. As he talked, Mama's face grew stern, and it seemed to grow more lean. Pepé finished. "I am a man now, Mama. The man said names to me I could not allow."

Mama nodded. "Yes, thou art a man, my poor little Pepé. Thou art a man. I have seen it coming on thee. I have watched you throwing the knife into the post, and I have been afraid." For a moment her face had softened, but now it grew stern again. "Come! We must get you ready. Go. Awaken Emilio and Rosy. Go quickly."

Pepé stepped over to the corner where his brother and sister slept among the sheepskins. He leaned down and shook them gently. "Come, Rosy! Come, Emilio! The mama says you must arise."

The little black ones sat up and rubbed their eyes in the candlelight. Mama was out of bed now, her long black skirt over her nightgown. "Emilio," she cried. "Go up and catch the other horse for Pepé. Quickly, now! Quickly." Emilio put his legs in his overalls and stumbled sleepily out the door.

"You heard no one behind you on the road?" Mama demanded.

"No, Mama. I listened carefully. No one was on the road."

Mama darted like a bird about the room. From a nail on the wall she took a canvas water bag and threw it on the floor. She stripped a blanket from her bed and rolled it into a tight tube and tied the ends with string. From a box beside the stove she lifted a flour sack half full of black stringy jerky. "Your father's black coat, Pepé. Here, put it on."

Pepé stood in the middle of the floor watching her

activity. She reached behind the door and brought out the rifle, a long 38-56, worn shiny the whole length of the barrel. Pepé took it from her and held it in the crook of his elbow. Mama brought a little leather bag and counted the cartridges into his hand. "Only ten left," she warned. "You must not waste them."

Emilio put his head in the door. "*'Qui 'st 'l caballo,* Mama."

"Put on the saddle from the other horse. Tie on the blanket. Here, tie the jerky to the saddle horn."

Still Pepé stood silently watching his mother's frantic activity. His chin looked hard, and his sweet mouth was drawn and thin. His little eyes followed Mama about the room almost suspiciously.

Rosy asked softly, "Where goes Pepé?"

Mama's eyes were fierce. "Pepé goes on a journey. Pepé is a man now. He has a man's thing to do."

Pepé straightened his shoulders. His mouth changed until he looked very much like Mama.

At last the preparation was finished. The loaded horse stood outside the door. The water bag dripped a line of moisture down the bay shoulder.

The moonlight was being thinned by the dawn and the big white moon was near down to the sea. The family stood by the shack. Mama confronted Pepé. "Look, my son! Do not stop until it is dark again. Do not sleep even though you are tired. Take care of the horse in order that he may not stop of weariness. Remember to be careful with the bullets—there are only ten. Do not fill thy stomach with jerky or it will make thee sick. Eat a little jerky and fill thy stomach with grass. When thou comest to the high mountains, if thou seest any of the dark watching men, go not near to them nor try to speak to them. And forget not thy prayers." She put her lean hands on Pepé's shoulders, stood on her toes and kissed him formally on both cheeks, and Pepé kissed her on both cheeks. Then he went to Emilio and Rosy and kissed both of their cheeks.

Pepé turned back to Mama. He seemed to look for a little softness, a little weakness in her. His eyes were searching, but Mama's face remained fierce. "Go now," she said. "Do not wait to be caught like a chicken."

Pepé pulled himself into the saddle. "I am a man," he said.

It was the first dawn when he rode up the hill toward the little canyon which let a trail into the mountains. Moonlight and daylight fought with each other, and the two warring qualities made it difficult to see. Before Pepé had gone a hundred yards, the outlines of his figure were misty; and long before he entered the canyon, he had become a grey, indefinite shadow.

Mama stood stiffly in front of her doorstep, and on either side of her stood Emilio and Rosy. They cast furtive glances at Mama now and then.

When the grey shape of Pepé melted into the hillside and disappeared, Mama relaxed. She began the high, whining keen of the death wail. "Our beautiful—our brave," she cried. "Our protector, our son is gone." Emilio and Rosy moaned beside her. "Our beautiful—our brave, he is gone." It was the formal wail. It rose to a high piercing whine and subsided to a moan. Mama raised it three times and then she turned and went into the house and shut the door.

Emilio and Rosy stood wondering in the dawn. They

heard Mama whimpering in the house. They went out to sit on the cliff above the ocean. They touched shoulders. "When did Pepé come to be a man?" Emilio asked.

"Last night," said Rosy. "Last night in Monterey." The ocean clouds turned red with the sun that was behind the mountains.

"We will have no breakfast," said Emilio. "Mama will not want to cook." Rosy did not answer him. "Where is Pepé gone?" he asked.

Rosy looked around at him. She drew her knowledge from the quiet air. "He has gone on a journey. He will never come back."

"Is he dead? Do you think he is dead?"

Rosy looked back at the ocean again. A little steamer, drawing a line of smoke sat on the edge of the horizon. "He is not dead," Rosy explained. "Not yet."

Pepé rested the big rifle across the saddle in front of him. He let the horse walk up the hill and he didn't look back. The stony slope took on a coat of short brush so that Pepé found the entrance to a trail and entered it.

When he came to the canyon opening, he swung once in his saddle and looked back, but the houses were swallowed in the misty light. Pepé jerked forward again. The high shoulder of the canyon closed in on him. His horse stretched out its neck and sighed and settled to the trail.

It was a well-worn path, dark soft leaf-mould earth strewn with broken pieces of sandstone. The trail rounded the shoulder of the canyon and dropped steeply into the bed of the stream. In the shallows the water ran smoothly, glinting in the first morning sun. Small round stones on the bottom were as brown as rust with sun moss. In the sand along the edges of the stream the tall, rich wild mint grew, while in the water itself the cress, old and tough, had gone to heavy seed.

The path went into the stream and emerged on the other side. The horse sloshed into the water and stopped. Pepé dropped his bridle and let the beast drink of the running water.

Soon the canyon sides became steep and the first giant sentinel redwoods guarded the trail, great round red trunks bearing foliage as green and lacy as ferns. Once Pepé was among the trees, the sun was lost. A perfumed and purple light lay in the pale green of the underbrush. Gooseberry bushes and blackberries and tall ferns lined the stream, and overhead the branches of the redwoods met and cut off the sky.

Pepé drank from the water bag, and he reached into the flour sack and brought out a black string of jerky. His white teeth gnawed at the string until the tough meat parted. He chewed slowly and drank occasionally from the water bag. His little eyes were slumberous and tired, but the muscles of his face were hard set. The earth of the trail was black now. It gave up a hollow sound under the walking hoofbeats.

The stream fell more sharply. Little waterfalls splashed on the stones. Five-fingered ferns hung over the water and dripped spray from their fingertips. Pepé rode half over in his saddle, dangling one leg loosely. He picked a bay leaf from a tree beside the way and put it into his mouth for a moment to flavor the dry jerky. He held the gun loosely across the pommel.

Suddenly he squared in his saddle, swung the horse from the trail and kicked it hurriedly up behind a big redwood tree. He pulled up the reins tight against the bit to keep the horse from whinnying. His face was intent and his nostrils quivered a little.

A hollow pounding came down the trail, and a horseman rode by, a fat man with red cheeks and a white stubble beard. His horse put down its head and blubbered at the trail when it came to the place where Pepé had turned off. "Hold up!" said the man and he pulled up his horse's head.

When the last sound of the hoofs died away, Pepé came back into the trail again. He did not relax in the saddle any more. He lifted the big rifle and swung the lever to throw a shell into the chamber, and then he let down the hammer to half cock.

The trail grew very steep. Now the redwood trees were smaller and their tops were dead, bitten dead where the wind reached them. The horse plodded on; the sun went slowly overhead and started down toward the afternoon.

Where the stream came out of a side canyon, the trail left it. Pepé dismounted and watered his horse and filled up his water bag. As soon as the trail had parted from the stream, the trees were gone and only the thick brittle sage and manzanita and chaparral edged the trail. And the soft black earth was gone, too, leaving only the light tan broken rock for the trail bed. Lizards scampered away into the brush as the horse rattled over the little stones.

Pepé turned in his saddle and looked back. He was in the open now: he could be seen from a distance. As he ascended the trail the country grew more rough and terrible and dry. The way wound about the bases of great square rocks. Little grey rabbits skittered in the brush. A bird made a monotonous high creaking. Eastward the bare rock mountaintops were pale and powder-dry under the dropping sun. The horse plodded up and up the trail toward a little V in the ridge which was the pass.

Pepé looked suspiciously back every minute or so, and his eyes sought the tops of the ridges ahead. Once, on a white barren spur, he saw a black figure for a moment, but he looked quickly away, for it was one of the dark watchers. No one knew who the watchers were, nor where they lived, but it was better to ignore them and never to show interest in them. They did not bother one who stayed on the trail and minded his own business.

The air was parched and full of light dust blown by the breeze from the eroding mountains. Pepé drank sparingly from his bag and corked it tightly and hung it on the horn again. The trail moved up the dry shale hillside, avoiding rocks, dropping under clefts, climbing in and out of old water scars. When he arrived at the little pass he stopped and looked back for a long time. No dark watchers were to be seen now. The trail behind was empty. Only the high tops of the redwoods indicated where the stream flowed.

Pepé rode on through the pass. His little eyes were nearly closed with weariness, but his face was stern, relentless and manly. The high mountain wind coasted sighing through the pass and whistled on the edges of the big blocks of broken granite. In the air, a red-tailed hawk sailed over close to the ridge and screamed angrily. Pepé went slowly through the broken jagged pass and looked down on the other side.

The trail dropped quickly, staggering among broken rock. At the bottom of the slope there was a dark crease, thick with brush, and on the other side of the crease a little flat, in which a grove of oak trees grew. A scar of green grass cut across the flat. And behind the flat another mountain rose, desolate with dead rocks and starving little black bushes. Pepé drank from the bag again for the air was so dry that it encrusted his nostrils and burned his lips. He put the horse down the trail. The hooves slipped and struggled on the steep way, starting little stones that rolled off into the brush. The sun was gone behind the westward mountain now, but still it glowed brilliantly on the oaks and on the grassy flat. The rocks and the hillsides still sent up waves of the heat they had gathered from the day's sun.

Pepé looked up to the top of the next dry withered ridge. He saw a dark form against the sky, a man's figure standing on top of a rock, and he glanced away quickly not to appear curious. When a moment later he looked up again, the figure was gone.

Downward the trail was quickly covered. Sometimes the horse floundered for footing, sometimes set his feet and slid a little way. They came at last to the bottom where the dark chaparral was higher than Pepé's head. He held up his rifle on one side and his arm on the other to shield his face from the sharp brittle fingers of the brush.

Up and out of the crease he rode, and up a little cliff. The grassy flat was before him, and the round comfortable oaks. For a moment he studied the trail down which he had come, but there was no movement and no sound from it. Finally he rode out over the flat, to the green streak, and at the upper end of the damp he found a little spring welling out of the earth and dropping into a dug basin before it seeped out over the flat.

Pepé filled his bag first, and then he let the thirsty horse drink out of the pool. He led the horse to the clump of oaks, and in the middle of the grove, fairly protected from sight on all sides, he took off the saddle and the bridle and laid them on the ground. The horse stretched his jaws sideways and yawned. Pepé knotted the lead rope about the horse's neck and tied him to a sapling among the oaks, where he could graze in a fairly large circle.

When the horse was gnawing hungrily at the dry grass, Pepé went to the saddle and took a black string of jerky from the sack and strolled to an oak tree on the edge of the grove, from under which he could watch the trail. He sat down in the crisp dry oak leaves and automatically felt for his big black knife to cut the jerky, but he had no knife. He leaned back on his elbow and gnawed at the tough strong meat. His face was blank, but it was a man's face.

The bright evening light washed the eastern ridge, but the valley was darkening. Doves flew down from the hills to the spring, and the quail came running out of the brush and joined them, calling clearly to one another.

Out of the corner of his eye Pepé saw a shadow grow out of the bushy crease. He turned his head slowly. A big spotted wildcat was creeping toward the spring, belly to the ground, moving like thought.

Pepé cocked his rifle and edged the muzzle slowly around. Then he looked apprehensively up the trail and dropped the hammer again. From the ground beside him he picked an oak twig and threw it toward the spring. The quail flew up with a roar and the doves whistled away. The big cat stood up: for a long moment he looked at Pepé with cold yellow eyes, and then fearlessly walked back into the gulch.

The dusk gathered quickly in the deep valley. Pepé muttered his prayers, put his head down on his arm and went instantly to sleep.

The moon came up and filled the valley with cold blue light, and the wind swept rustling down from the peaks. The owls worked up and down the slopes looking for rabbits. Down in the brush of the gulch a coyote gabbled. The oak trees whispered softly in the night breeze.

Pepé started up, listening. His horse had whinnied. The moon was just slipping behind the western ridge, leaving the valley in darkness behind it. Pepé sat tensely gripping his rifle. From far up the trail he heard an answering whinny and the crash of shod hooves on the broken rock. He jumped to his feet, ran to his horse and led it under the trees. He threw on the saddle and cinched it tight for the steep trail, caught the unwilling head and forced the bit into the mouth. He felt the saddle to make sure the water bag and the sack of jerky were there. Then he mounted and turned up the hill.

It was velvet dark. The horse found the entrance to the trail where it left the flat, and started up, stumbling and slipping on the rocks. Pepé's hand rose up to his head. His hat was gone. He had left it under the oak tree.

The horse had struggled far up the trail when the first change of dawn came into the air, a steel greyness as light mixed thoroughly with dark. Gradually the sharp snaggled edge of the ridge stood out above them, rotten granite tortured and eaten by the winds of time. Pepé had dropped his reins on the horn, leaving direction to the horse. The brush grabbed at his legs in the dark until one knee of his jeans was ripped.

Gradually the light flowed down over the ridge. The starved brush and rocks stood out in the half light, strange and lonely in high perspective. Then there came warmth into the light. Pepé drew up and looked back, but he could see nothing in the darker valley below. The sky turned blue over the coming sun. In the waste of the mountainside, the poor dry brush grew only three feet high. Here and there, big outcroppings of unrotted granite stood up like mouldering houses. Pepé relaxed a little. He drank from his water bag and bit off a piece of jerky. A single eagle flew over, high in the light.

Without warning Pepé's horse screamed and fell on its side. He was almost down before the rifle crash echoed up from the valley. From a hole behind the struggling shoulder, a stream of bright crimson blood pumped and stopped and pumped and stopped. The hooves threshed on the ground. Pepé lay half stunned beside the horse. He looked slowly down the hill. A piece of sage clipped off beside his head and another crash echoed up from side to side of the canyon. Pepé flung himself frantically behind a bush.

He crawled up the hill on his knees and one hand. His right hand held the rifle up off the ground and pushed it ahead of him. He moved with the instinctive care of an animal. Rapidly he wormed his way toward one of the big outcroppings of granite on the hill above him. Where the brush was high he doubled up and ran, but where the cover was slight he wriggled forward on his stomach, pushing the rifle ahead of him. In the last little distance there was no cover at all. Pepé poised and then he darted across the space and flashed around the corner of the rock.

He leaned panting against the stone. When his breath came easier he moved along behind the big rock until he came to a narrow split that offered a thin section of vision down the hill. Pepé lay on his stomach and pushed the rifle barrel through the slit and waited.

The sun reddened the western ridges now. Already the buzzards were settling down toward the place where the horse lay. A small brown bird scratched in the dead sage leaves directly in front of the rifle muzzle. The coasting eagle flew back toward the rising sun.

Pepé saw a little movement in the brush far below. His grip tightened on the gun. A little brown doe stepped daintily out on the trail and crossed it and disappeared into the brush again. For a long time Pepé waited. Far below he could see the little flat and the oak trees and the slash of green. Suddenly his eyes flashed back at the trail again. A quarter of a mile down there had been a quick movement in the chaparral. The rifle swung over. The front sight nestled in the v of the rear sight. Pepé studied for a moment and then raised the rear sight a notch. The little movement in the brush came again. The sight settled on it. Pepé squeezed the trigger. The explosion crashed down the mountain and up the other side, and came rattling back. The whole side of the slope grew still. No more movement. And then a white streak cut into the granite of the slit and a bullet whined away and a crash sounded up from below. Pepé felt a sharp pain in his right hand. A sliver of granite was sticking out from between his first and second knuckles and the point protruded from his palm. Carefully he pulled out the sliver of stone. The wound bled evenly and gently. No vein nor artery was cut.

Pepé looked into a little dusty cave in the rock and gathered a handful of spider web, and he pressed the mass into the cut, plastering the soft web into the blood. The flow stopped almost at once.

The rifle was on the ground. Pepé picked it up, levered a new shell into the chamber. And then he slid into the brush on his stomach. Far to the right he crawled, and then up the hill, moving slowly and carefully, crawling to cover and resting and then crawling again.

In the mountains the sun is high in its arc before it penetrates the gorges. The hot face looked over the hill and brought instant heat with it. The white light beat on the rocks and reflected from them and rose up quivering from the earth again, and the rocks and bushes seemed to quiver behind the air.

Pepé crawled in the general direction of the ridge peak, zig-zagging for cover. The deep cut between his knuckles began to throb. He crawled close to a rattlesnake before he saw it, and when it raised its dry head and made a soft beginning whirr, he backed up and took another way. The quick grey lizards flashed in front of him, raising a tiny line of dust. He found another mass of spider web and pressed it against his throbbing hand.

Pepé was pushing the rifle with his left hand now.

Little drops of sweat ran to the ends of his coarse black hair and rolled down his cheeks. His lips and tongue were growing thick and heavy. His lips writhed to draw saliva into his mouth. His little dark eyes were uneasy and suspicious. Once when a grey lizard paused in front of him on the parched ground and turned its head sideways he crushed it flat with a stone.

When the sun slid past noon he had not gone a mile. He crawled exhaustedly a last hundred yards to a patch of high sharp manzanita, crawled desperately, and when the patch was reached he wriggled in among the tough gnarly trunks and dropped his head on his left arm. There was little shade in the meager brush, but there was cover and safety. Pepé went to sleep as he lay and the sun beat on his back. A few little birds hopped close to him and peered and hopped away. Pepé squirmed in his sleep and he raised and dropped his wounded hand again and again.

The sun went down behind the peaks and the cool evening came, and then the dark. A coyote yelled from the hillside, Pepé started awake and looked about with misty eyes. His hand was swollen and heavy; a little thread of pain ran up the inside of his arm and settled in a pocket in his armpit. He peered about and then stood up, for the mountains were black and the moon had not yet risen. Pepé stood up in the dark. The coat of his father pressed on his arm. His tongue was swollen until it nearly filled his mouth. He wriggled out of the coat and dropped it in the brush, and then he struggled up the hill, falling over rocks and tearing his way through the brush. The rifle knocked against stones as he went.

Little dry avalanches of gravel and shattered stone went whispering down the hill behind him.

After a while the old moon came up and showed the jagged ridge top ahead of him. By moonlight Pepé traveled more easily. He bent forward so that his throbbing arm hung away from his body. The journey uphill was made in dashes and rests, a frantic rush up a few yards and then a rest. The wind coasted down the slope rattling the dry stems of the bushes.

The moon was at meridian when Pepé came at last to the sharp backbone of the ridge top. On the last hundred yards of the rise no soil had clung under the wearing winds. The way was on solid rock. He clambered to the top and looked down on the other side. There was a draw like the last below him, misty with moonlight, brushed with dry struggling sage and chaparral. On the other side the hill rose up sharply and at the top the jagged rotten teeth of the mountain showed against the sky. At the bottom of the cut the brush was thick and dark.

Pepé stumbled down the hill. His throat was almost closed with thirst. At first he tried to run, but immediately he fell and rolled. After that he went more carefully. The moon was just disappearing behind the mountains when he came to the bottom. He crawled into the heavy brush feeling with his fingers for water. There was no water in the bed of the stream, only damp earth. Pepé laid his gun down and scooped up a handful of mud and put it in his mouth, and then he spluttered and scraped the earth from his tongue with his finger, for the mud drew at his mouth like a poultice. He dug a hole in the stream bed with his fingers, dug a little basin to catch water; but before it was very deep his head fell forward on the damp ground and he slept.

The dawn came and the heat of the day fell on the earth, and still Pepé slept. Late in the afternoon his head jerked up. He looked slowly around. His eyes were slits of wariness. Twenty feet away in the heavy brush a big tawny mountain lion stood looking at him. Its long thick tail waved gracefully, its ears were erect with interest, not laid back dangerously. The lion squatted down on its stomach and watched him.

Pepé looked at the hole he had dug in the earth. A half inch of muddy water had collected in the bottom. He tore the sleeve from his hurt arm, with his teeth ripped out a little square, soaked it in the water and put it in his mouth. Over and over he filled the cloth and sucked it.

Still the lion sat and watched him. The evening came down but there was no movement on the hills. No birds visited the dry bottom of the cut. Pepé looked occasionally at the lion. The eyes of the yellow beast drooped as though he were about to sleep. He yawned and his long thin red tongue curled out. Suddenly his head jerked around and his nostrils quivered. His big tail lashed. He stood up and slunk like a tawny shadow into the thick brush.

A moment later Pepé heard the sound, the faint far crash of horses' hooves on gravel. And he heard something else, a high whining yelp of a dog.

Pepé took his rifle in his left hand and he glided into the brush almost as quietly as the lion had. In the darkening evening he crouched up the hill toward the next ridge. Only when the dark came did he stand up. His energy was short. Once it was dark he fell over the rocks and slipped to his knees on the steep slope, but he moved on and on up the hill, climbing and scrabbling over the broken hillside.

When he was far up toward the top, he lay down and slept for a little while. The withered moon, shining on his face, awakened him. He stood up and moved up the hill. Fifty yards away he stopped and turned back, for he had forgotten his rifle. He walked heavily down and poked about in the brush, but he could not find his gun. At last he lay down to rest. The pocket of pain in his armpit had grown more sharp. His arm seemed to swell out and fall with every heartbeat. There was no position lying down where the heavy arm did not press against his armpit.

With the effort of a hurt beast, Pepé got up and moved again toward the top of the ridge. He held his swollen arm away from his body with his left hand. Up the steep hill he dragged himself, a few steps and a rest, and a few more steps. At last he was nearing the top. The moon showed the uneven sharp back of it against the sky.

Pepé's brain spun in a big spiral up and away from him. He slumped to the ground and lay still. The rock ridge top was only a hundred feet above him.

The moon moved over the sky. Pepé half turned on his back. His tongue tried to make words, but only a thick hissing came from between his lips.

When the dawn came, Pepé pulled himself up. His eyes were sane again. He drew his great puffed arm in front of him and looked at the angry wound. The black line ran up from his wrist to his armpit. Automatically he reached in his pocket for the big black knife, but it was not there. His eyes searched the ground. He picked up a sharp blade of stone and scraped at the wound, sawed at the proud flesh and then squeezed the green juice out in big drops. Instantly he threw back his head and whined like a dog. His whole right side shuddered at the pain, but the pain cleared his head.

In the grey light he struggled up the last slope to the ridge and crawled over and lay down behind a line of rocks. Below him lay a deep canyon exactly like the last, waterless and desolate. There was no flat, no oak trees, not even heavy brush in the bottom of it. And on the other side a sharp ridge stood up, thinly brushed with starving sage, littered with broken granite. Strewn over the hill there were giant outcroppings, and on the top the granite teeth stood out against the sky.

The new day was light now. The flame of the sun came over the ridge and fell on Pepé where he lay on the ground. His coarse black hair was littered with twigs and bits of spider web. His eyes had retreated back into his head. Between his lips the tip of his black tongue showed.

He sat up and dragged his great arm into his lap and nursed it, rocking his body and moaning in his throat. He threw back his head and looked up into the pale sky. A big black bird circled nearly out of sight, and far to the left another was sailing near.

He lifted his head to listen, for a familiar sound had come to him from the valley he had climbed out of; it was the crying yelp of hounds, excited and feverish, on a trail.

Pepé bowed his head quickly. He tried to speak rapid

words but only a thick hiss came from his lips. He drew a shaky cross on his breast with his left hand. It was a long struggle to get to his feet. He crawled slowly and mechanically to the top of a big rock on the ridge peak. Once there, he arose slowly, swaying to his feet, and stood erect. Far below he could see the dark brush where he had slept. He braced his feet and stood there, black against the morning sky.

There came a ripping sound at his feet. A piece of stone flew up and a bullet droned off into the next gorge. The hollow crash echoed up from below. Pepé looked down for a moment and then pulled himself straight again.

His body jarred back. His left hand fluttered helplessly toward his breast. The second crash sounded from below. Pepé swung forward and toppled from the rock. His body struck and rolled over and over, starting a little avalanche. And when at last he stopped against a bush, the avalanche slid slowly down and covered up his head.

THE SNAKE

THE SNAKE

IT WAS almost dark when young Dr. Phillips swung his sack to his shoulder and left the tide pool. He climbed up over the rocks and squashed along the street in his rubber boots. The street lights were on by the time he arrived at his little commercial laboratory on the cannery street of Monterey. It was a tight little building, standing partly on piers over the bay water and partly on the land. On both sides the big corrugated-iron sardine canneries crowded in on it.

Dr. Phillips climbed the wooden steps and opened the door. The white rats in their cages scampered up and down the wire, and the captive cats in their pens mewed for milk. Dr. Phillips turned on the glaring light over the dissection table and dumped his clammy sack on the floor. He walked to the glass cages by the window where the rattlesnakes lived, leaned over and looked in.

The snakes were bunched and resting in the corners of the cage, but every head was clear; the dusty eyes seemed to look at nothing, but as the young man leaned over the cage the forked tongues, black on the ends and pink behind, twittered out and waved slowly up and down. Then the snakes recognized the man and pulled in their tongues.

Dr. Phillips threw off his leather coat and built a fire

in the tin stove; he set a kettle of water on the stove and dropped a can of beans into the water. Then he stood staring down at the sack on the floor. He was a slight young man with the mild, preoccupied eyes of one who looks through a microscope a great deal. He wore a short blond beard.

The draft ran breathily up the chimney and a glow of warmth came from the stove. The little waves washed quietly about the piles under the building. Arranged on shelves about the room were tier above tier of museum jars containing the mounted marine specimens the laboratory dealt in.

Dr. Phillips opened a side door and went into his bedroom, a book-lined cell containing an army cot, a reading light and an uncomfortable wooden chair. He pulled off his rubber boots and put on a pair of sheepskin slippers. When he went back to the other room the water in the kettle was already beginning to hum.

He lifted his sack to the table under the white light and emptied out two dozen common starfish. These he laid out side by side on the table. His preoccupied eyes turned to the busy rats in the wire cages. Taking grain from a paper sack, he poured it into the feeding troughs. Instantly the rats scrambled down from the wire and fell upon the food. A bottle of milk stood on a glass shelf between a small mounted octopus and a jellyfish. Dr. Phillips lifted down the milk and walked to the cat cage, but before he filled the containers he reached in the cage and gently picked out a big rangy alley tabby. He stroked her for a moment and then dropped her in a small black painted box, closed the lid and bolted it and then turned on a petcock which admitted gas into the killing chamber. While the short soft struggle went on in the black box he filled the saucers with milk. One of the cats arched against his hand and he smiled and petted her neck.

The box was quiet now. He turned off the petcock, for the airtight box would be full of gas.

On the stove the pan of water was bubbling furiously about the can of beans. Dr. Phillips lifted out the can with a big pair of forceps, opened it, and emptied the beans into a glass dish. While he ate he watched the starfish on the table. From between the rays little drops of milky fluid were exuding. He bolted his beans and when they were gone he put the dish in the sink and stepped to the equipment cupboard. From this he took a microscope and a pile of little glass dishes. He filled the dishes one by one with sea water from a tap and arranged them in a line beside the starfish. He took out his watch and laid it on the table under the pouring white light. The waves washed with little sighs against the piles under the floor. He took an eyedropper from a drawer and bent over the starfish.

At that moment there were quick soft steps on the wooden stairs and a strong knocking at the door. A slight grimace of annoyance crossed the young man's face as he went to open. A tall, lean woman stood in the doorway. She was dressed in a severe dark suit—her straight black hair, growing low on a flat forehead, was mussed as though the wind had been blowing it. Her black eyes glittered in the strong light.

She spoke in a soft throaty voice, "May I come in? I want to talk to you."

"I'm very busy just now," he said half-heartedly. "I

have to do things at times." But he stood away from the door. The tall woman slipped in.

"I'll be quiet until you can talk to me."

He closed the door and brought the uncomfortable chair from the bedroom. "You see," he apologized, "the process is started and I must get to it." So many people wandered in and asked questions. He had little routines of explanations for the commoner processes. He could say them without thinking. "Sit here. In a few minutes I'll be able to listen to you."

The tall woman leaned over the table. With the eye-dropper the young man gathered fluid from between the rays of the starfish and squirted it into a bowl of water, and then he drew some milky fluid and squirted it in the same bowl and stirred the water gently with the eyedropper. He began his little patter of explanation.

"When starfish are sexually mature they release sperm and ova when they are exposed at low tide. By choosing mature specimens and taking them out of the water, I give them a condition of low tide. Now I've mixed the sperm and eggs. Now I put some of the mixture in each one of these ten watch glasses. In ten minutes I will kill those in the first glass with menthol, twenty minutes later I will kill the second group and then a new group every twenty minutes. Then I will have arrested the process in stages, and I will mount the series on microscope slides for biologic study." He paused. "Would you like to look at this first group under the microscope?"

"No, thank you."

He turned quickly to her. People always wanted to look through the glass. She was not looking at the table at all, but at him. Her black eyes were on him, but they did not seem to see him. He realized why—the irises were as dark as the pupils, there was no color line between the two. Dr. Phillips was piqued at her answer. Although answering questions bored him, a lack of interest in what he was doing irritated him. A desire to arouse her grew in him.

"While I'm waiting the first ten minutes I have something to do. Some people don't like to see it. Maybe you'd better step into that room until I finish."

"No," she said in her soft flat tone. "Do what you wish. I will wait until you can talk to me." Her hands rested side by side on her lap. She was completely at rest. Her eyes were bright but the rest of her was almost in a state of suspended animation. He thought, "Low metabolic rate, almost as low as a frog's, from the looks." The desire to shock her out of her inanition possessed him again.

He brought a little wooden cradle to the table, laid out scalpels and scissors and rigged a big hollow needle to a pressure tube. Then from the killing chamber he brought the limp dead cat and laid it in the cradle and tied its legs to hooks in the sides. He glanced sidewise at the woman. She had not moved. She was still at rest.

The cat grinned up into the light, its pink tongue stuck out between its needle teeth. Dr. Phillips deftly snipped open the skin at the throat; with a scalpel he slit through and found an artery. With flawless technique he put the needle in the vessel and tied it in with gut. "Embalming fluid," he explained. "Later I'll inject yellow mass into the veinous system and red mass into the arterial system—for bloodstream dissection—biology classes."

He looked around at her again. Her dark eyes seemed veiled with dust. She looked without expression at the cat's open throat. Not a drop of blood had escaped. The incision was clean. Dr. Phillips looked at his watch. "Time for the first group." He shook a few crystals of menthol into the first watch-glass.

The woman was making him nervous. The rats climbed about on the wire of their cage again and squeaked softly. The waves under the building beat with little shocks on the piles.

The young man shivered. He put a few lumps of coal in the stove and sat down. "Now," he said. "I haven't anything to do for twenty minutes." He noticed how short her chin was between lower lip and point. She seemed to awaken slowly, to come up out of some deep pool of consciousness. Her head raised and her dark dusty eyes moved about the room and then came back to him.

"I was waiting," she said. Her hands remained side by side on her lap. "You have snakes?"

"Why, yes," he said rather loudly. "I have about two dozen rattlesnakes. I milk out the venom and send it to the anti-venom laboratories."

She continued to look at him but her eyes did not center on him, rather they covered him and seemed to see in a big circle all around him. "Have you a male snake, a male rattlesnake?"

"Well, it just happens I know I have. I came in one morning and found a big snake in—in coition with a smaller one. That's very rare in captivity. You see, I do know I have a male snake."

"Where is he?"

"Why, right in the glass cage by the window there."

Her head swung slowly around but her two quiet hands did not move. She turned back toward him. "May I see?"

He got up and walked to the case by the window. On the sand bottom the knot of rattlesnakes lay entwined, but their heads were clear. The tongues came out and flickered a moment and then waved up and down feeling the air for vibrations. Dr. Phillips nervously turned his head. The woman was standing beside him. He had not heard her get up from the chair. He had heard only the splash of water among the piles and the scampering of the rats on the wire screen.

She said softly, "Which is the male you spoke of?"

He pointed to a thick, dusty grey snake lying by itself in one corner of the cage. "That one. He's nearly five feet long. He comes from Texas. Our Pacific coast snakes are usually smaller. He's been taking all the rats, too. When I want the others to eat I have to take him out."

The woman stared down at the blunt dry head. The forked tongue slipped out and hung quivering for a long moment. "And you're sure he's a male."

"Rattlesnakes are funny," he said glibly. "Nearly every generalization proves wrong. I don't like to say anything definite about rattlesnakes, but—yes—I can assure you he's a male."

Her eyes did not move from the flat head. "Will you sell him to me?"

"Sell him?" he cried. "Sell him to you?"

"You do sell specimens, don't you?"

"Oh—yes. Of course I do. Of course I do."

"How much? Five dollars? Ten?"

"Oh! Not more than five. But—do you know anything about rattlesnakes? You might be bitten."

She looked at him for a moment. "I don't intend to take him. I want to leave him here, but—I want him to be mine. I want to come here and look at him and feed him and to know he's mine." She opened a little purse and took out a five-dollar bill. "Here! Now he is mine."

Dr. Phillips began to be afraid. "You could come to look at him without owning him."

"I want him to be mine."

"Oh, Lord!" he cried. "I've forgotten the time." He ran to the table. "Three minutes over. It won't matter much." He shook menthol crystals into the second watch-glass. And then he was drawn back to the cage where the woman still stared at the snake.

She asked, "What does he eat?"

"I feed them white rats, rats from the cage over there."

"Will you put him in the other cage? I want to feed him."

"But he doesn't need food. He's had a rat already this week. Sometimes they don't eat for three or four months. I had one that didn't eat for over a year."

In her low monotone she asked, "Will you sell me a rat?"

He shrugged his shoulders. "I see. You want to watch how rattlesnakes eat. All right. I'll show you. The rat will cost twenty-five cents. It's better than a bullfight if you look at it one way, and it's simply a snake eating his dinner if you look at it another." His tone had become acid. He hated people who made sport of natural processes. He was not a sportsman but a biologist. He could kill a thousand animals for knowledge, but not an insect for pleasure. He'd been over this in his mind before.

She turned her head slowly toward him and the beginning of a smile formed on her thin lips. "I want to feed my snake," she said. "I'll put him in the other cage." She had opened the top of the cage and dipped her hand in before he knew what she was doing. He leaped forward and pulled her back. The lid banged shut.

"Haven't you any sense," he asked fiercely. "Maybe he wouldn't kill you, but he'd make you damned sick in spite of what I could do for you."

"You put him in the other cage then," she said quietly.

Dr. Phillips was shaken. He found that he was avoiding the dark eyes that didn't seem to look at anything. He felt that it was profoundly wrong to put a rat into the cage, deeply sinful; and he didn't know why. Often he had put rats in the cage when someone or other had wanted to see it, but this desire tonight sickened him. He tried to explain himself out of it.

"It's a good thing to see," he said. "It shows you how a snake can work. It makes you have a respect for a rattlesnake. Then, too, lots of people have dreams about the terror of snakes making the kill. I think because it is a subjective rat. The person is the rat. Once you see it the whole matter is objective. The rat is only a rat and the terror is removed."

He took a long stick equipped with a leather noose from the wall. Opening the trap he dropped the noose over the big snake's head and tightened the thong. A piercing dry rattle filled the room. The thick body writhed and slashed about the handle of the stick as he lifted the snake out and dropped it in the feeding cage.

It stood ready to strike for a time, but the buzzing gradually ceased. The snake crawled into a corner, made a big figure eight with its body and lay still.

"You see," the young man explained, "these snakes are quite tame. I've had them a long time. I suppose I could handle them if I wanted to, but everyone who does handle rattlesnakes gets bitten sooner or later. I just don't want to take the chance." He glanced at the woman. He hated to put in the rat. She had moved over in front of the new cage; her black eyes were on the stony head of the snake again.

She said, "Put in a rat."

Reluctantly he went to the rat cage. For some reason he was sorry for the rat, and such a feeling had never come to him before. His eyes went over the mass of swarming white bodies climbing up the screen toward him. "Which one?" he thought. "Which one shall it be?" Suddenly he turned angrily to the woman. "Wouldn't you rather I put in a cat? Then you'd see a real fight. The cat might even win, but if it did it might kill the snake. I'll sell you a cat if you like."

She didn't look at him. "Put in a rat," she said. "I want him to eat."

He opened the rat cage and thrust his hand in. His fingers found a tail and he lifted a plump, red-eyed rat out of the cage. It struggled up to try to bite his fingers and, failing, hung spread out and motionless from its tail. He walked quickly across the room, opened the feeding cage and dropped the rat in on the sand floor. "Now, watch it," he cried.

The woman did not answer him. Her eyes were on the

snake where it lay still. Its tongue flicking in and out rapidly, tasted the air of the cage.

The rat landed on its feet, turned around and sniffed at its pink naked tail and then unconcernedly trotted across the sand, smelling as it went. The room was silent. Dr. Phillips did not know whether the water sighed among the piles or whether the woman sighed. Out of the corner of his eye he saw her body crouch and stiffen.

The snake moved out smoothly, slowly. The tongue flicked in and out. The motion was so gradual, so smooth that it didn't seem to be motion at all. In the other end of the cage the rat perked up in a sitting position and began to lick down the fine white hair on its chest. The snake moved on, keeping always a deep S curve in its neck.

The silence beat on the young man. He felt the blood drifting up in his body. He said loudly, "See! He keeps the striking curve ready. Rattlesnakes are cautious, almost cowardly animals. The mechanism is so delicate. The snake's dinner is to be got by an operation as deft as a surgeon's job. He takes no chances with his instruments."

The snake had flowed to the middle of the cage by now. The rat looked up, saw the snake and then unconcernedly went back to licking its chest.

"It's the most beautiful thing in the world," the young man said. His veins were throbbing. "It's the most terrible thing in the world."

The snake was close now. Its head lifted a few inches from the sand. The head weaved slowly back and forth, aiming, getting distance, aiming. Dr. Phillips glanced again at the woman. He turned sick. She was weaving too, not much, just a suggestion.

The rat looked up and saw the snake. It dropped to four feet and back up, and then—the stroke. It was impossible to see, simply a flash. The rat jarred as though under an invisible blow. The snake backed hurriedly into the corner from which it had come, and settled down, its tongue working constantly.

"Perfect!" Dr. Phillips cried. "Right between the shoulder blades. The fangs must almost have reached the heart."

The rat stood still, breathing like a little white bellows. Suddenly it leaped in the air and landed on its side. Its legs kicked spasmodically for a second and it was dead.

The woman relaxed, relaxed sleepily.

"Well," the young man demanded, "it was an emotional bath, wasn't it?"

She turned her misty eyes to him. "Will he eat it now?" she asked.

"Of course he'll eat it. He didn't kill it for a thrill. He killed it because he was hungry."

The corners of the woman's mouth turned up a trifle again. She looked back at the snake. "I want to see him eat it."

Now the snake came out of its corner again. There was no striking curve in its neck, but it approached the rat gingerly, ready to jump back in case it attacked. It nudged the body gently with its blunt nose, and drew away. Satisfied that it was dead, the snake touched the body all over with its chin, from head to tail. It seemed to measure the body and to kiss it. Finally it opened its mouth and unhinged its jaws at the corners.

Dr. Phillips put his will against his head to keep it

from turning toward the woman. He thought, "If she's opening her mouth, I'll be sick. I'll be afraid." He succeeded in keeping his eyes away.

The snake fitted its jaws over the rat's head and then with a slow peristaltic pulsing, began to engulf the rat. The jaws gripped and the whole throat crawled up, and the jaws gripped again.

Dr. Phillips turned away and went to his work table. "You've made me miss one of the series," he said bitterly. "The set won't be complete." He put one of the watch glasses under a low-power microscope and looked at it, and then angrily he poured the contents of all the dishes into the sink. The waves had fallen so that only a wet whisper came up through the floor. The young man lifted a trapdoor at his feet and dropped the starfish down into the black water. He paused at the cat, crucified in the cradle and grinning comically into the light. Its body was puffed with embalming fluid. He shut off the pressure, withdrew the needle and tied the vein.

"Would you like some coffee?" he asked.

"No, thank you. I shall be going pretty soon."

He walked to her where she stood in front of the snake cage. The rat was swallowed, all except an inch of pink tail that stuck out of the snake's mouth like a sardonic tongue. The throat heaved again and the tail disappeared. The jaws snapped back into their sockets, and the big snake crawled heavily to the corner, made a big eight and dropped its head on the sand.

"He's asleep now," the woman said. "I'm going now. But I'll come back and feed my snake every little while. I'll pay for the rats. I want him to have plenty. And sometime—I'll take him away with me." Her eyes came out of their dusty dream for a moment. "Remember, he's mine. Don't take his poison. I want him to have it. Good-night." She walked swiftly to the door and went out. He heard her footsteps on the stairs, but he could not hear her walk away on the pavement.

Dr. Phillips turned a chair around and sat down in front of the snake cage. He tried to comb out his thought as he looked at the torpid snake. "I've read so much about psychological sex symbols," he thought. "It doesn't seem to explain. Maybe I'm too much alone. Maybe I should kill the snake. If I knew—no, I can't pray to anything."

For weeks he expected her to return. "I will go out and leave her alone here when she comes," he decided. "I won't see the damned thing again."

She never came again. For months he looked for her when he walked about in the town. Several times he ran after some tall woman thinking it might be she. But he never saw her again—ever.

BREAKFAST

BREAKFAST

THIS THING fills me with pleasure. I don't know why, I can see it in the smallest detail. I find myself recalling it again and again, each time bringing more detail out of a sunken memory, remembering brings the curious warm pleasure.

It was very early in the morning. The eastern mountains were black-blue, but behind them the light stood up faintly colored at the mountain rims with a washed red, growing colder, greyer and darker as it went up and overhead until, at a place near the west, it merged with pure night.

And it was cold, not painfully so, but cold enough so that I rubbed my hands and shoved them deep into my pockets, and I hunched my shoulders up and scuffled my feet on the ground. Down in the valley where I was, the earth was that lavender grey of dawn. I walked along a country road and ahead of me I saw a tent that was only a little lighter grey than the ground. Beside the tent there was a flash of orange fire seeping out of the cracks of an old rusty iron stove. Grey smoke spurted up out of the stubby stovepipe, spurted up a long way before it spread out and dissipated.

I saw a young woman beside the stove, really a girl. She was dressed in a faded cotton skirt and waist. As I came close I saw that she carried a baby in a crooked arm and the baby was nursing, its head under her waist out of the cold. The mother moved about, poking the fire, shifting the rusty lids of the stove to make a greater draft, opening the oven door; and all the time the baby was nursing, but that didn't interfere with the mother's work, nor with the light quick gracefulness of her movements. There was something very precise and practiced in her movements. The orange fire flicked out of the cracks in the stove and threw dancing reflections on the tent.

I was close now and I could smell frying bacon and baking bread, the warmest, pleasantest odors I know. From the east the light grew swiftly. I came near to the stove and stretched my hands out to it and shivered all over when the warmth struck me. Then the tent flap jerked up and a young man came out and an older man followed him. They were dressed in new blue dungarees and in new dungaree coats with the brass buttons shining. They were sharp-faced men, and they looked much alike.

The younger had a dark stubble beard and the older had a grey stubble beard. Their heads and faces were wet, their hair dripped with water, and water stood out on their stiff beards and their cheeks shone with water. Together they stood looking quietly at the lightening east; they yawned together and looked at the light on the hill rims. They turned and saw me.

"Morning," said the older man. His face was neither friendly nor unfriendly.

"Morning, sir," I said.

"Morning," said the young man.

The water was slowly drying on their faces. They came to the stove and warmed their hands at it.

The girl kept to her work, her face averted and her eyes on what she was doing. Her hair was tied back out of her eyes with a string and it hung down her back and swayed as she worked. She set tin cups on a big packing box, set tin plates and knives and forks out too. Then she scooped fried bacon out of the deep grease and laid it on a big tin platter, and the bacon cricked and rustled as it grew crisp. She opened the rusty oven door and took out a square pan full of high big biscuits.

When the smell of that hot bread came out, both of the men inhaled deeply. The young man said softly, "Keerist!"

The elder man turned to me, "Had your breakfast?"

"No."

"Well, sit down with us, then."

That was the signal. We went to the packing case and squatted on the ground about it. The young man asked, "Picking cotton?"

"No."

"We had twelve days' work so far," the young man said.

The girl spoke from the stove. "They even got new clothes."

The two men looked down at their new dungarees and they both smiled a little.

The girl set out the platter of bacon, the brown high biscuits, a bowl of bacon gravy and a pot of coffee, and then she squatted down by the box too. The baby was still nursing, its head up under her waist out of the cold. I could hear the sucking noises it made.

We filled our plates, poured bacon gravy over our biscuits and sugared our coffee. The older man filled his mouth full and he chewed and chewed and swallowed. Then he said, "God Almighty, it's good," and he filled his mouth again.

The young man said, "We been eating good for twelve days."

We all ate quickly, frantically, and refilled our plates and ate quickly again until we were full and warm. The hot bitter coffee scalded our throats. We threw the last little bit with the grounds in it on the earth and refilled our cups.

There was color in the light now, a reddish gleam that made the air seem colder. The two men faced the east and their faces were lighted by the dawn, and I looked up for a moment and saw the image of the mountain and the light coming over it reflected in the older man's eyes.

Then the two men threw the grounds from their cups on the earth and they stood up together. "Got to get going," the older man said.

The younger turned to me. " 'Fyou want to pick cotton, we could maybe get you on."

"No. I got to go along. Thanks for breakfast."

The older man waved his hand in a negative. "O. K. Glad to have you." They walked away together. The air was blazing with light at the eastern skyline. And I walked away down the country road.

That's all. I know, of course, some of the reasons why it was pleasant. But there was some element of great beauty there that makes the rush of warmth when I think of it.

THE RAID

THE RAID

IT WAS dark in the little California town when the two men stepped from the lunch car and strode arrogantly through the back streets. The air was full of the sweet smell of fermenting fruit from the packing plants. High over the corners, blue arc lights swung in the wind and put moving shadows of telephone wires on the ground. The old wooden buildings were silent and resting. The dirty windows dismally reflected the street lights.

The two men were about the same size, but one was much older than the other. Their hair was cropped, they wore blue jeans. The older man had on a peajacket, while the younger wore a blue turtle-neck sweater. As they swung down the dark street, footsteps echoed back loudly from the wooden buildings. The younger man began to whistle *Come to Me My Melancholy Baby*. He stopped abruptly. "I wish that damn tune would get out of my head. It's been going all day. It's an old tune, too."

His companion turned toward him. "You're scared, Root. Tell the truth. You're scared as hell."

They were passing under one of the blue street lights. Root's face put on its toughest look, the eyes squinted, the mouth went crooked and bitter. "No, I ain't scared." They were out of the light. His face relaxed again. "I wish I knew the ropes better. You been out before, Dick. You know what to expect. But I ain't ever been out."

"The way to learn is to do," Dick quoted sententiously. "You never really learn nothing from books."

They crossed a railroad track. A block tower up the line a little was starred with green lights. "It's awful dark," said Root. "I wonder if the moon will come up later. Usually does when it's so dark. You going to make the first speech, Dick?"

"No, you make it. I had more experience than you. I'll watch them while you talk and then I can smack them where I know they bite. Know what you're going to say?"

"Sure I do. I got it all in my head, every word. I wrote it out and learned it. I heard guys tell how they got up and couldn't think of a thing to say, and then all of a sudden they just started in like it was somebody else, and the words came out like water out of a hydrant. Big Mike Sheane said it was like that with him. But I wasn't taking no chances, so I wrote it out."

A train hooted mournfully, and in a moment it rounded a bend and pushed its terrible light down the track. The lighted coaches rattled past. Dick turned to watch it go by. "Not many people on that one," he said with satisfaction. "Didn't you say your old man worked on the railroad?"

Root tried to keep the bitterness out of his voice. "Sure, he works on the road. He's a brakeman. He kicked me out when he found out what I was doing. He was scared he'd lose his job. He couldn't see. I talked to him, but he just couldn't see. He kicked me right out." Root's voice was lonely. Suddenly he realized how he had weakened and how he sounded homesick. "That's the trouble with them," he went on harshly. "They can't see beyond their jobs. They can't see what's happening to them. They hang on to their chains."

"Save it," said Dick. "That's good stuff. Is that part of your speech?"

"No, but I guess I'll put it in if you say it's good."

The street lights were fewer now. A line of locust trees grew along the road, for the town was beginning to thin and the country took control. Along the unpaved road there were a few little houses with ill-kept gardens.

"Jesus! It's dark," Root said again. "I wonder if there'll be any trouble. It's a good night to get away if anything happens."

Dick snorted into the collar of his peajacket. They walked along in silence for a while.

"Do you think you'd try to get away, Dick?" Root asked.

"No, by God! It's against orders. If anything happens we got to stick. You're just a kid. I guess you'd run if I let you!"

Root blustered: "You think you're hell on wheels just because you been out a few times. You'd think you was a hundred to hear you talk."

"I'm dry behind the ears, anyway," said Dick.

Root walked with his head down. He said softly, "Dick, are you sure you wouldn't run? Are you sure you could just stand there and take it?"

"Of course I'm sure. I've done it before. It's the orders, ain't it? Why, it's good publicity." He peered through the darkness at Root. "What makes you ask, kid? You scared you'll run? If you're scared you got no business here."

Root shivered. "Listen, Dick, you're a good guy. You

won't tell nobody what I say, will you? I never been tried. How do I know what I'll do if somebody smacks me in the face with a club? How can anybody tell what he'd do? I don't think I'd run. I'd try not to run."

"All right, kid. Let it go at that. But you try running, and I'll turn your name in. We got no place for yellow bastards. You remember that, kid."

"Oh, lay off that kid stuff. You're running that in the ground."

The locust trees grew closer together as they went. The wind rustled gently in the leaves. A dog growled in one of the yards as the men went by. A light fog began to drift down through the air, and the stars were swallowed in it. "You sure you got everything ready?" Dick asked. "Got the lamps? Got the lit'ature? I left all that to you."

"I did it all this afternoon," said Root. "I didn't put the posters up yet, but I got them in a box out there."

"Got oil in the lamps?"

"They had plenty in. Say, Dick, I guess some bastard has squealed, don't you?"

"Sure. Somebody always squeals."

"Well, you didn't hear nothing about no raid, did you?"

"How the hell would I hear. You think they'd come and tell me they was going to knock my can off? Get hold of yourself, Root. You got the pants scared off you. You're going to make me nervous if you don't cut it out."

II

They approached a low, square building, black and heavy in the darkness. Their feet pounded on a wooden sidewalk. "Nobody here, yet," said Dick. "Let's open her up and get some light." They had come to a deserted store. The old show-windows were opaque with dirt. A Lucky Strike poster was stuck to the glass on one side while a big cardboard Coca-Cola lady stood like a ghost in the other. Dick threw open the double doors and walked in. He struck a match and lighted a kerosene lamp, got the chimney back in place, and set the lamp on on an up-ended apple box. "Come on, Root, we got to get things ready."

The walls of the building were scabrous with streaked whitewash. A pile of dusty newspapers had been kicked into a corner. The two back windows were laced with cobwebs. Except for three apple boxes, there was nothing at all in the store.

Root walked to one of the boxes and took out a large poster bearing a portrait of a man done in harsh reds and blacks. He tacked the portrait to the whitewashed wall behind the lamp. Then he tacked another poster beside it, a large red symbol on a white background. Last he up-ended another apple box and piled leaflets and little paper-bound books on it. His footsteps were loud on the bare wooden floor. "Light the other lamp, Dick! It's too damned dark in here."

"Scared of the dark, too, kid?"

"No. The men will be here pretty soon. We want to have more light when they come. What time is it?"

Dick looked at his watch. "Quarter to eight. Some of the guys ought to be here pretty soon now." He put his hands in the breast pockets of his peajacket and stood loosely by the box of pamphlets. There was nothing to sit on. The black and red portrait stared harshly out at the room. Root leaned against the wall.

The light from one of the lamps yellowed, and the flame slowly sank down. Dick stepped over to it. "I thought you said there was plenty of oil. This one's dry."

"I thought there was plenty. Look! The other one's nearly full. We can pour some of that oil in this lamp."

"How we going to do that? We got to put them both out to pour the oil. You got any matches?"

Root felt through his pockets. "Only two."

"Now, you see? We got to hold this meeting with only one lamp. I should've looked things over this afternoon. I was busy in town, though. I thought I could leave it to you."

"Maybe we could quick pour some of this oil in a can and then pour it into the other lamp."

"Yeah, and then set the joint on fire. You're a hell of a helper."

Root leaned back against the wall again. "I wish they'd come. What time is it, Dick?"

"Five after eight."

"Well, what's keeping them? What are they waiting for? Did you tell them eight o'clock?"

"Oh! Shut up, kid. You'll get my goat pretty soon. I don't know what's keeping them. Maybe they got cold feet. Now shut up for a little while." He dug his hands into the pockets of his jacket again. "Got a cigarette, Root?"

"No."

It was very still. Nearer the center of the town, automobiles were moving; the mutter of their engines and an occasional horn sounded. A dog barked unexcitedly at one of the houses nearby. The wind ruffled the locust trees in whishing gusts.

"Listen, Dick! Do you hear voices? I think they're coming." They turned their heads and strained to listen.

"I don't hear nothing. You just thought you heard it."

Root walked to one of the dirty windows and looked out. Coming back, he paused at the pile of pamphlets and straightened them neatly. "What time is it now, Dick?"

"Keep still, will you? You'll drive me nuts. You got to have guts for this job. For God's sake show some guts."

"Well, I never been out before, Dick."

"Do you think anybody couldn't tell that? You sure make it plain enough."

The wind gusted sharply in the locust trees. The front doors clicked and one of them opened slowly, squeaking a little at the hinges. The breeze came in, ruffled the pile of dusty newspapers in the corner and sailed the posters out from the wall like curtains.

"Shut that door, Root. . . . No, leave it open. Then we can hear them coming better." He looked at his watch. "It's nearly half-past eight."

"Do you think they'll come? How long we going to wait, if they don't show up?"

The older man stared at the open door. "We ain't going to leave here before nine-thirty at the earliest. We got orders to hold this meeting."

The night sounds came in more clearly through the open door—the dance of dry locust leaves on the road, the slow steady barking of the dog. On the wall the red and black portrait was menacing in the dim light. It floated out at the bottom again. Dick looked around at it. "Listen, kid," he said quietly. "I know you're scared. When you're scared, just take a look at him." He indicated the picture with his thumb. "He wasn't scared. Just remember about what he did."

The boy considered the portrait. "You suppose he wasn't ever scared?"

Dick reprimanded him sharply. "If he was, nobody ever found out about it. You take that for a lesson and don't go opening up for everybody to show them how you feel."

"You're a good guy, Dick. I don't know what I'll do when I get sent out alone."

"You'll be all right, kid. You got stuff in you. I can tell that. You just never been under fire."

Root glanced quickly at the door. "Listen! You hear somebody coming?"

"Lay off that stuff! When they get here, they'll get here."

"Well—let's close the door. It's kind of cold in here. Listen! There *is* somebody coming."

Quick footsteps sounded on the road, broke into a run and crossed the wooden sidewalk. A man in overalls and a painter's cap ran into the room. He was panting and winded. "You guys better scram," he said. "There's a raiding party coming. None of the boys is coming to the meeting. They was going to let you take it, but I wouldn't do that. Come on! Get your stuff together and get out. That party's on the way."

Root's face was pale and tight. He looked nervously at Dick. The older man shivered. He thrust his hands into his breast pockets and slumped his shoulders.

"Thanks," he said. "Thanks for telling us. You run along. We'll be all right."

"The others was just going to leave you take it," the man said.

Dick nodded. "Sure, they can't see the future. They can't see beyond their nose. Run along now before you get caught."

"Well, ain't you guys coming? I'll help carry some of your stuff."

"We're going to stay," Dick said woodenly. "We got orders to stay. We got to take it."

The man was moving toward the door. He turned back. "Want me to stay with you?"

"No, you're a good guy. No need for you to stay. We could maybe use you some other time."

"Well, I did what I could."

III

Dick and Root heard him cross the wooden sidewalk and trot off into the darkness. The night resumed its sounds. The dead leaves scraped along the ground. The motors hummed from the centre of the town.

Root looked at Dick. He could see that the man's fists were doubled up in his breast pockets. The face muscles were stiff, but he smiled at the boy. The posters drifted out from the wall and settled back again.

"Scared, kid?"

Root bristled to deny it, and then gave it up. "Yes, I'm scared. Maybe I won't be no good at this."

"Take hold, kid!" Dick said fiercely. "You take hold!"

Dick quoted to him, " 'The men of little spirit must have an example of stead—steadfastness. The people at large must have an example of injustice.' There it is, Root. That's orders." He relapsed into silence. The barking dog increased his tempo.

"I guess that's them," said Root. "Will they kill us, do you think?"

"No, they don't very often kill anybody."

"But they'll hit us and kick us, won't they? They'll hit us in the face with sticks and break our nose. Big Mike, they broke his jaw in three places."

"Take hold, kid! You take hold! And listen to me; if some one busts you, it isn't him that's doing it, it's the System. And it isn't you he's busting. He's taking a crack at the Principle. Can you remember that?"

"I don't want to run, Dick. Honest to God I don't. If I start to run, you hold me, will you?"

Dick walked near and touched him on the shoulder. "You'll be all right. I can tell a guy that will stick."

"Well, hadn't we better hide the lit'ature so it won't all get burned?"

"No—somebody might put a book in his pocket and read it later. Then it would be doing some good. Leave the books there. And shut up now! Talking only makes it worse."

The dog had gone back to his slow, spiritless barking. A rush of wind brought a scurry of dead leaves in the open door. The portrait poster blew out and came loose at one corner. Root walked over and pinned it back. Somewhere in the town, an automobile squealed its brakes.

"Hear anything, Dick? Hear them coming yet?"

"No."

"Listen, Dick. Big Mike lay two days with his jaw broke before anybody'd help him."

The older man turned angrily on him. One doubled fist came out of his peajacket pocket. His eyes narrowed as he looked at the boy. He walked close and put an arm about his shoulders. "Listen to me close, kid," he said. "I don't know much, but I been through this mill before. I can tell you this for sure. When it comes—it won't hurt. I don't know why, but it won't. Even if they kill you it won't hurt." He dropped his arm and moved toward the front door. He looked out and listened in two directions before he came back into the room.

"Hear anything?"

"No. Not a thing."

"What—do you think is keeping them?"

"How do you suppose I'd know?"

Root swallowed thickly. "Maybe they won't come. Maybe it was all a lie that fella told us, just a joke."

"Maybe."

"Well, are—we going to wait all night to get our cans knocked off?"

Dick mimicked him. "Yes, we're going to wait all night to get our cans knocked off."

The wind sounded in one big fierce gust and then dropped away completely. The dog stopped barking. A train screamed for the crossing and went crashing by, leaving the night more silent than before. In a house nearby, an alarm clock went off. Dick said, "Somebody goes to work early. Night watchman, maybe." His voice was too loud in the stillness. The front door squeaked slowly shut.

"What time is it now, Dick?"

"Quarter-past nine."

"Jesus! Only that? I thought it was about morning. . . . Don't you wish they'd come and get it over, Dick? Listen, Dick!—I thought I heard voices."

They stood stiffly, listening. Their heads were bent forward. "You hear voices, Dick?"

"I think so. Like they're talking low."

The dog barked again, fiercely this time. A little quiet murmur of voices could be heard. "Look, Dick! I thought I saw somebody out the back window."

The older man chuckled uneasily. "That's so we can't get away. They got the place surrounded. Take hold, kid! They're coming now. Remember about it's not them, it's the System."

There came a rushing clatter of footsteps. The doors burst open. A crowd of men thronged in, roughly dressed men, wearing black hats. They carried clubs and sticks in their hands. Dick and Root stood erect, their chins out, their eyes dropped and nearly closed.

Once inside, the raiders were uneasy. They stood in a half-circle about the two men, scowling, waiting for some one to move.

Young Root glanced sidewise at Dick and saw that the older man was looking at him coldly, critically, as though he judged his deportment. Root shoved his trembling hands in his pockets. He forced himself forward. His voice was shrill with fright. "Comrades," he shouted, "you're just men like we are. We're all brothers——" A piece of two-by-four lashed out and struck him on the side of the head with a fleshy thump. Root went down to his knees and steadied himself with his hands.

The men stood still, glaring.

Root climbed slowly to his feet. His split ear spilled a red stream down his neck. The side of his face was mushy and purple. He got himself erect again. His breath burst passionately. His hands were steady now, his voice sure and strong. His eyes were hot with an ecstasy. "Can't you see?" he shouted. "It's all for you. We're doing it for you. All of it. You don't know what you're doing."

"Kill the red rats!"

Some one giggled hysterically. And then the wave came. As he went down, Root caught a moment's glimpse of Dick's face smiling a tight, hard smile.

IV

He came near the surface several times, but didn't quite make it into consciousness. At last he opened his eyes and knew things. His face and head were heavy with bandages. He could only see a line of light between his puffed eyelids. For a time he lay, trying to think his way out. Then he heard Dick's voice near to him.

"You awake, kid?"

Root tried his voice and found that it croaked pretty badly. "I guess so."

"They sure worked out on your head. I thought you was gone. You was right about your nose. It ain't going to be very pretty."

"What'd they do to you, Dick?"

"Oh, they bust my arm and a couple of ribs. You got to learn to turn your face down to the ground. That saves your eyes." He paused and drew a careful breath. "Hurts some to breathe when you get a rib bust. We are lucky. The cops picked us up and took us in."

"Are we in jail, Dick?"

"Yeah! Hospital cell."

"What they got on the book?"

He heard Dick try to chuckle, and gasp when it hurt him. "Inciting to riot. We'll get six months, I guess. The cops got the lit'ature."

"You won't tell them I'm under age, will you, Dick?"

"No. I won't. You better shut up. Your voice don't sound so hot. Take it easy."

Root lay silent, muffled in a coat of dull pain. But in a moment he spoke again. "It didn't hurt, Dick. It was funny. I felt all full up—and good."

"You done fine, kid. You done as good as anybody I ever seen. I'll give you a blow to the committee. You just done fine."

Root struggled to get something straight in his head. "When they was busting me I wanted to tell them I didn't care."

"Sure, kid. That's what I told you. It wasn't them. It was the System. You don't want to hate them. They don't know no better."

Root spoke drowsily. The pain was muffling him under. "You remember in the Bible, Dick, how it says something like 'Forgive them because they don't know what they're doing'?"

Dick's reply was stern. "You lay off that religion stuff, kid." He quoted, " 'Religion is the opium of the people.' "

"Sure, I know," said Root. "But there wasn't no religion to it. It was just—I felt like saying that. It was just kind of the way I felt."

THE HARNESS

THE HARNESS

PETER RANDALL was one of the most highly respected farmers of Monterey County. Once, before he was to make a little speech at a Masonic convention, the brother who introduced him referred to him as an example for young Masons of California to emulate. He was nearing fifty; his manner was grave and restrained, and he wore a carefully tended beard. From every gathering he reaped the authority that belongs to the bearded man. Peter's eyes were grave, too; blue and grave almost to the point of sorrowfulness. People knew there was force in him, but force held caged. Sometimes, for no apparent reason, his eyes grew sullen and mean, like the eyes of a bad dog; but that look soon passed, and the restraint and probity came back into his face. He was tall and broad. He held his shoulders back as though they were braced, and he sucked in his stomach like a soldier. Inasmuch as farmers are usually slouchy men, Peter gained an added respect because of his posture.

Concerning Peter's wife, Emma, people generally agreed that it was hard to see how such a little skin-and-bones woman could go on living, particularly when she was sick most of the time. She weighed eighty-seven pounds. At forty-five, her face was as wrinkled and brown as that of an old, old woman, but her dark eyes were feverish with a determination to live. She was a proud woman, who complained very little. Her father had been a thirty-third degree Mason and Worshipful Master of the Grand Lodge of California. Before he died he had taken a great deal of interest in Peter's Masonic career.

Once a year Peter went away for a week, leaving his wife alone on the farm. To neighbors who called to keep her company she invariably explained, "He's away on a business trip."

Each time Peter returned from a business trip, Emma was ailing for a month or two, and this was hard on Peter, for Emma did her own work and refused to hire a girl. When she was ill, Peter had to do the housework.

The Randall ranch lay across the Salinas River, next to the foothills. It was an ideal balance of bottom and upland. Forty-five acres of rich level soil brought from the cream of the county by the river in old times and spread out as flat as a board; and eighty acres of gentle upland for hay and orchard. The white farmhouse was as neat and restrained as its owners. The immediate yard was fenced, and in the garden, under Emma's direction, Peter raised button dahlias and immortelles, carnations and pinks.

From the front porch one could look down over the flat to the river with its sheath of willows and cottonwoods, and across the river to the beet fields, and past the fields to the bulbous dome of the Salinas courthouse. Often in the afternoon Emma sat in a rocking-chair on the front porch, until the breeze drove her in. She knitted constantly, looking up now and then to watch Peter working on the flat or in the orchard, or on the slope below the house.

The Randall ranch was no more encumbered with mortgage than any of the others in the valley. The crops, judiciously chosen and carefully tended, paid the interest, made a reasonable living and left a few hundred dollars every year toward paying off the principal. It was no wonder that Peter Randall was respected by his neighbors, and that his seldom spoken words were given attention even when they were about the weather or the way things were going. Let Peter say, "I'm going to kill a pig Saturday," and nearly every one of his hearers went home and killed a pig on Saturday. They didn't know why, but if Peter Randall was going to kill a pig, it seemed like a good, safe, conservative thing to do.

Peter and Emma were married for twenty-one years. They collected a houseful of good furniture, a number of framed pictures, vases of all shapes, and books of a sturdy type. Emma had no children. The house was unscarred, uncarved, unchalked. On the front and back porches footscrapers and thick cocoa-fiber mats kept dirt out of the house.

In the intervals between her illnesses, Emma saw to it that the house was kept up. The hinges of doors and cupboards were oiled, and no screws were gone from the catches. The furniture and woodwork were freshly varnished once a year. Repairs were usually made after Peter came home from his yearly business trips.

Whenever the word went around among the farms that Emma was sick again, the neighbors waylaid the doctor as he drove by on the river road.

"Oh, I guess she'll be all right," he answered their questions. "She'll have to stay in bed for a couple of weeks."

The good neighbors took cakes to the Randall farm, and they tiptoed into the sickroom, where the little skinny bird of a woman lay in a tremendous walnut bed. She looked at them with her bright little dark eyes.

"Wouldn't you like the curtains up a little, dear?" they asked.

"No, thank you. The light worries my eyes."

"Is there anything we can do for you?"

"No, thank you. Peter does for me very well."

"Just remember, if there's anything you think of——"

Emma was such a tight woman. There was nothing you could do for her when she was ill, except to take pies and cakes to Peter. Peter would be in the kitchen, wearing a neat, clean apron. He would be filling a hot water bottle or making junket.

And so, one fall, when the news traveled that Emma was down, the farm-wives baked for Peter and prepared to make their usual visits.

Mrs. Chappell, the next farm neighbor, stood on the river road when the doctor drove by. "How's Emma Randall, doctor?"

"I don't think she's so very well, Mrs. Chappell. I think she's a pretty sick woman."

Because to Dr. Marn anyone who wasn't actually a corpse was well on the road to recovery, the word went about among the farms that Emma Randall was going to die.

It was a long, terrible illness. Peter himself gave enemas and carried bedpans. The doctor's suggestion that a nurse be employed met only beady, fierce refusal in the eyes of the patient; and, ill as she was, her demands were respected. Peter fed her and bathed her, and made up the great walnut bed. The bedroom curtains remained drawn.

It was two months before the dark, sharp bird eyes veiled, and the sharp mind retired into unconsciousness. And only then did a nurse come to the house. Peter was lean and sick himself, not far from collapse. The neighbors brought him cakes and pies, and found them uneaten in the kitchen when they called again.

Mrs. Chappell was in the house with Peter the afternoon Emma died. Peter became hysterical immediately. Mrs. Chappell telephoned the doctor, and then she called her husband to come and help her, for Peter was wailing like a crazy man, and beating his bearded cheeks with his fists. Ed Chappell was ashamed when he saw him.

Peter's beard was wet with his tears. His loud sobbing could be heard throughout the house. Sometimes he sat by the bed and covered his head with a pillow, and sometimes he paced the floor of the bedroom bellowing like a calf. When Ed Chappell self-consciously put a hand on his shoulder and said, "Come on, Peter, come on, now," in a helpless voice, Peter shook his hand off. The doctor drove out and signed the certificate.

When the undertaker came, they had a devil of a time with Peter. He was half mad. He fought them when they tried to take the body away. It was only after Ed Chappell and the undertaker held him down while the doctor stuck him with a hypodermic, that they were able to remove Emma.

The morphine didn't put Peter to sleep. He sat hunched in the corner, breathing heavily and staring at the floor.

"Who's going to stay with him?" the doctor asked. "Miss Jack?" to the nurse.

"I couldn't handle him, doctor, not alone."

"Will you stay, Chappell?"

"Sure, I'll stay."

"Well, look. Here are some triple bromides. If he gets going again, give him one of these. And if they don't work, here's some sodium amytal. One of these capsules will calm him down."

Before they went away, they helped the stupefied Peter into the sitting-room and laid him gently down on a sofa. Ed Chappell sat in an easy-chair and watched him. The bromides and a glass of water were on the table beside him.

The little sitting-room was clean and dusted. Only that morning Peter had swept the floor with pieces of damp newspaper. Ed built a little fire in the grate, and put on a couple of pieces of oak when the flames were well started. The dark had come early. A light rain spattered against the windows when the wind drove it. Ed trimmed the kerosene lamps and turned the flames low. In the grate the blaze snapped and crackled and the flames curled like hair over the oak. For a long time Ed sat in his easy-chair watching Peter where he lay drugged on the couch. At last Ed dozed off to sleep.

It was about ten o'clock when he awakened. He started up and looked toward the sofa. Peter was sitting up, looking at him. Ed's hand went out toward the bromide bottle, but Peter shook his head.

"No need to give me anything, Ed. I guess the doctor slugged me pretty hard, didn't he? I feel all right now, only a little dopey."

"If you'll just take one of these, you'll get some sleep."

"I don't want sleep." He fingered his draggled beard and then stood up. "I'll go out and wash my face, then I'll feel better."

Ed heard him running water in the kitchen. In a moment he came back into the living-room, still drying his face on a towel. Peter was smiling curiously. It was an expression Ed had never seen on him before, a quizzical, wondering smile. "I guess I kind of broke loose when she died, didn't I?" Peter said.

"Well—yes, you carried on some."

"It seemed like something snapped inside of me," Peter explained. "Something like a suspender strap. It made me all come apart. I'm all right, now, though."

Ed looked down at the floor and saw a little brown spider crawling, and stretched out his foot and stomped it.

Peter asked suddenly, "Do you believe in an after-life?"

Ed Chappell squirmed. He didn't like to talk about such things, for to talk about them was to bring them up in his mind and think about them. "Well, yes. I suppose if you come right down to it, I do."

"Do you believe that somebody that's—passed on—can look down and see what we're doing?"

"Oh, I don't know as I'd go that far—I don't know."

Peter went on as though he were talking to himself. "Even if she could see me, and I didn't do what she wanted, she ought to feel good because I did it when she was here. It ought to please her that she made a good man of me. If I wasn't a good man when she wasn't here, that'd prove she did it all, wouldn't it? I was a good man, wasn't I, Ed?"

"What do you mean, 'was'?"

"Well, except for one week a year I was good. I don't know what I'll do now. . . ." His face grew angry. "Except one thing." He stood up and stripped off his coat and his shirt. Over his underwear there was a web harness that pulled his shoulders back. He unhooked the harness and threw it off. Then he dropped his trousers, disclosing a wide elastic belt. He shucked this off over his feet, and then he scratched his stomach luxuriously before he put on his clothes again. He smiled at Ed, the strange, wondering smile, again. "I don't know how she got me to do things, but she did. She didn't seem to boss me, but she always made me do things. You know, I don't think I believe in an after-life. When she was alive, even when she was sick, I had to do things she wanted, but just the minute she died, it was—why like that harness coming off! I couldn't stand it. It was all over. I'm going to have to get used to going without that harness." He shook his finger in Ed's direction. "My stomach's going to stick out," he said positively. "I'm going to let it stick out. Why, I'm fifty years old."

Ed didn't like that. He wanted to get away. This sort of thing wasn't very decent. "If you'll just take one of these, you'll get some sleep," he said weakly.

Peter had not put his coat on. He was sitting on the sofa in an open shirt. "I don't want to sleep. I want to talk. I guess I'll have to put that belt and harness on for the funeral, but after that I'm going to burn them. Listen, I've got a bottle of whiskey in the barn. I'll go get it."

"Oh no," Ed protested quickly. "I couldn't drink now, not at a time like this."

Peter stood up. "Well, I could. You can sit and watch me if you want. I tell you, it's all over." He went out the door, leaving Ed Chappell unhappy and scandalized. It was only a moment before he was back. He started talking as he came through the doorway with the whiskey. "I only got one thing in my life, those trips. Emma was a pretty bright woman. She knew I'd've gone crazy if I didn't get away once a year. God, how she worked on my conscience when I came back!" His voice lowered confidentially. "You know what I did on those trips?"

Ed's eyes were wide open now. Here was a man he didn't know, and he was becoming fascinated. He took the glass of whiskey when it was handed to him. "No, what did you do?"

Peter gulped his drink and coughed, and wiped his mouth with his hand. "I got drunk," he said. "I went to fancy houses in San Francisco. I was drunk for a week, and I went to a fancy house every night." He poured his glass full again. "I guess Emma knew, but she never said anything. I'd've *busted* if I hadn't got away."

Ed Chappell sipped his whiskey gingerly. "She always said you went on business."

Peter looked at his glass and drank it, and poured it full again. His eyes had begun to shine. "Drink your drink, Ed. I know you think it isn't right—so soon, but no one'll know but you and me. Kick up the fire. I'm not sad."

Chappell went to the grate and stirred the glowing wood until lots of sparks flew up the chimney like little shining birds. Peter filled the glasses and retired to the sofa again. When Ed went back to the chair he sipped from his glass and pretended he didn't know it was filled up. His cheeks were flushing. It didn't seem so terrible, now, to be drinking. The afternoon and the death had receded into an indefinite past.

"Want some cake?" Peter asked. "There's half a dozen cakes in the pantry."

"No, I don't think I will thank you for some."

"You know," Peter confessed, "I don't think I'll eat cake again. For ten years, every time Emma was sick, people sent cakes. It was nice of 'em, of course, only now cake means sickness to me. Drink your drink."

Something happened in the room. Both men looked up, trying to discover what it was. The room was somehow different than it had been a moment before. Then Peter smiled sheepishly. "It was that mantel clock stopped. I don't think I'll start it any more. I'll get a little quick alarm clock that ticks fast. That clack-clack-clack is too mournful." He swallowed his whiskey. "I guess you'll be telling around that I'm crazy, won't you?"

Ed looked up from his glass, and smiled and nodded. "No, I will not. I can see pretty much how you feel about things. I didn't know you wore that harness and belt."

"A man ought to stand up straight," Peter said. "I'm a natural sloucher." Then he exploded: "I'm a natural fool! For twenty years I've been pretending I was a wise, good man—except for that one week a year." He said loudly, "Things have been dribbled to me. My life's been dribbled out to me. Here, let me fill your glass. I've got another bottle out in the barn, way down under a pile of sacks."

Ed held out his glass to be filled. Peter went on, "I thought how it would be nice to have my whole river flat in sweet peas. Think how it'd be to sit on the front porch and see all those acres of blue and pink, just solid. And when the wind came up over them, think of the big smell. A big smell that would almost knock you over."

"A lot of men have gone broke on sweet peas. 'Course you get a big price for the seed, but too many things can happen to your crop."

"I don't give a damn," Peter shouted. "I want a lot of everything. I want forty acres of color and smell. I want fat women, with breasts as big as pillows. I'm hungry, I tell you, I'm hungry for everything, for a lot of everything."

Ed's face became grave under the shouting. "If you'd just take one of these, you'd get some sleep."

Peter looked ashamed. "I'm all right. I didn't mean to yell like that. I'm not just thinking these things for the first time. I been thinking about them for years, the way a kid thinks of vacation. I was always afraid I'd be too old. Or that I'd go first and miss everything. But I'm only fifty, I've got plenty of vinegar left. I told Emma about the sweet peas, but she wouldn't let me. I don't know how she made me do things," he said wonderingly. "I can't remember. She had a way of doing it. But she's gone. I can feel she's gone just like that harness is gone. I'm going to slouch, Ed—slouch all over the place. I'm going to track dirt into the house. I'm going to get a big fat housekeeper—a big fat one from San Francisco. I'm going to have a bottle of brandy on the shelf all the time."

Ed Chappell stood up and stretched his arms over his head. "I guess I'll go home now, if you feel all right. I got to get some sleep. You better wind that clock, Peter. It don't do a clock any good to stand not running."

The day after the funeral Peter Randall went to work on his farm. The Chappells, who lived on the next place, saw the lamp in his kitchen long before daylight, and they saw his lantern cross the yard to the barn half an hour before they even got up.

Peter pruned his orchard in three days. He worked from first light until he couldn't see the twigs against the sky any more. Then he started to shape the big piece of river flat. He plowed and rolled and harrowed. Two strange men dressed in boots and riding breeches came out and looked at his land. They felt the dirt with their fingers and ran a post-hole digger deep down under the surface, and when they went away they took little paper bags of the dirt with them.

Ordinarily, before planting time, the farmers did a good deal of visiting back and forth. They sat on their haunches, picking up handsful of dirt and breaking little clods between their fingers. They discussed markets and crops, recalled other years when beans had done well in a good market, and other years when field peas didn't bring enough to pay for the seed hardly. After a great number of these discussions it usually happened that all the farmers planted the same things. There were certain men whose ideas carried weight. If Peter Randall or Clark DeWitt thought they would put in pink beans and barley, most of the crops would turn out to be pink beans and barley that year; for, since such men were respected and fairly successful, it was conceded that their plans must be based on something besides chance choice. It was generally believed but never stated that Peter Randall and Clark DeWitt had extra reasoning powers and special prophetic knowledge.

When the usual visits started, it was seen that a change had taken place in Peter Randall. He sat on his plow and talked pleasantly enough. He said he hadn't decided yet what to plant, but he said it in such a guilty way that it was plain he didn't intend to tell. When he had rebuffed a few inquiries, the visits to his place stopped and the farmers went over in a body to Clark DeWitt. Clark was putting in Chevalier barley. His decision dictated the major part of the planting in the vicinity.

But because the questions stopped, the interest did not. Men driving by the forty-five acre flat of the Randall place studied the field to try to figure out from the type of work what the crop was going to be. When Peter drove the seeder back and forth across the land no one came in, for Peter had made it plain that his crop was a secret.

Ed Chappell didn't tell on him, either. Ed was a little ashamed when he thought of that night; ashamed of Peter for breaking down, and ashamed of himself for having sat there and listened. He watched Peter narrowly to see whether his vicious intentions were really there or whether the whole conversation had been the result of loss and hysteria. He did notice that Peter's shoulders weren't back and that his stomach stuck out a little. He went to Peter's house and was relieved when he saw no dirt on the floor and when he heard the mantel clock ticking away.

Mrs. Chappell spoke often of the afternoon. "You'd've thought he lost his mind the way he carried on. He just howled. Ed stayed with him part of the night, until he quieted down. Ed had to give him some whiskey to get him to sleep. But," she said brightly, "hard work is the thing to kill sorrow. Peter Randall is getting up at three o'clock every morning. I can see the light in his kitchen window from my bedroom."

The pussywillows burst out in silver drops, and the little weeds sprouted up along the roadside. The Salinas River ran dark water, flowed for a month, and then subsided into green pools again. Peter Randall had shaped his land beautifully. It was smooth and black; no clod was larger than a small marble, and under the rains it looked purple with richness.

And then the little weak lines of green stretched out across the black field. In the dusk a neighbor crawled under the fence and pulled one of the tiny plants. "Some kind of legume," he told his friends. "Field peas, I guess. What did he want to be so quiet about it for? I asked him right out what he was planting, and he wouldn't tell me."

The word ran through the farms, "It's sweet peas. The whole God-damn' forty-five acres is in sweet peas!" Men called on Clark DeWitt then, to get his opinion.

His opinion was this: "People think because you can get twenty to sixty cents a pound for sweet peas you can get rich on them. But it's the most ticklish crop in the world. If the bugs don't get it, it might do good. And then come a hot day and bust the pods and lose your crop on the ground. Or it might come up a little rain and spoil the whole kaboodle. It's all right to put in a few acres and take a chance, but not the whole place. Peter's touched in the head since Emma died."

This opinion was widely distributed. Every man used it as his own. Two neighbors often said it to each other, each one repeating half of it. When too many people said it to Peter Randall he became angry. One day he cried, "Say, whose land is this? If I want to go broke, I've got a damn good right to, haven't I?" And that changed the whole feeling. Men remembered that Peter was a good farmer. Perhaps he had special knowledge. Why, that's who those two men in boots were—soil chemists! A good many of the farmers wished they'd put in a few acres of sweet peas.

They wished it particularly when the vines spread out, when they met each other across the rows and hid the dark earth from sight, when the buds began to form and it was seen the crop was rich. And then the blooms came; forty-five acres of color, forty-five acres of perfume. It was said that you could smell them in Salinas, four miles away. Busses brought the school children out to look at them. A group of men from a seed company spent all day looking at the vines and feeling the earth.

Peter Randall sat on his porch in a rocking-chair every afternoon. He looked down on the great squares of pink and blue, and on the mad square of mixed colors. When the afternoon breeze came up, he inhaled deeply. His blue shirt was open at the throat, as though he wanted to get the perfume down next his skin.

Men called on Clark DeWitt to get his opinion now. He said, "There's about ten things that can happen to spoil that crop. He's welcome to his sweet peas." But the men knew from Clark's irritation that he was a little jealous. They looked up over the fields of color to where Peter sat on his porch, and they felt a new admiration and respect for him.

Ed Chappell walked up the steps to him one afternoon. "You got a crop there, mister."

"Looks that way," said Peter.

"I took a look. Pods are setting fine."

Peter sighed. "Blooming's nearly over," he said. "I'll hate to see the petals drop off."

"Well, I'd be glad to see 'em drop. You'll make a lot of money, if nothing happens."

Peter took out a bandana handkerchief and wiped his nose, and jiggled it sideways to stop an itch. "I'll be sorry when the smell stops," he said.

Then Ed made his reference to the night of the death. One of his eyes drooped secretly. "Found somebody to keep house for you?"

"I haven't looked," said Peter. "I haven't had time." There were lines of worry about his eyes. But who wouldn't worry, Ed thought, when a single shower could ruin his whole year's crop.

If the year and the weather had been manufactured for sweet peas, they couldn't have been better. The fog lay close to the ground in the mornings when the vines were pulled. When the great piles of vines lay safely on spread canvasses, the hot sun shone down and crisped the pods for the threshers. The neighbors watched the long cotton sacks filling with round black seeds, and they went home and tried to figure out how much money Peter would make on his tremendous crop. Clark DeWitt lost a good part of his following. The men decided to find out what Peter was going to plant next year if they had to follow him around. How did he know, for instance, that this year'd be good for sweet peas? He *must* have some kind of special knowledge.

When a man from the upper Salinas Valley goes to San Francisco on business or for a vacation, he takes a room in the Ramona Hotel. This is a nice arrangement, for in the lobby he can usually find someone from home. They can sit in the soft chairs of the lobby and talk about the Salinas Valley.

Ed Chappell went to San Francisco to meet his wife's cousin who was coming out from Ohio for a trip. The train was not due until the next morning. In the lobby of the Ramona, Ed looked for someone from the Salinas Valley, but he could see only strangers sitting in the soft chairs. He went out to a moving picture show. When he returned, he looked again for someone from home, and still there were only strangers. For a moment he considered glancing over the register, but it was quite late. He sat down to finish his cigar before he went to bed.

There was a commotion at the door. Ed saw the clerk motion with his hand. A bellhop ran out. Ed squirmed around in his chair to look. Outside a man was being helped out of a taxicab. The bellhop took him from the driver and guided him in the door. It was Peter Randall. His eyes were glassy, and his mouth open and wet. He had no hat on his mussed hair. Ed jumped up and strode over to him.

"Peter!"

Peter was batting helplessly at the bellhop. "Let me alone," he explained. "I'm all right. You let me alone, and I'll give you two bits."

Ed called again, "Peter!"

The glassy eyes turned slowly to him, and then Peter fell into his arms. "My old friend," he cried. "Ed Chappell, my old, good friend. What you doing here? Come up to my room and have a drink."

Ed set him back on his feet. "Sure I will," he said. "I'd like a little night-cap."

"Night-cap, hell. We'll go out and see a show, or something."

Ed helped him into the elevator and got him to his room. Peter dropped heavily to the bed and struggled up to a sitting position. "There's a bottle of whiskey in the bathroom. Bring me a drink, too."

Ed brought out the bottle and the glasses. "What you doing, Peter, celebrating the crop? You must've made a pile of money."

Peter put out his palm and tapped it impressively with a forefinger. "Sure I made money—but it wasn't a bit better than gambling. It was just like straight gambling."

"But you got the money."

Peter scowled thoughtfully. "I might've lost my pants," he said. "The whole time, all the year, I been worrying. It was just like gambling."

"Well, you got it, anyway."

Peter changed the subject, then. "I been sick," he said. "I been sick right in the taxicab. I just came from a fancy house on Van Ness Avenue," he explained apologetically, "I just had to come up to the city. I'd'a busted if I hadn't come up and got some of the vinegar out of my system."

Ed looked at him curiously. Peter's head was hanging loosely between his shoulders. His beard was draggled and rough. "Peter—" Ed began, "the night Emma—passed on, you said you was going to—change things."

Peter's swaying head rose up slowly. He stared owlishly at Ed Chappell. "She didn't die dead," he said thickly. "She won't let me do things. She's worried me all year about those peas." His eyes were wondering. "I don't know how she does it." Then he frowned. His palm came out, and he tapped it again. "But you mark, Ed Chappell, I won't wear that harness, and I damn well won't ever wear it. You remember that." His head dropped forward again. But in a moment he looked up. "I been drunk," he said seriously. "I been to fancy houses." He edged out confidentially toward Ed. His voice dropped to a heavy whisper. "But it's all right, I'll fix it. When I get back, you know what I'm going to do? I'm going to put in electric lights. Emma always wanted electric lights." He sagged sideways on the bed.

Ed Chappell stretched Peter out and undressed him before he went to his own room.

[illegible] I remember, and get some of the [illegible] out of my reason."

Ed looked at him curiously. Peter's head was [illegible] between his shoulders. He [illegible] and laugh. [illegible] "The [illegible] [illegible] to—things."

Peter's [illegible] rose up slowly. He [illegible] suddenly. "Ed Chappell, [illegible] didn't die dead," he [illegible]. "She won't let me [illegible] about [illegible]." His [illegible]. "I don't know [illegible]." He frowned. His [illegible] came [illegible] and he [illegible]. "But you mark, Ed [illegible] I [illegible] wear that [illegible] and I damn well won't [illegible] it [illegible] after that." His head dropped forward again [illegible] he looked up. "I been [illegible]," he said [illegible]. "[illegible] to [illegible]." He [illegible] out [illegible] fell. His [illegible] "What'd [illegible] know what I'm going to do? I'm going to [illegible]. Emma always wanted [illegible]." He [illegible] on the bed.

Ed Chappell [illegible] Peter out and undressed him before he went to his own room.

THE VIGILANTE

THE VIGILANTE

THE great surge of emotion, the milling and shouting of the people fell gradually to silence in the town park. A crowd of people still stood under the elm trees, vaguely lighted by a blue street light two blocks away. A tired quiet settled on the people; some members of the mob began to sneak away into the darkness. The park lawn was cut to pieces by the feet of the crowd.

Mike knew it was all over. He could feel the let-down in himself. He was as heavily weary as though he had gone without sleep for several nights, but it was a dream-like weariness, a grey comfortable weariness. He pulled his cap down over his eyes and moved away, but before leaving the park he turned for one last look.

In the center of the mob someone had lighted a twisted newspaper and was holding it up. Mike could see how the flame curled about the feet of the grey naked body hanging from the elm tree. It seemed curious to him that negroes turn a bluish grey when they are dead. The burning newspaper lighted the heads of the up-looking men, silent men and fixed; they didn't move their eyes from the hanged man.

Mike felt a little irritation at whoever it was who was trying to burn the body. He turned to a man who stood beside him in the near-darkness. "That don't do no good," he said.

The man moved away without replying.

The newspaper torch went out, leaving the park almost black by contrast. But immediately another twisted paper was lighted and held up against the feet. Mike moved to another watching man. "That don't do no good," he repeated. "He's dead now. They can't hurt him none."

The second man grunted but did not look away from the flaming paper. "It's a good job," he said. "This'll save the county a lot of money and no sneaky lawyers getting in."

"That's what I say," Mike agreed. "No sneaky lawyers. But it don't do no good to try to burn him."

The man continued staring toward the flame. "Well, it can't do much harm, either."

Mike filled his eyes with the scene. He felt that he was dull. He wasn't seeing enough of it. Here was a thing he would want to remember later so he could tell about it, but the dull tiredness seemed to cut the sharpness off the picture. His brain told him this was a terrible and important affair, but his eyes and his feelings didn't agree. It was just ordinary. Half an hour before, when he had been howling with the mob and fighting for a chance to help pull on the rope, then his chest had been so full that he had found he was crying. But now everything was dead, everything unreal; the dark mob was made up of stiff lay-figures. In the flamelight the faces were as expressionless as wood. Mike felt the stiffness, the unreality in himself, too. He turned away at last and walked out of the park.

The moment he left the outskirts of the mob a cold loneliness fell upon him. He walked quickly along the street wishing that some other man might be walking beside him. The wide street was deserted, empty, as unreal as the park had been. The two steel lines of the car tracks stretched glimmering away down the street under the electroliers, and the dark store windows reflected the midnight globes.

A gentle pain began to make itself felt in Mike's chest. He felt with his fingers; the muscles were sore. Then he remembered. He was in the front line of the mob when it rushed the closed jail door. A driving line forty men deep had crashed Mike against the door like the head of a ram. He had hardly felt it then, and even now the pain seemed to have the dull quality of loneliness.

Two blocks ahead the burning neon word BEER hung over the sidewalk. Mike hurried toward it. He hoped there would be people there, and talk, to remove this silence; and he hoped the men wouldn't have been to the lynching.

The bartender was alone in his little bar, a small, middle-aged man with a melancholy moustache and an expression like an aged mouse, wise and unkempt and fearful.

He nodded quickly as Mike came in. "You look like you been walking in your sleep," he said.

Mike regarded him with wonder. "That's just how I feel, too, like I been walking in my sleep."

"Well, I can give you a shot if you want."

Mike hesitated. "No—I'm kind of thirsty. I'll take a beer. . . . Was you there?"

The little man nodded his mouse-like head again. "Right at the last, after he was all up and it was all over. I figured a lot of the fellas would be thirsty, so I came back and opened up. Nobody but you so far. Maybe I was wrong."

"They might be along later," said Mike. "There's a lot of them still in the park. They cooled off, though. Some of them trying to burn him with newspapers. That don't do no good."

"Not a bit of good," said the little bartender. He twitched his thin moustache.

Mike knocked a few grains of celery salt into his beer and took a long drink. "That's good," he said. "I'm kind of dragged out."

The bartender leaned close to him over the bar, his eyes were bright. "Was you there all the time—to the jail and everything?"

Mike drank again and then looked through his beer and watched the beads of bubbles rising from the grains of salt in the bottom of the glass. "Everything," he said. "I was one of the first in the jail, and I helped pull on the rope. There's times when citizens got to take the law in their own hands. Sneaky lawyer comes along and gets some fiend out of it."

The mousy head jerked up and down. "You God-dam' right," he said. "Lawyers can get them out of anything. I guess the nigger was guilty all right."

"Oh, sure! Somebody said he even confessed."

The head came close over the bar again. "How did it start, mister? I was only there after it was all over, and then I only stayed a minute and then came back to open up in case any of the fellas might want a glass of beer."

Mike drained his glass and pushed it out to be filled. "Well, of course everybody knew it was going to happen. I was in a bar across from the jail. Been there all afternoon. A guy came in and says, 'What are we waiting for?' So we went across the street, and a lot more guys was there and a lot more come. We all stood there and yelled. Then the sheriff come out and made a speech, but we yelled him down. A guy with a twenty-two rifle went along the street and shot out the street lights. Well, then we rushed the jail doors and bust them. The sheriff wasn't going to do nothing. It wouldn't do him no good to shoot a lot of honest men to save a nigger fiend."

"And election coming on, too," the bartender put in.

"Well, the sheriff started yelling, 'Get the right man, boys, for Christ's sake get the right man. He's in the fourth cell down.'

"It was kind of pitiful," Mike said slowly. "The other prisoners was so scared. We could see them through the bars. I never seen such faces."

The bartender excitedly poured himself a small glass of whiskey and poured it down. "Can't blame 'em much. Suppose you was in for thirty days and a lynch mob came through. You'd be scared they'd get the wrong man."

"That's what I say. It was kind of pitiful. Well, we got to the nigger's cell. He just stood stiff with his eyes closed like he was dead drunk. One of the guys slugged him down and he got up, and then somebody else socked him and he went over and hit his head on the cement floor." Mike leaned over the bar and tapped the polished wood with his forefinger. " 'Course this is only my idea, but I think that killed him. Because I helped get his clothes off, and he never made a wiggle, and when we strung him up he didn't jerk around none. No, sir. I think he was dead all the time, after that second guy smacked him."

"Well, it's all the same in the end."

"No, it ain't. You like to do the thing right. He had it coming to him, and he should have got it." Mike reached into his trousers pocket and brought out a piece of torn blue denim. "That's a piece of the pants he had on."

The bartender bent close and inspected the cloth. He jerked his head up at Mike. "I'll give you a buck for it."

"Oh no, you won't!"

"All right. I'll give you two bucks for half of it."

Mike looked suspiciously at him. "What you want it for?"

"Here! Give me your glass! Have a beer on me. I'll pin it up on the wall with a little card under it. The fellas that come in will like to look at it."

Mike haggled the piece of cloth in two with his pocket knife and accepted two silver dollars from the bartender.

"I know a show card writer," the little man said. "Comes in every day. He'll print me up a nice little card to go under it." He looked wary. "Think the sheriff will arrest anybody?"

" 'Course not. What's he want to start any trouble for? There was a lot of votes in that crowd tonight. Soon as they all go away, the sheriff will come and cut the nigger down and clean up some."

The bartender looked toward the door. "I guess I was wrong about the fellas wanting a drink. It's getting late."

"I guess I'll get along home. I feel tired."

"If you go south, I'll close up and walk a ways with you. I live on south Eighth."

"Why, that's only two blocks from my house. I live

on south Sixth. You must go right past my house. Funny I never saw you around."

The bartender washed Mike's glass and took off the long apron. He put on his hat and coat, walked to the door and switched off the red neon sign and the house lights. For a moment the two men stood on the sidewalk looking back toward the park. The city was silent. There was no sound from the park. A policeman walked along a block away, turning his flash into the store windows.

"You see?" said Mike. "Just like nothing happened."

"Well, if the fellas wanted a glass of beer they must have gone someplace else."

"That's what I told you," said Mike.

They swung along the empty street and turned south, out of the business district. "My name's Welch," the bartender said. "I only been in this town about two years."

The loneliness had fallen on Mike again. "It's funny—" he said, and then, "I was born right in this town, right in the house I live in now. I got a wife but no kids. Both of us born right in this town. Everybody knows us."

They walked on for a few blocks. The stores dropped behind and the nice houses with bushy gardens and cut lawns lined the street. The tall shade trees were shadowed on the sidewalk by the street lights. Two night dogs went slowly by, smelling at each other.

Welch said softly—"I wonder what kind of a fella he was—the nigger, I mean."

Mike answered out of his loneliness. "The papers all said he was a fiend. I read all the papers. That's what they all said."

"Yes, I read them, too. But it makes you wonder about him. I've known some pretty nice niggers."

Mike turned his head and spoke protestingly. "Well, I've knew some dam' fine niggers myself. I've worked right 'longside some niggers and they was as nice as any white man you could want to meet. —But not no fiends."

His vehemence silenced little Welch for a moment. Then he said, "You couldn't tell, I guess, what kind of a fella he was?"

"No—he just stood there stiff, with his mouth shut and his eyes tight closed and his hands right down at his sides. And then one of the guys smacked him. It's my idea he was dead when we took him out."

Welch sidled close on the walk. "Nice gardens along here. Must take a lot of money to keep them up." He walked even closer, so that his shoulder touched Mike's arm. "I never been to a lynching. How's it make you feel —afterwards?"

Mike shied away from the contact. "It don't make you feel nothing." He put down his head and increased his pace. The little bartender had nearly to trot to keep up. The street lights were fewer. It was darker and safer. Mike burst out, "Makes you feel kind of cut off and tired, but kind of satisfied, too. Like you done a good job—but tired and kind of sleepy." He slowed his steps. "Look, there's a light in the kitchen. That's where I live. My old lady's waiting up for me." He stopped in front of his little house.

Welch stood nervously beside him. "Come into my place when you want a glass of beer—or a shot. Open till midnight. I treat my friends right." He scampered away like an aged mouse.

Mike called, "Good night."

He walked around the side of his house and went in the back door. His thin, petulant wife was sitting by the open gas oven warming herself. She turned complaining eyes on Mike where he stood in the doorway.

Then her eyes widened and hung on his face. "You been with a woman," she said hoarsely. "What woman you been with?"

Mike laughed. "You think you're pretty slick, don't you? You're a slick one, ain't you? What makes you think I been with a woman?"

She said fiercely, "You think I can't tell by the look on your face that you been with a woman?"

"All right," said Mike. "If you're so slick and know-it-all, I won't tell you nothing. You can just wait for the morning paper."

He saw doubt come into the dissatisfied eyes. "Was it the nigger?" she asked. "Did they get the nigger? Everybody said they was going to."

"Find out for yourself if you're so slick. I ain't going to tell you nothing."

He walked through the kitchen and went into the bathroom. A little mirror hung on the wall. Mike took off his cap and looked at his face. "By God, she was right," he thought. "That's just exactly how I do feel."

JOHNNY BEAR

JOHNNY BEAR

THE VILLAGE of Loma is built, as its name implies, on a low round hill that rises like an island out of the flat mouth of the Salinas Valley in central California. To the north and east of the town a black tule swamp stretches for miles, but to the south the marsh has been drained. Rich vegetable land has been the result of the draining, land so black with wealth that the lettuce and cauliflowers grow to giants.

The owners of the swamp to the north of the village began to covet the black land. They banded together and formed a reclamation district. I work for the company which took the contract to put a ditch through. The floating clam-shell digger arrived, was put together and started eating a ditch of open water through the swamp.

I tried living in the floating bunkhouse with the crew for a while, but the mosquitoes that hung in banks over the dredger and the heavy pestilential mist that sneaked out of the swamp every night and slid near to the ground drove me into the village of Loma, where I took a furnished room, the most dismal I have ever seen, in the house of Mrs. Ratz. I might have looked farther, but the idea of having my mail come in care of Mrs. Ratz decided me. After all, I only slept in the bare cold room. I ate my meals in the galley of the floating bunkhouse.

There aren't more than two hundred people in Loma. The Methodist church has the highest place on the hill; its spire is visible for miles. Two groceries, a hardware store, an ancient Masonic Hall and the Buffalo Bar comprise the public buildings. On the side of the hills are the small wooden houses of the population, and on the rich southern flats are the houses of the landowners, small yards usually enclosed by high walls of clipped cypress to keep out the driving afternoon winds.

There was nothing to do in Loma in the evening except to go to the saloon, an old board building with swinging doors and a wooden sidewalk awning. Neither prohibition nor repeal had changed its business, its clientele, or the quality of its whiskey. In the course of an evening every male inhabitant of Loma over fifteen years old came at least once to the Buffalo Bar, had a drink, talked a while and went home.

Fat Carl, the owner and bartender, greeted every newcomer with a phlegmatic sullenness which nevertheless inspired familiarity and affection. His face was sour, his tone downright unfriendly, and yet—I don't know how he did it. I know I felt gratified and warm when Fat Carl knew me well enough to turn his sour pig face to me and say with some impatience, "Well, what's it going to be?" He always asked that although he served only whiskey, and only one kind of whiskey. I have seen him flatly refuse to squeeze some lemon juice into it for a stranger. Fat Carl didn't like fumadiddles. He wore a big towel tied about his middle and he polished the glasses on it as he moved about. The floor was bare wood sprinkled with sawdust, the bar an old store counter, the chairs were hard and straight; the only decorations were the posters and cards and pictures stuck to the wall by candidates for county elections, salesmen and auctioneers. Some of these were many years old. The card of Sheriff Rittal still begged for re-election although Rittal had been dead for seven years.

The Buffalo Bar sounds, even to me, like a terrible place, but when you walked down the night street, over the wooden sidewalks, when the long streamers of swamp fog, like waving, dirty bunting, flapped in your face, when finally you pushed open the swinging doors of Fat Carl's and saw men sitting around talking and drinking, and Fat Carl coming along toward you, it seemed pretty nice. You couldn't get away from it.

There would be a game of the mildest kind of poker going on. Timothy Ratz, the husband of my landlady, would be playing solitaire, cheating pretty badly because he took a drink only when he got it out. I've seen him get it out five times in a row. When he won he piled the cards neatly, stood up and walked with great dignity to the bar. Fat Carl, with a glass half filled before he arrived, asked, "What'll it be?"

"Whiskey," said Timothy gravely.

In the long room, men from the farms and the town sat in the straight hard chairs or stood against the old counter. A soft, monotonous rattle of conversation went on except at times of elections or big prize fights, when there might be orations or loud opinions.

I hated to go out into the damp night, and to hear far off in the swamp the chuttering of the Diesel engine on the dredger and the clang of the bucket, and then to go to my own dismal room at Mrs. Ratz'.

Soon after my arrival in Loma I scraped an acquaintance with Mae Romero, a pretty half-Mexican girl. Sometimes in the evenings I walked with her down the south side of the hill, until the nasty fog drove us back into town. After I escorted her home I dropped in at the bar for a while.

I was sitting in the bar one night talking to Alex Hartnell, who owned a nice little farm. We were talking about black bass fishing, when the front doors opened and swung closed. A hush fell on the men in the room. Alex nudged me and said, "It's Johnny Bear." I looked around.

His name described him better than I can. He looked like a great, stupid, smiling bear. His black matted head bobbed forward and his long arms hung out as though he should have been on all fours and was only standing upright as a trick. His legs were short and bowed, ending with strange, square feet. He was dressed in dark blue denim, but his feet were bare; they didn't seem to be crippled or deformed in any way, but they were square, just as wide as they were long. He stood in the doorway, swinging his arms jerkily the way half-wits do. On his face there was a foolish happy smile. He moved forward and for all his bulk and clumsiness, he seemed to creep. He didn't move like a man, but like some prowling night animal. At the bar he stopped, his little bright eyes went about from face to face expectantly, and he asked, "Whiskey?"

Loma was not a treating town. A man might buy a drink for another if he were pretty sure the other would immediately buy one for him. I was surprised when one of the quiet men laid a coin on the counter. Fat Carl filled the glass. The monster took it and gulped the whiskey.

"What the devil——" I began. But Alex nudged me and said, "Sh."

There began a curious pantomime. Johnny Bear moved to the door and then he came creeping back. The foolish smile never left his face. In the middle of the room he crouched down on his stomach. A voice came from his throat, a voice that seemed familiar to me.

"But you are too beautiful to live in a dirty little town like this."

The voice rose to a soft throaty tone, with just a trace of accent in the words. "You just tell me that."

I'm sure I nearly fainted. The blood pounded in my ears. I flushed. It was my voice coming out of the throat of Johnny Bear, my words, my intonation. And then it was the voice of Mae Romero—exact. If I had not seen the crouching man on the floor I would have called to her. The dialogue went on. Such things sound silly when someone else says them. Johnny Bear went right on, or rather I should say I went right on. He said things and made sounds. Gradually the faces of the men turned from Johnny Bear, turned toward me, and they grinned at me. I could do nothing. I knew that if I tried to stop him I would have a fight on my hands, and so the scene went on, to a finish. When it was over I was cravenly glad Mae Romero had no brothers. What obvious, forced, ridiculous words had come from Johnny Bear. Finally he stood up, still smiling the foolish smile, and he asked again, "Whiskey?"

I think the men in the bar were sorry for me. They looked away from me and talked elaborately to one another. Johnny Bear went to the back of the room, crawled under a round cardtable, curled up like a dog and went to sleep.

Alex Hartnell was regarding me with compassion. "First time you ever heard him?"

"Yes, what in hell is he?"

Alex ignored my question for a moment. "If you're worrying about Mae's reputation, don't. Johnny Bear has followed Mae before."

"But how did he hear us? I didn't see him."

"No one sees or hears Johnny Bear when he's on business. He can move like no movement at all. Know what our young men do when they go out with girls? They take a dog along. Dogs are afraid of Johnny and they can smell him coming."

"But good God! Those voices——"

Alex nodded. "I know. Some of us wrote up to the university about Johnny, and a young man came down. He took a look and then he told us about Blind Tom. Ever hear of Blind Tom?"

"You mean the negro piano player? Yes, I've heard of him."

"Well, Blind Tom was a half-wit. He could hardly talk, but he could imitate anything he heard on the piano, long pieces. They tried him with fine musicians and he reproduced not only the music but every little personal emphasis. To catch him they made little mistakes, and he played the mistakes. He photographed the playing in the tiniest detail. The man says Johnny Bear is the same, only he can photograph words and voices. He tested Johnny with a long passage in Greek and Johnny did it exactly. He doesn't know the words he's saying, he just says them. He hasn't brains enough to make anything up, so you know that what he says is what he heard."

"But why does he do it? Why is he interested in listening if he doesn't understand?"

Alex rolled a cigarette and lighted it. "He isn't, but he loves whiskey. He knows if he listens in windows and comes here and repeats what he hears, someone will give him whiskey. He tries to palm off Mrs. Ratz' conversation in the store, or Jerry Noland arguing with his mother, but he can't get whiskey for such things."

I said, "It's funny somebody hasn't shot him while he was peeking in windows."

Alex picked at his cigarette. "Lots of people have tried, but you just don't see Johnny Bear, and you don't catch him. You keep your windows closed, and even then you talk in a whisper if you don't want to be repeated. You were lucky it was dark tonight. If he had seen you, he might have gone through the action too. You should see Johnny Bear screw up his face to look like a young girl. It's pretty awful."

I looked toward the sprawled figure under the table. Johnny Bear's back was turned to the room. The light fell on his black matted hair. I saw a big fly land on his head, and then I swear I saw the whole scalp shiver the way the skin of a horse shivers under flies. The fly landed again and the moving scalp shook it off. I shuddered too, all over.

Conversation in the room had settled to the bored monotone again. Fat Carl had been polishing a glass on his apron towel for the last ten minutes. A little group of men near me was discussing fighting dogs and fighting cocks, and they switched gradually to bullfighting.

Alex, beside me, said, "Come have a drink."

We walked to the counter. Fat Carl put out two glasses. "What'll it be?"

Neither of us answered. Carl poured out the brown whiskey. He looked sullenly at me and one of his thick, meaty eyelids winked at me solemnly. I don't know why, but I felt flattered. Carl's head twitched back toward the card table. "Got you, didn't he?"

I winked back at him. "Take a dog next time." I imitated his clipped sentences. We drank our whiskey and went back to our chairs. Timothy Ratz won a game of solitaire and piled his cards and moved up on the bar.

I looked back at the table under which Johnny Bear lay. He had rolled over on his stomach. His foolish, smiling face looked out at the room. His head moved and he peered all about, like an animal about to leave its den. And then he came sliding out and stood up. There was a paradox about his movement. He looked twisted and shapeless, and yet he moved with complete lack of effort.

Johnny Bear crept up the room toward the bar, smiling about at the men he passed. In front of the bar his insistent question arose. "Whiskey? Whiskey?" It was like a bird call. I don't know what kind of bird, but I've heard it—two notes on a rising scale, asking a question over and over, "Whiskey? Whiskey?"

The conversation in the room stopped, but no one came forward to lay money on the counter. Johnny smiled plaintively. "Whiskey?"

Then he tried to cozen them. Out of his throat an angry woman's voice issued. "I tell you it was all bone. Twenty cents a pound, and half bone." And then a man, "Yes, ma'am. I didn't know it. I'll give you some sausage to make it up."

Johnny Bear looked around expectantly. "Whiskey?" Still none of the men offered to come forward. Johnny crept to the front of the room and crouched. I whispered, "What's he doing?"

Alex said, "Sh. Looking through a window. Listen!"

A woman's voice came, a cold, sure voice, the words clipped. "I can't quite understand it. Are you some kind of monster? I wouldn't have believed it if I hadn't seen you."

Another woman's voice answered her, a voice low and hoarse with misery. "Maybe I am a monster. I can't help it. I can't help it."

"You *must* help it," the cold voice broke in. "Why you'd be better dead."

I heard a soft sobbing coming from the thick smiling lips of Johnny Bear. The sobbing of a woman in hopelessness. I looked around at Alex. He was sitting stiffly, his eyes wide open and unblinking. I opened my mouth to whisper a question, but he waved me silent. I glanced about the room. All the men were stiff and listening. The sobbing stopped. "Haven't you ever felt that way, Emalin?"

Alex caught his breath sharply at the name. The cold voice announced, "Certainly not."

"Never in the night? Not ever—ever in your life?"

"If I had," the cold voice said, "if ever I had, I would cut that part of me away. Now stop your whining, Amy. I won't stand for it. If you don't get control of your nerves I'll see about having some medical treatment for you. Now go to your prayers."

Johnny Bear smiled on. "Whiskey?"

Two men advanced without a word and put down coins. Fat Carl filled two glasses and, when Johnny Bear tossed off one after the other, Carl filled one again. Everyone knew by that how moved he was. There were no drinks on the house at the Buffalo Bar. Johnny Bear smiled about the room and then he went out with that creeping gait of his. The doors folded together after him, slowly and without a sound.

Conversation did not spring up again. Everyone in the room seemed to have a problem to settle in his own mind. One by one they drifted out and the back-swing of the doors brought in little puffs of tule fog. Alex got up and walked out and I followed him.

The night was nasty with the evil-smelling fog. It seemed to cling to the buildings and to reach out with free arms into the air. I doubled my pace and caught up with Alex. "What was it?" I demanded. "What was it all about?"

For a moment I thought he wouldn't answer. But then he stopped and turned to me. "Oh, damn it. Listen! Every town has its aristocrats, its family above reproach. Emalin and Amy Hawkins are our aristocrats, maiden ladies, kind people. Their father was a congressman. I don't like this. Johnny Bear shouldn't do it. Why! they feed him. Those men shouldn't give him whiskey. He'll haunt that house now. . . . Now he knows he can get whiskey for it."

I asked, "Are they relatives of yours?"

"No, but they're—why, they aren't like other people. They have the farm next to mine. Some Chinese farm it on shares. You see, it's hard to explain. The Hawkins women, they're symbols. They're what we tell our kids when we want to—well, to describe good people."

"Well," I protested, "Nothing Johnny Bear said would hurt them, would it?"

"I don't know. I don't know what it means. I mean, I kind of know. Oh! Go on to bed. I didn't bring the Ford. I'm going to walk out home." He turned and hurried into that slow squirming mist.

I walked along to Mrs. Ratz' boarding house. I could hear the chuttering of the Diesel engine off in the swamp and the clang of the big steel mouth that ate its way through the ground. It was Saturday night. The dredger would stop at seven Sunday morning and rest until midnight Sunday. I could tell by the sound that everything was all right. I climbed the narrow stairs to my room. Once in bed I left the light burning for a while and stared at the pale insipid flowers on the wallpaper. I thought of those two voices speaking out of Johnny Bear's mouth. They were authentic voices, not reproductions. Remembering the tones, I could see the women who had spoken, the chill-voiced Emalin, and the loose, misery-broken face of Amy. I wondered what caused the misery. Was it just the lonely suffering of a middle-aged woman? It hardly seemed so to me, for there was too much fear in the voice. I went to sleep with the light on and had to get up later and turn it off.

About eight the next morning I walked down across the swamp to the dredger. The crew was busy bending some new wire to the drums and coiling the worn cable for removal. I looked over the job and at about eleven o'clock walked back to Loma. In front of Mrs. Ratz' boarding house Alex Hartnell sat in a model T Ford touring car. He called to me, "I was just going to the dredger to get you. I knocked off a couple of chickens this morning. Thought you might like to come out and help with them."

I accepted joyfully. Our cook was a good cook, a big pasty man; but lately I had found a dislike for him arising in me. He smoked Cuban cigarettes in a bamboo holder. I didn't like the way his fingers twitched in the morning. His hands were clean—floury like a miller's hands. I never knew before why they called them moth millers, those little flying bugs. Anyway I climbed into the Ford beside Alex and we drove down the hill to the rich land of the southwest. The sun shone brilliantly on the black earth. When I was little, a Catholic boy told me that the sun always shone on Sunday, if only for a moment, because it was God's day. I always meant to keep track to see if it were true. We rattled down to the level plain.

Alex shouted, "Remember about the Hawkinses?"

"Of course I remember."

He pointed ahead. "That's the house."

Little of the house could be seen, for a high thick hedge of cypress surrounded it. There must be a small garden inside the square too. Only the roof and the tops of the windows showed over the hedge. I could see that the house was painted tan, trimmed with dark brown, a combination favored for railroad stations and schools in California. There were two wicket gates in the front and side of the hedge. The barn was outside the green barrier to the rear of the house. The hedge was clipped square. It looked incredibly thick and strong.

"The hedge keeps the wind out," Alex shouted above the roar of the Ford.

"It doesn't keep Johnny Bear out," I said.

A shadow crossed his face. He waved at a whitewashed square building standing out in the field. "That's where the Chink share-croppers live. Good workers. I wish I had some like them."

At that moment from behind the corner of the hedge a horse and buggy appeared and turned into the road. The grey horse was old but well groomed, the buggy shiny and the harness polished. There was a big silver H on the outside of each blinder. It seemed to me that the check-rein was too short for such an old horse.

Alex cried, "There they are now, on their way to church."

We took off our hats and bowed to the women as they went by, and they nodded formally to us. I had a good look at them. It was a shock to me. They looked almost exactly as I thought they would. Johnny Bear was more monstrous even than I had known, if by the tone of voice he could describe the features of his people. I didn't have to ask which was Emalin and which was Amy. The clear straight eyes, the sharp sure chin, the mouth cut with the precision of a diamond, the stiff, curveless figure, that was Emalin. Amy was very like her, but so unlike. Her edges were soft. Her eyes were warm, her mouth full. There was a swell to her breast, and yet she did look like Emalin. But whereas Emalin's mouth was straight by nature, Amy *held* her mouth straight. Emalin must have been fifty or fifty-five and Amy about ten years younger. I had only a moment to look at them, and I never saw them again. It seems strange that I don't know anyone in the world better than those two women.

Alex was shouting, "You see what I meant about aristocrats?"

I nodded. It was easy to see. A community would feel kind of—safe, having women like that about. A place like Loma with its fogs, with its great swamp like a hideous sin, needed, really needed, the Hawkins women. A few years there might do things to a man's mind if those women weren't there to balance matters.

It was a good dinner. Alex's sister fried the chicken in butter and did everything else right. I grew more suspicious and uncharitable toward our cook. We sat around in the dining-room and drank really good brandy.

I said, "I can't see why you ever go into the Buffalo. That whiskey is——"

"I know," said Alex. "But the Buffalo is the mind of Loma. It's our newspaper, our theatre and our club."

This was so true that when Alex started the Ford and prepared to take me back I knew, and he knew, we would go for an hour or two to the Buffalo Bar.

We were nearly into town. The feeble lights of the car splashed about on the road. Another car rattled toward us. Alex swung across the road and stopped. "It's the doctor, Doctor Holmes," he explained. The oncoming car pulled up because it couldn't get around us. Alex called, "Say, Doc, I was going to ask you to take a look at my sister. She's got a swelling on her throat."

Doctor Holmes called back, "All right, Alex, I'll take a look. Pull out, will you? I'm in a hurry."

Alex was deliberate. "Who's sick, Doc?"

"Why, Miss Amy had a little spell. Miss Emalin phoned in and asked me to hurry. Get out of the way, will you?"

Alex squawked his car back and let the doctor by. We drove on. I was about to remark that the night was clear when, looking ahead, I saw the rags of fog creeping around the hill from the swamp side and climbing like slow snakes on the top of Loma. The Ford shuddered to a stop in front of the Buffalo. We went in.

Fat Carl moved toward us, wiping a glass on his apron. He reached under the bar for the nearby bottle. "What'll it be?"

"Whiskey."

For a moment a faint smile seemed to flit over the fat sullen face. The room was full. My dredger crew was there, all except the cook. He was probably on the scow, smoking his Cuban cigarettes in a bamboo holder. He didn't drink. That was enough to make me suspicious of him. Two deck hands and an engineer and three levermen were there. The levermen were arguing about a cutting. The old lumber adage certainly held for them: "Women in the woods and logging in the honky-tonk."

That was the quietest bar I ever saw. There weren't any fights, not much singing and no tricks. Somehow the sullen baleful eyes of Fat Carl made drinking a quiet, efficient business rather than a noisy game. Timothy Ratz was playing solitaire at one of the round tables. Alex and I drank our whiskey. No chairs were available, so we just stayed leaning against the bar, talking about sports and markets and adventures we had had or pretended we had—just a casual barroom conversation. Now and then we bought another drink. I guess we hung around for a couple of hours. Alex had already said he was going home, and I felt like it. The dredger crew trooped out, for they had to start to work at midnight.

The doors unfolded silently, and Johnny Bear crept into the room, swinging his long arms, nodding his big hairy head and smiling foolishly about. His square feet were like cats' feet.

"Whiskey?" he chirruped. No one encouraged him. He got out his wares. He was down on his stomach the way he had been when he got me. Sing-song nasal words came out, Chinese I thought. And then it seemed to me that the same words were repeated in another voice, slower and not nasally. Johnny Bear raised his shaggy head and asked, "Whiskey?" He got to his feet with effortless ease. I was interested. I wanted to see him perform. I slid a quarter along the bar. Johnny gulped his drink. A moment later I wished I hadn't. I was afraid to look at Alex; for Johnny Bear crept to the middle of the room and took that window pose of his.

The chill voice of Emalin said, "She's in here, doctor." I closed my eyes against the looks of Johnny Bear, and the moment I did he went out. It was Emalin Hawkins who had spoken.

I had heard the doctor's voice in the road, and it was his veritable voice that replied, "Ah—you said a fainting fit?"

"Yes, doctor."

There was a little pause, and then the doctor's voice again, very softly, "Why did she do it, Emalin?"

"Why did she do what?" There was almost a threat in the question.

"I'm your doctor, Emalin. I was your father's doctor. You've got to tell me things. Don't you think I've seen that kind of a mark on the neck before? How long was she hanging before you got her down?"

There was a longer pause then. The chill left the woman's voice. It was soft, almost a whisper. "Two or three minutes. Will she be all right, doctor?"

"Oh, yes, she'll come around. She's not badly hurt. Why did she do it?"

The answering voice was even colder than it had been at first. It was frozen. "I don't know, sir."

"You mean you won't tell me?"

"I mean what I say."

Then the doctor's voice went on giving directions for treatment, rest, milk and a little whiskey. "Above all, be gentle," he said. "Above everything, be gentle with her."

Emalin's voice trembled a little. "You would never—tell, doctor?"

"I'm your doctor," he said softly. "Of course I won't tell. I'll send down some sedatives tonight."

"Whiskey?" My eyes jerked open. There was the horrible Johnny Bear smiling around the room.

The men were silent, ashamed. Fat Carl looked at the floor. I turned apologetically to Alex, for I was really responsible. "I didn't know he'd do that," I said. "I'm sorry."

I walked out the door and went to the dismal room at Mrs. Ratz'. I opened the window and looked out into that coiling, pulsing fog. Far off in the marsh I heard the Diesel engine start slowly and warm up. And after a while I heard the clang of the big bucket as it went to work on the ditch.

The next morning one of those series of accidents so common in construction landed on us. One of the new wires parted on the in-swing and dropped the bucket on one of the pontoons, sinking it and the works in eight feet of ditch water. When we sunk a dead man and got a line out to it to pull us from the water, the line parted and clipped the legs neatly off one of the deck hands. We bound the stumps and rushed him to Salinas. And then little accidents happened. A leverman developed blood poisoning from a wire scratch. The cook finally justified my opinion by trying to sell a little can of marijuana to the engineer. Altogether there wasn't much peace in the outfit. It was two weeks before we were going again with a new pontoon, a new deck hand and a new cook.

The new cook was a sly, dark, little long-nosed man, with a gift for subtle flattery.

My contact with the social life of Loma had gone to pot, but when the bucket was clanging into the mud again and the big old Diesel was chuttering away in the swamp I walked out to Alex Hartnell's farm one night. Passing the Hawkins place, I peered in through one of the little wicket gates in the cypress hedge. The house was dark, more than dark because a low light glowed in one window. There was a gentle wind that night, blowing balls of fog like tumbleweeds along the ground. I walked in the clear a moment, and then was swallowed in a thick mist, and then was in the clear again. In the starlight I could see those big silver fog balls moving like elementals across the fields. I thought I heard a soft moaning in the Hawkins yard behind the hedge, and once when I came suddenly out of the fog I saw a dark figure hurrying along in the field, and I knew from the dragging footsteps that it was one of the Chinese field hands walking in sandals. The Chinese eat a great many things that have to be caught at night.

Alex came to the door when I knocked. He seemed glad to see me. His sister was away. I sat down by his stove and he brought out a bottle of that nice brandy. "I heard you were having some trouble," he said.

I explained the difficulty. "It seems to come in series. The men have it figured out that accidents come in groups of three, five, seven and nine."

Alex nodded. "I kind of feel that way myself."

"How are the Hawkins sisters?" I asked. "I thought I heard someone crying as I went by."

Alex seemed reluctant to talk about them, and at the same time eager to talk about them. "I stopped over about a week ago. Miss Amy isn't feeling very well. I didn't see her. I only saw Miss Emalin." Then Alex broke out, "There's something hanging over those people, something——"

"You almost seem to be related to them," I said.

"Well, their father and my father were friends. We called the girls Aunt Amy and Aunt Emalin. They can't do anything bad. It wouldn't be good for any of us if the Hawkins sisters weren't the Hawkins sisters."

"The community conscience?" I asked.

"The safe thing," he cried. "The place where a kid can get gingerbread. The place where a girl can get re-assurance. They're proud, but they believe in things we hope are true. And they live as though—well, as though honesty really is the best policy and charity really is its own reward. We need them."

"I see."

"But Miss Emalin is fighting something terrible and—I don't think she's going to win."

"What do you mean?"

"I don't know what I mean. But I've thought I should shoot Johnny Bear and throw him in the swamp. I've really thought about doing it."

"It's not his fault," I argued. "He's just a kind of recording and reproducing device, only you use a glass of whiskey instead of a nickel."

We talked of some other things then, and after a while I walked back to Loma. It seemed to me that that fog was clinging to the cypress hedge of the Hawkins house, and it seemed to me that a lot of the fog balls were clustered about it and others were slowly moving in. I smiled as I walked along at the way a man's thought can rearrange nature to fit his thoughts. There was no light in the house as I went by.

A nice steady routine settled on my work. The big bucket cut out the ditch ahead of it. The crew felt the trouble was over too, and that helped, and the new cook flattered the men so successfully that they would have eaten fried cement. The personality of a cook has a lot more to do with the happiness of a dredger crew than his cooking has.

In the evening of the second day after my visit to Alex I walked down the wooden sidewalk trailing a streamer of fog behind me and went into the Buffalo Bar. Fat Carl moved toward me polishing the whiskey glass. I cried, "Whiskey," before he had a chance to ask what it would be. I took my glass and went to one of the straight chairs. Alex was not there. Timothy Ratz was playing solitaire and having a phenomenal run of luck. He got it out four times in a row and had a drink each time. More and more men arrived. I don't know what we would have done without the Buffalo Bar.

At about ten o'clock the news came. Thinking about such things afterwards, you never can remember quite what transpired. Someone comes in; a whisper starts; suddenly everyone knows what has happened, knows details. Miss Amy had committed suicide. Who brought in the story? I don't know. She had hanged herself. There wasn't much talk in the barroom about it. I could see the men were trying to get straight on it. It was a thing that didn't fit into their schemes. They stood in groups, talking softly.

The swinging doors opened slowly and Johnny Bear crept in, his great hairy head rolling, and that idiot smile on his face. His square feet slid quietly over the floor. He looked about and chirruped, "Whiskey? Whiskey for Johnny?"

Now those men really wanted to know. They were ashamed of wanting to know, but their whole mental system required the knowledge. Fat Carl poured out a drink. Timothy Ratz put down his cards and stood up. Johnny Bear gulped the whiskey. I closed my eyes.

The doctor's tone was harsh. "Where is she, Emalin?"

I've never heard a voice like that one that answered, cold control, layer and layer of control, but cold penetrated by the most awful heartbreak. It was a monotonous tone, emotionless, and yet the heartbreak got into the vibrations. "She's in here, doctor."

"H-m-m." A long pause. "She was hanging a long time."

"I don't know how long, doctor."

"Why did she do it, Emalin?"

The monotone again. "I don't—know, doctor."

A longer pause, and then, "H-m-m. Emalin, did you know she was going to have a baby?"

The chill voice cracked and a sigh came through. "Yes, doctor," very softly.

"If that was why you didn't find her for so long—— No, Emalin, I didn't mean that, poor dear."

The control was back in Emalin's voice. "Can you make out the certificate without mentioning——"

"Of course I can, sure I can. And I'll speak to the undertaker, too. You needn't worry."

"Thank you, doctor."

"I'll go and telephone now. I won't leave you here alone. Come into the other room, Emalin. I'm going to fix you a sedative. . . ."

"Whiskey? Whiskey for Johnny?" I saw the smile and the rolling hairy head. Fat Carl poured out another glass. Johnny Bear drank it and then crept to the back of the room and crawled under a table and went to sleep.

No one spoke. The men moved up to the bar and laid down their coins silently. They looked bewildered, for a system had fallen. A few minutes later Alex came into the silent room. He walked quickly over to me. "You've heard?" he asked softly.

"Yes."

"I've been afraid," he cried. "I told you a couple of nights ago. I've been afraid."

I said, "Did you know she was pregnant?"

Alex stiffened. He looked around the room and then back at me. "Johnny Bear?" he asked.

I nodded.

Alex ran his palm over his eyes. "I don't believe it."

I was about to answer when I heard a little scuffle and looked to the back of the room. Johnny Bear crawled like a badger out of his hole and stood up and crept toward the bar.

"Whiskey?" He smiled expectantly at Fat Carl.

Then Alex stepped out and addressed the room. "Now you guys listen! This has gone far enough. I don't want any more of it." If he had expected opposition he was disappointed. I saw the men nodding to one another.

"Whiskey for Johnny?"

Alex turned on the idiot. "You ought to be ashamed. Miss Amy gave you food, and she gave you all the clothes you ever had."

Johnny smiled at him. "Whiskey?"

He got out his tricks. I heard the sing-song nasal language that sounded like Chinese. Alex looked relieved.

And then the other voice, slow, hesitant, repeating the words without the nasal quality.

Alex sprang so quickly that I didn't see him move. His fist splatted into Johnny Bear's smiling mouth. "I told you there was enough of it," he shouted.

Johnny Bear recovered his balance. His lips were split and bleeding, but the smile was still there. He moved slowly and without effort. His arms enfolded Alex as the tentacles of an anemone enfold a crab. Alex bent backward. Then I jumped and grabbed one of the arms and wrenched at it, and could not tear it loose. Fat Carl came rolling over the counter with a bung-starter in his hand. And he beat the matted head until the arms relaxed and Johnny Bear crumpled. I caught Alex and helped him to a chair. "Are you hurt?"

He tried to get his breath. "My back's wrenched, I guess," he said. "I'll be all right."

"Got your Ford outside? I'll drive you home."

Neither of us looked at the Hawkins place as we went by. I didn't lift my eyes off the road. I got Alex to his own dark house and helped him to bed and poured a hot brandy into him. He hadn't spoken all the way home. But after he was propped in the bed he demanded, "You don't think anyone noticed, do you? I caught him in time, didn't I?"

"What are you talking about? I don't know yet why you hit him."

"Well, listen," he said. "I'll have to stay close for a little while with this back. If you hear anyone say anything, you stop it, won't you? Don't let them say it."

"I don't know what you're talking about."

He looked into my eyes for a moment. "I guess I can trust you," he said. "That second voice—that was Miss Amy."

THE MURDER

THE MURDER

THIS HAPPENED a number of years ago in Monterey County, in central California. The Cañon del Castillo is one of those valleys in the Santa Lucia range which lie between its many spurs and ridges. From the main Cañon del Castillo a number of little arroyos cut back into the mountains, oak-wooded canyons, heavily brushed with poison oak and sage. At the head of the canyon there stands a tremendous stone castle, buttressed and towered like those strongholds the Crusaders put up in the path of their conquests. Only a close visit to the castle shows it to be a strange accident of time and water and erosion working on soft, stratified sandstone. In the distance the ruined battlements, the gates, the towers, even the arrow slits, require little imagination to make out.

Below the castle, on the nearly level floor of the canyon, stand the old ranch house, a weathered and mossy barn and a warped feeding-shed for cattle. The house is deserted; the doors, swinging on rusted hinges, squeal and bang on nights when the wind courses down from the castle. Not many people visit the house. Sometimes a crowd of boys tramp through the rooms, peering into empty closets and loudly defying the ghosts they deny.

Jim Moore, who owns the land, does not like to have people about the house. He rides up from his new house, farther down the valley, and chases the boys away. He has put "No Trespassing" signs on his fences to keep curious and morbid people out. Sometimes he thinks of burning the old house down, but then a strange and powerful relation with the swinging doors, the blind and desolate windows, forbids the destruction. If he should burn the house he would destroy a great and important piece of his life. He knows that when he goes to town with his plump and still pretty wife, people turn and look at his retreating back with awe and some admiration.

Jim Moore was born in the old house and grew up in it. He knew every grained and weathered board of the barn, every smooth, worn manger-rack. His mother and father were both dead when he was thirty. He celebrated his majority by raising a beard. He sold the pigs and decided never to have any more. At last he bought a fine Guernsey bull to improve his stock, and he began to go to Monterey on Saturday nights, to get drunk and to talk with the noisy girls of the Three Star.

Within a year Jim Moore married Jelka Sepic, a Jugo-Slav girl, daughter of a heavy and patient farmer of Pine Canyon. Jim was not proud of her foreign family, of her many brothers and sisters and cousins, but he delighted in her beauty. Jelka had eyes as large and questioning as a doe's eyes. Her nose was thin and sharply faceted, and her lips were deep and soft. Jelka's skin always startled Jim, for between night and night he forgot how beautiful it was. She was so smooth and quiet and gentle, such a good housekeeper, that Jim often thought with disgust of her father's advice on the wedding day. The old man, bleary and bloated with festival beer, elbowed Jim in the ribs and grinned suggestively, so that his little dark eyes almost disappeared behind puffed and wrinkled lids.

"Don't be big fool, now," he said. "Jelka is Slav girl. He's not like American girl. If he is bad, beat him. If he's good too long, beat him too. I beat his mama. Papa beat my mama. Slav girl! He's not like a man that don't beat hell out of him."

"I wouldn't beat Jelka," Jim said.

The father giggled and nudged him again with his elbow, "Don't be big fool," he warned. "Sometime you see." He rolled back to the beer barrel.

Jim found soon enough that Jelka was not like American girls. She was very quiet. She never spoke first, but only answered his questions, and then with soft short replies. She learned her husband as she learned passages of Scripture. After they had been married a while, Jim never wanted for any habitual thing in the house but Jelka had it ready for him before he could ask. She was a fine wife, but there was no companionship in her. She never talked. Her great eyes followed him, and when he smiled, sometimes she smiled too, a distant and covered smile. Her knitting and mending and sewing were interminable. There she sat, watching her wise hands, and she seemed to regard with wonder and pride the little white hands that could do such nice and useful things. She was so much like an animal that sometimes Jim patted her head and neck under the same impulse that made him stroke a horse.

In the house Jelka was remarkable. No matter what time Jim came in from the hot dry range or from the bottom farm land, his dinner was exactly, steamingly ready for him. She watched while he ate, and pushed the dishes close when he needed them, and filled his cup when it was empty.

Early in the marriage he told her things that happened on the farm, but she smiled at him as a foreigner does who wishes to be agreeable even though he doesn't understand.

"The stallion cut himself on the barbed wire," he said.

And she replied, "Yes," with a downward inflection that held neither question nor interest.

He realized before long that he could not get in touch with her in any way. If she had a life apart, it was so remote as to be beyond his reach. The barrier in her eyes was not one that could be removed, for it was neither hostile nor intentional.

At night he stroked her straight black hair and her unbelievably smooth golden shoulders, and she whimpered a little with pleasure. Only in the climax of his embrace did she seem to have a life apart, fierce and passionate. And then immediately she lapsed into the alert and painfully dutiful wife.

"Why don't you ever talk to me?" he demanded. "Don't you want to talk to me?"

"Yes," she said. "What do you want me to say?" She spoke the language of his race out of a mind that was foreign to his race.

When a year had passed, Jim began to crave the company of women, the chattery exchange of small talk, the shrill pleasant insults, the shame-sharpened vulgarity. He began to go again to town, to drink and to play with the noisy girls of the Three Star. They liked him there for his firm, controlled face and for his readiness to laugh.

"Where's your wife?" they demanded.

"Home in the barn," he responded. It was a never-failing joke.

Saturday afternoons he saddled a horse and put a rifle in the scabbard in case he should see a deer. Always he asked, "You don't mind staying alone?"

"No. I don't mind."

At once he asked, "Suppose someone should come?"

Her eyes sharpened for a moment, and then she smiled. "I would send them away," she said.

"I'll be back about noon tomorrow. It's too far to ride in the night." He felt that she knew where he was going, but she never protested nor gave any sign of disapproval. "You should have a baby," he said.

Her face lighted up. "Some time God will be good," she said eagerly.

He was sorry for her loneliness. If only she visited with the other women of the canyon she would be less lonely, but she had no gift for visiting. Once every month or so she put horses to the buckboard and went to spend an afternoon with her mother, and with the brood of brothers and sisters and cousins who lived in her father's house.

"A fine time you'll have," Jim said to her. "You'll gabble your crazy language like ducks for a whole afternoon. You'll giggle with that big grown cousin of yours with the embarrassed face. If I could find any fault with you, I'd call you a damn foreigner." He remembered how she blessed the bread with the sign of the cross before she put it in the oven, how she knelt at the bedside every night, how she had a holy picture tacked to the wall in the closet.

One Saturday of a hot dusty June, Jim cut oats in the farm flat. The day was long. It was after six o'clock when the mower tumbled the last band of oats. He drove the clanking machine up into the barnyard and backed it into the implement shed, and there he unhitched the horses and turned them out to graze on the hills over Sunday. When he entered the kitchen Jelka was just putting his dinner on the table. He washed his hands and face and sat down to eat.

"I'm tired," he said, "but I think I'll go to Monterey anyway. There'll be a full moon."

Her soft eyes smiled.

"I'll tell you what I'll do," he said. "If you would like to go, I'll hitch up a rig and take you with me."

She smiled again and shook her head. "No, the stores would be closed. I would rather stay here."

"Well, all right, I'll saddle the horse then. I didn't think I was going. The stock's all turned out. Maybe I can catch a horse easy. Sure you don't want to go?"

"If it was early, and I could go to the stores—but it will be ten o'clock when you get there."

"Oh, no—well, anyway, on horseback I'll make it a little after nine."

Her mouth smiled to itself, but her eyes watched him for the development of a wish. Perhaps because he was tired from the long day's work, he demanded, "What are you thinking about?"

"Thinking about? I remember, you used to ask that nearly every day when we were first married."

"But what are you?" he insisted irritably.

"Oh—I'm thinking about the eggs under the black hen." She got up and went to the big calendar on the wall. "They will hatch tomorrow or maybe Monday."

It was almost dusk when he had finished shaving and putting on his blue serge suit and his new boots. Jelka had the dishes washed and put away. As Jim went through the kitchen he saw that she had taken the lamp to the table near the window, and that she sat beside it knitting a brown wool sock.

"Why do you sit there tonight?" he asked. "You always sit over here. You do funny things sometimes."

Her eyes arose slowly from her flying hands. "The moon," she said quietly. "You said it would be full tonight. I want to see the moon rise."

"But you're silly. You can't see it from that window I thought you knew direction better than that."

She smiled remotely. "I will look out of the bedroom window, then."

Jim put on his black hat and went out. Walking through the dark empty barn, he took a halter from the rack. On the grassy sidehill he whistled high and shrill. The horses stopped feeding and moved slowly in towards him, and stopped twenty feet away. Carefully he approached his bay gelding and moved his hand from its rump along its side and up and over its neck. The halter-strap clicked in its buckle. Jim turned and led the horse back to the barn. He threw his saddle on and cinched it tight, put his silver-bound bridle over the stiff ears, buckled the throat latch, knotted the tie-rope about the gelding's neck and fastened the neat coil-end to the saddle string. Then he slipped the halter and led the horse to the house. A radiant crown of soft red light lay over the eastern hills. The full moon would rise before the valley had completely lost the daylight.

In the kitchen Jelka still knitted by the window. Jim strode to the corner of the room and took up his 30-30 carbine. As he rammed cartridges into the magazine, he said, "The moon glow is on the hills. If you are going to see it rise, you better go outside now. It's going to be a good red one at rising."

"In a moment," she replied, "when I come to the end here." He went to her and patted her sleek head.

"Good night. I'll probably be back by noon tomorrow." Her dusky black eyes followed him out of the door.

Jim thrust the rifle into his saddle-scabbard, and mounted and swung his horse down the canyon. On his right, from behind the blackening hills, the great red moon slid rapidly up. The double light of the day's last afterglow and the rising moon thickened the outlines of the trees and gave a mysterious new perspective to the hills. The dusty oaks shimmered and glowed, and the shade under them was black as velvet. A huge, long-legged shadow of a horse and half a man rode to the left and slightly ahead of Jim. From the ranches near and distant came the sound of dogs tuning up for a night of song. And the roosters crowed, thinking a new dawn had come too quickly. Jim lifted the gelding to a trot. The spattering hoof-steps echoed back from the castle behind him. He thought of blond May at the Three Star in Monterey. "I'll be late. Maybe someone else'll have her," he thought. The moon was clear of the hills now.

Jim had gone a mile when he heard the hoofbeats of a horse coming towards him. A horseman cantered up and pulled to a stop. "That you, Jim?"

"Yes. Oh, hello, George."

"I was just riding up to your place. I want to tell you—you know the springhead at the upper end of my land?"

"Yes, I know."

"Well, I was up there this afternoon. I found a dead campfire and a calf's head and feet. The skin was in the fire, half burned, but I pulled it out and it had your brand."

"The hell," said Jim. "How old was the fire?"

"The ground was still warm in the ashes. Last night, I guess. Look, Jim, I can't go up with you. I've got to go to town, but I thought I'd tell you, so you could take a look around."

Jim asked quietly, "Any idea how many men?"

"No. I didn't look close."

"Well, I guess I better go up and look. I was going to town too. But if there are thieves working, I don't want to lose any more stock. I'll cut up through your land if you don't mind, George."

"I'd go with you, but I've got to go to town. You got a gun with you?"

"Oh yes, sure. Here under my leg. Thanks for telling me."

"That's all right. Cut through any place you want. Good night." The neighbour turned his horse and cantered back in the direction from which he had come.

For a few moments Jim sat in the moonlight, looking down at his stilted shadow. He pulled his rifle from its scabbard, levered a cartridge into the chamber, and held the gun across the pommel of his saddle. He turned left from the road, went up the little ridge, through the oak grove, over the grassy hogback and down the other side into the next canyon.

In half an hour he had found the deserted camp. He turned over the heavy, leathery calf's head and felt its dusty tongue to judge by the dryness how long it had been dead. He lighted a match and looked at his brand on the half-burned hide. At last he mounted his horse again, rode over the bald grassy hills and crossed into his own land.

A warm summer wind was blowing on the hilltops. The moon, as it quartered up the sky, lost its redness and turned the colour of strong tea. Among the hills the coyotes were singing, and the dogs at the ranch houses below joined them with broken-hearted howling. The dark green oaks below and the yellow summer grass showed their colours in the moonlight.

Jim followed the sound of the cowbells to his herd, and found them eating quietly, and a few deer feeding with them. He listened for the sound of hoofbeats or the voices of men on the wind.

It was after eleven when he turned his horse towards home. He rounded the west tower of the sandstone castle, rode through the shadow and out into the moonlight again. Below, the roofs of his barn and house shone dully. The bedroom window cast back a streak of reflection.

The feeding horses lifted their heads as Jim came down through the pasture. Their eyes glinted redly when they turned their heads.

Jim had almost reached the corral fence—he heard a horse stamping in the barn. His hand jerked the gelding down. His listened. It came again, the stamping from the barn. Jim lifted his rifle and dismounted silently. He turned his horse loose and crept towards the barn.

In the blackness he could hear the grinding of the horse's teeth as it chewed hay. He moved along the barn until he came to the occupied stall. After a moment of listening he scratched a match on the butt of his rifle. A saddled and bridled horse was tied in the stall. The bit was slipped under the chin and the cinch loosened. The horse stopped eating and turned its head towards the light.

Jim blew out the match and walked quickly out of the barn. He sat on the edge of the horse trough and looked into the water. His thoughts came so slowly that he put them into words and said them under his breath.

"Shall I look through the window? No. My head would throw a shadow in the room."

He regarded the rifle in his hand. Where it had been rubbed and handled, the black gun finish had worn off, leaving the metal silvery.

At last he stood up with decision and moved towards the house. At the steps, an extended foot tried each board tenderly before he put his weight on it. The three ranch dogs came out from under the house and shook themselves, stretched and sniffed, wagged their tails and went back to bed.

The kitchen was dark, but Jim knew where every piece of furniture was. He put out his hand and touched the corner of the table, a chair back, the towel hanger, as he went along. He crossed the room so silently that even he could hear only his breath and the whisper of his trouser legs together, and the beating of his watch in his pocket.

The bedroom door stood open and spilled a patch of moonlight on the kitchen floor. Jim reached the door at last and peered through.

The moonlight lay on the white bed. Jim saw Jelka lying on her back, one soft bare arm flung across her forehead and eyes. He could not see who the man was, for his head was turned away. Jim watched, holding his breath. Then Jelka twitched in her sleep and the man rolled his head and sighed—Jelka's cousin, her grown, embarrassed cousin.

Jim turned and quickly stole back across the kitchen and down the back steps. He walked up the yard to the water-trough again, and sat down on the edge of it. The moon was white as chalk, and it swam in the water, and lighted the straws and barley dropped by the horses' mouths. Jim could see the mosquito wigglers, tumbling up and down, end over end, in the water, and he could see a newt lying in the sun moss in the bottom of the trough.

He cried a few dry, hard, smothered sobs, and wondered why, for his thought was of the grassed hilltops and of the lonely summer wind whisking along.

His thought turned to the way his mother used to hold a bucket to catch the throat blood when his father killed a pig. She stood as far away as possible and held the bucket at arms'-length to keep her clothes from getting spattered.

Jim dipped his hand into the trough and stirred the moon to broken, swirling streams of light. He wetted his forehead with his damp hands and stood up. This time he did not move so quietly, but he crossed the kitchen on tiptoe and stood in the bedroom door. Jelka moved her arm and opened her eyes a little. Then the eyes sprang wide, then they glistened with moisture. Jim looked into her eyes; his face was empty of expression. A little drop ran out of Jelka's nose and lodged in the hollow of her upper lip. She stared back at him.

Jim cocked the rifle. The steel click sounded through the house. The man on the bed stirred uneasily in his sleep. Jim's hands were quivering. He raised the gun to his shoulder and held it tightly to keep from shaking. Over the sights he saw the little white square between the man's brows and hair. The front sight wavered a moment and then came to rest.

The gun crash tore the air. Jim, still looking down the barrel, saw the whole bed jolt under the blow. A small, black, bloodless hole was in the man's forehead. But behind, the hollow-point took brain and bone and splashed them on the pillow.

Jelka's cousin gurgled in his throat. His hands came crawling out from under the covers like big white spiders, and they walked for a moment, then shuddered and fell quiet.

Jim looked slowly back at Jelka. Her nose was running. Her eyes had moved from him to the end of the rifle. She whined softly, like a cold puppy.

Jim turned in panic. His boot heels beat on the kitchen floor, but outside, he moved slowly towards the water-trough again. There was a taste of salt in his throat, and his heart heaved painfully. He pulled his hat off and dipped his head into the water. Then he leaned over and vomited on the ground. In the house he could hear Jelka moving about. She whimpered like a puppy. Jim straightened up, weak and dizzy.

He walked tiredly through the corral and into the pasture. His saddled horse came at his whistle. Automatically he tightened the cinch, mounted and rode away, down the road to the valley. The squat black shadow traveled under him. The moon sailed high and white. The uneasy dogs barked monotonously.

At daybreak a buckboard and pair trotted up to the ranch yard, scattering the chickens. A deputy sheriff and a coroner sat in the seat. Jim Moore half reclined against his saddle in the wagon-box. His tired gelding followed behind. The deputy sheriff set the brake and wrapped the lines around it. The men dismounted.

Jim asked, "Do I have to go in? I'm too tired and wrought up to see it now."

The coroner pulled his lip and studied. "Oh, I guess not. We'll tend to things and look around."

Jim sauntered away towards the water-trough. "Say," he called, "kind of clean up a little, will you? You know."

The men went on into the house.

In a few minutes they emerged, carrying the stiffened body between them. It was wrapped up in a comforter. They eased it up into the wagon-box. Jim walked back towards them. "Do I have to go in with you now?"

"Where's your wife, Mr. Moore?" the deputy sheriff demanded.

"I don't know," he said wearily. "She's somewhere around."

"You're sure you didn't kill her too?"

"No. I didn't touch her. I'll find her and bring her in this afternoon. That is, if you don't want me to go in with you now."

"We've got your statement," the coroner said. "And by God, we've got eyes, haven't we, Will? Of course there's a technical charge of murder against you, but it'll be dismissed. Always is in this part of the country. Go kind of light on your wife, Mr. Moore."

"I won't hurt her," said Jim.

He stood and watched the buckboard jolt away. He kicked his feet reluctantly in the dust. The hot June sun showed its face over the hills and flashed viciously on the bedroom window.

Jim went slowly into the house, and brought out a nine-foot, loaded bull whip. He crossed the yard and walked into the barn. And as he climbed the ladder to the hayloft, he heard the high, puppy whimpering start.

When Jim came out of the barn again, he carried Jelka over his shoulder. By the water-trough he set her tenderly on the ground. Her hair was littered with bits of hay. The back of her shirtwaist was streaked with blood.

Jim wetted his bandana at the pipe and washed her bitten lips, and washed her face and brushed back her hair. Her dusty black eyes followed every move he made.

"You hurt me," she said. "You hurt me bad."

He nodded gravely. "Bad as I could without killing you."

The sun shone hotly on the ground. A few blowflies buzzed about, looking for the blood.

Jelka's thickened lips tried to smile. "Did you have any breakfast at all?"

"No," he said. "None at all."

"Well, then, I'll fry you up some eggs." She struggled painfully to her feet.

"Let me help you," he said. "I'll help you get your shirtwaist off. It's drying stuck to your back. It'll hurt."

"No. I'll do it myself." Her voice had a peculiar resonance in it. Her dark eyes dwelt warmly on him for a moment, and then she turned and limped into the house.

Jim waited, sitting on the edge of the water-trough. He saw the smoke start out of the chimney and sail straight up into the air. In a very few moments Jelka called him from the kitchen door.

"Come, Jim. Your breakfast."

Four fried eggs and four thick slices of bacon lay on a warmed plate for him. "The coffee will be ready in a minute," she said.

"Won't you eat?"

"No. Not now. My mouth's too sore."

He ate his eggs hungrily and then looked up at her. Her black hair was combed smooth. She had on a fresh white shirtwaist. "We're going to town this afternoon," he said. "I'm going to order lumber. We'll build a new house farther down the canyon."

Her eyes darted to the closed bedroom door and then back to him. "Yes," she said. "That will be good." And then, after a moment, "Will you whip me any more—for this?"

"No, not any more, for this."

Her eyes smiled. She sat down on a chair beside him, and Jim put out his hand and stroked her hair and the back of her neck.